CONOR'S QUEST

THE BOOK OF WORDS TRILOGY BOOK TWO

KE MEUIR

IRISH VIKING PUBLISHING

ALSO BY KE MEUIR

The Book of Words Trilogy, Book One

The Mountain Fog

Conor's Quest

Book Two of the Book of Words Trilogy

Softcover ISBN: 979-9-218-25872-6

Library of Congress Control Number: 202-391-4688

Cover Art and Design by Ivan Zann at www.BookCoversArt.com

For more information on K E Meuir's projects, go to her website at www.kemeuir.com

ACKNOWLEDGEMENTS

"Writing is utter solitude, the descent into the cold abyss of oneself."

Franz Kafka (1883-1924)

It's just you and the words you form in your imagination, and it can be a lonely pursuit. Somewhere along the way, you fall in love with your characters, and the world is a joyous place again. Writing can be the most magical art; building worlds, stringing together characters, creating problems that only you dream up and solve, and finally writing endings that leave your readers wishing for more. It can just as easily frustrate you when you doubt your ability to craft even the simplest sentence that moves your story forward.

But you persist, and you persevere. You write like mad and erase half of it. You pace the room and write and rewrite. Then you turn it all over to an editor, and that's when it becomes truly humbling.

I praise the authors whose words have filled me with wonder. Someday, I hope to do the same, but for now, I am grateful to be one of them, a writer.

My eternal love and gratitude go to my partner and fellow writer, Mark David Albertson. Whenever I think of walking away, his example brings me back to the writing again. His ideas and encouragement are everywhere in this book and in my life.

I am grateful to Irish Viking Publishing Co. for their willingness to publish my work yet again.

I owe a debt of gratitude to Ivan Zann at BookCoversArt.com. He takes my disjointed ideas and turns them into beautiful artwork that brings my story to life.

PROLOGUE

The mountain stood as it had for thousands of years, silently overlooking the village in the valley below. Dark clouds hid the topmost peak, the clouds swirling around and around but never blowing away, never stopping their constant movement. There were no sounds of insects or creatures of flight at the top of the mountain, only the stiff wind as it whistled around the rocks, sending small clouds of dust from the path that led to the cave. The constant wind stripped the clearing outside the cave of dirt, scouring it down to the bare rock, leaving no trace of footsteps entering or leaving the cave.

The entrance to the cave did not invite a weary traveler, for the air inside was cold and stale, and dank water ran in small streamlets down the sides of the cave and across the floor. Stone platforms stood in rows as far as the dim light from the entrance allowed. Beyond that, the cave was nothing but darkness, so thick it felt as if you could grasp it in your hands.

The last row of stone platforms held two shapes, each covered with a cloth; one shape with long black hair that cascaded past the end of the platform. A faint light made its way through the heavy darkness from a hallway beyond. A man fussed around the shapes, adjusting the cloths, muttering to himself as he moved from one shape to the other. Satisfied with his efforts in the material's arrangement, he took up a brush and with long strokes, ran it over the black hair, brushing it until it was soft and gleaming. His own hair was unkept, long and shaggy, and hung in lank strands around the frayed collar of his shirt while his face was barely visible above his beard, as black as the hair he brushed. Badly sewn patches covered his shirt and pants, and the soles of his boots showed his socks through holes worn thin on the rock floor of the cave. His eyes held the faraway look of madness in them, and they darted from side to side, always searching for something.

At last, he finished his work and, bending over the covered figure with the raven hair, he gently kissed the forehead. Backing away as if the form might rise and follow him, he stumbled down what seemed like a natural hallway, taking him deeper into the cave. There, he entered a smaller chamber and kicked at a small bed of coals to bring them to life. Gathering sticks from the far corner, he carefully built up a fire to warm the space and give him much needed light. As the fire grew and warmed him, he sat beside it and held his head in his hands. His shoulders shook with quiet sobs until finally spent, he rubbed his face with a dirty sleeve and sat back against the rock wall. Smoke curled around him until it finally found a small hole in the cave's ceiling and made its way up and out. As the fire grew, so did the light, and he looked around the cave at the piles of silver dishes and candlesticks tumbled about in no particular order. Nearby, plates and cups of pewter stood in rows, as did sacks of coins piled high. Here and there a jeweled dagger or a ring twinkled and caught the firelight. Glimpses of gold showed among the piles, but mostly it was silver that stood silently waiting.

The man rubbed his forehead again and muttered, "What good did it do us, Mara? What good is all of this to us now? We're stuck here, you asleep and me tending to you. The Darkness take you for your greed and impatience. I knew we should have left this Light forsaken mountain long before they came for the children. Would you listen, you stubborn old witch? No! You always know what's best, don't you? Now what? I am forced to lay traps for rats and mice to keep myself alive, and all this wealth sits here and mocks me. May the Darkness take you and swallow you up!"

The man leaned his head against the wall and stretched his legs to the fire. Slowly, his eyes closed and his head nodded in sleep. As he drifted away, a figure slid silently into the far end of the cave. He stood for a moment, allowing his eyes to adjust to the brighter light from the fire. He approached the sleeping man, whistling tunelessly until he stood over him, looking down thoughtfully.

Dressed in black breeches tucked into leather boots with a white linen shirt, and his cloak flung back off his shoulders, he looked strong and elegant. His hand, with long, tapered fingers, stroked a beard that was trimmed short and neat. It was only when you looked closely would you see that the cuffs of his shirt were threadbare and worn. His cloak looked as if the patches sewn together made up a whole new cloak. Leather boots, though polished until shiny, showed wear at the toes and heels. His face carried a powerful jaw and a good straight nose, but his eyes were small and set too close together to be handsome. His mouth turned down in a constant sneer that belied any good nature, making the whole of his face unpleasant.

He fingered the sphere in his pocket as he continued to stroke his beard. "I think it's time, Jebez," he whispered. "Time to wake Mara and get back to work. Greedy and weak as you are, I believe someone has a use for you both. Why he thinks you will be useful to him is beyond me, but he does. Not for what you can do but for what you can bring him." He raised his foot as if to send a swift kick aimed at the sleeping man's head but thought better of it. He stared down at him for a moment before he turned away with a snarl and made his way down the stone hallway taking him deeper into the belly of the earth.

Chapter One

The Peddler

The wagon swayed back and forth on the dirt road; the wheels groaning as they dipped down into the ruts that ran across it at angles impossible to avoid. Leatherleaf trees along the road grew so thick with their summer leaves of green that there was no view to be seen on either side.

The driver of the wagon held the reins loosely in his hands, flapping them now and then against the back of his mule to coax more speed from him. Snorting and pinning his ears against his head, the mule expressed his dislike for the act. Chuckling to himself, the man loosened his grip on the reins. "You're right Jasper. We will get there when we get there no matter what I think."

Tall and lean, the man wore a good woolen shirt, open at the throat with his sleeves rolled up to expose sunburnt arms, strong and corded with muscles. His hair was the dark grey of strong iron, and he wore it long and tied back with a piece of braided leather. A neatly trimmed beard, long enough to touch the front of his shirt, was decorated with colorful beads woven through the strands. His face was brown from the sun, with wrinkles at his eyes and along his mouth so that it was difficult to determine his age. With eyes the color of the June sky, he startled most people when he directed his piercing gaze at them. Altogether, the man gave the impression of quiet strength.

The girl on the wagon seat next to him was the opposite of him in every way. Flaming red hair curled down her back and blew across her face with the breeze. Her green eyes darted from side to side, searching for something to see past the wall of trees that hid everything from sight. She gathered up her heavy red hair with one hand and fanned her neck with the other, her mouth twisting into a pout as she did so. The skin on her arms showed freckles against alabaster white, and her face was smooth save for the frown she wore between her eyes. Her feet were bare, and she tapped them impatiently on the floorboards of the wagon as she hummed a tune. Dropping her hair back on her neck, she slapped at her legs and kept time to the tune she hummed.

Pausing her music, she squinted up at the sun. "Why in the Light are we going to this little or nothing village, Da? They are so far from anywhere, and I doubt they have two coins to rub together. June is the best month for selling our wares, but out here in the middle of nowhere, I doubt we sell two pots. This seems like a waste of time to me." She sat back against the wagon seat and crossed her arms over her chest.

"I have my reasons, girl," he said through gritted teeth. "I am here for more than selling this wagon load of junk. You never mind where we go and when we get there. I will let you know when I need something from you. And when we get to this little or nothing village, as you call it, you put on your best smile and pour out the charm like cream from a pitcher, do you hear?" He looked sideways at her in a manner that stilled the words she had on the tip of her tongue. She sighed quietly and sat back against the boards of the wagon, the music in her head all but forgotten.

The mule pulled a wagon that looked as if it could well use an entire team of mules to get it down the road, loaded as it was. Besides the two people sitting on the front seat, the back of the wagon carried piles of goods covered with heavy tarps. A frame built along the edges and back of the wagon bed held hooks and ropes from which dangled shovels, hoes, rakes, scythes, and other tools for gardens and fields. On the other side hung axes, poles for turning logs, harnesses, pots and pans, and assorted household goods. They banged and beat against each other with the swaying of the wagon, sending out a musical tune that sounded as if children were banging on their mothers' pots and pans with sticks.

At the back of the wagon, sacks of onions and potatoes were piled on top of each other to form a wall, all lashed together by more rope to keep them from falling onto the roadbed. Wooden casks stood upright along the sides and chests with heavy locks held them in place. The wagon had a prosperous look about it, and it was no surprise that villagers came rushing out to greet it whenever it rolled into their towns and villages.

The mule plodded down the rutted road, finding a bend that brought them out of the woods and into the edge of the valley, bright with sunlight. Spread out in front of the travelers, the valley floor was lush with grasses and dotted with groves of ash and alders. The man pulled hard on the reins and brought the mule up short. He seemed to hold his breath as his gaze crossed the valley and took in the hills and the high mountains beyond them. Back and forth, his eyes traveled until he settled on the highest mountain peak, rising above the valley like an ancient sentinel. The peak was hidden from view by heavy black clouds that moved in a constant motion around and around the mountaintop but never seemed to blow away as if held in place by an invisible force. He let out his breath in one long exhalation as he continued to stare at the black mass of clouds. Slowly, he sat back and closed his eyes. Relaxing his body so that the reins drifted down from his hands, he let his mind go free, free to travel through the valley and into the mountains beyond.

The girl slid her eyes sideways to look at him, but she seemed to know better than to disturb him in his present state. Sighing again, she jumped down from the wagon seat to explore the surrounding land.

At last, the man opened his eyes and, shaking his head as if to clear it, picked up the reins. Only then did he notice the empty seat beside him. "Roisin, get here now, girl. I'm ready."

The girl hurried back from where she was picking early summer flowers and climbed back into the wagon. Snatching the flowers from her hand with a frown, the man threw them aside and snapped, "Stop wasting my time. I've found what I've been looking for, at least part of it. And if one part is here, the other part is surely nearby. Let's get on."

Chapter Two

THE VILLAGE AT THE VALLEY'S EDGE

Erik Tamen stepped out on his front porch with a cup of tea in one hand and a large hunk of white cheese wrapped in his wife's excellent bread in the other. He leaned against the upright support at the edge of the steps, looking down to an expanse of green grass and flowers leading out to the village road. He chuckled to himself as he eyed the flowers, hot and dusty in the June morning sun. *If I don't haul some water for that woman so she can keep these flowers alive, my head might as well go on a pike by itself!*

He raised a hand and brushed back his hair, red and worn long around his neck. Pulling a large white handkerchief out of his back pocket, he cleaned the crumbs from his beard, stowing the last small bit of his bread in his pocket. *It's going to be a fine, quiet day.* A quiet day was always a good one, as far as Erik Tamen was concerned. As the mayor and constable of the Village at the Valley's Edge, the less fuss he found, the better.

There had been no wolves to trouble the village since last winter, and they were so far off the main road, travelers were few. While the village tavern served hard cider and an occasional beer when the tavern owner could get the recipe right, his only customers were the farmers and villagers who had little coin to spend on drink. The men of the village mostly used the tavern as a place to sit by the fire, away from the occasional sharp tongues of their wives. There they told old stories heard half a dozen times, each time embellished a bit more for their audience. This was exactly the way Erik Tamen liked it.

He thought back to the troubles two years before when Jebez and Mara raised the mountain fog and stole their children from their own beds in the night. He shook his head again as he recalled the last scene in the cave; Mara was screaming for Ceobhran to rise. Someone, probably Ronan, jerking frantically on his arm, pulling him out of the cave with all her might. His heart broke all over again for the boy, Conor, when he realized the woman responsible for so much pain was his own mother. How must it have felt to discover his own flesh and blood had harmed the girl he had loved since he was a small boy running wild in the village? And Sean? What of Sean, he thought. In the end, he might have been the saving grace they needed to escape. *I never thought much of the man. Never had much use for him, but it seems he made something of himself in the end.* Erik shook his head as the memories came to him. The memory of Ceobhran overtaking Sean while they all fled, running for their lives out of that Light forsaken cave. *I haven't checked on Doiranne for a while. We owe her something for Sean's death; I know. It's a task I put off and for good reason.*

Erik shrugged and pulled the last small bit of bread out of his pocket. "There you are, little one. I thought you weren't coming this morning." He tossed the bread out to a bright red cardinal who cocked his head, grabbed the offering, and flew off.

Bringing his hand up to shade his eyes, he squinted in the bright morning sun as he looked down the road that led away from the village. He could see a speck of something and a cloud of dust around it. Shading his eyes against the sun, he watched as the speck and dust cloud grew larger. *Looks like we'll have some visitors after all. Who would come here so far off the main road?*

Erik Tamen turned from the porch to set his teacup on the kitchen table. "Guin, it looks like we've got company coming our way."

His wife stopped drying her dishes and turned to the door. Stepping out on the porch, she shaded her eyes against the morning sun and looked in the direction he pointed. "What on this good green earth would bring a wagon way out here? Oh, I hope it's a peddler. We haven't had one of those in years, and I could certainly use some new kitchen tools and a good digging trowel for my garden. Invite them to stay on the green, will you, my love?"

Erik Tamen stepped down from the porch and made his way across the village to the center green. The villagers built their cottages around the edge of the green with the tavern at the center of everything. A blacksmith shop stood next to the tavern, and there was a gristmill built to take advantage of the stream that flowed nearby. The water wheel turned slowly as the water flowed over the wooden paddles, turning the giant stone inside to grind the wheat and rye for the villagers. Since the completion of the mill a year ago, the men of the village had taken to turning their pastures into grain fields. Now the sheep turned out of their former grazing areas, bunched up around the green, gobbling soft grass as fast as they could.

Erik Tamen watched as the wagon pulled into the village, raising a small cloud of dust along the way. Small, barefoot boys chased after the wagon, kicking up their own clouds of dust.

The man pulled on the reins, stopping the mule just outside the green. He set the brake with his left foot and climbed down from the wagon. Bending over, he stretched and slapped the dust from his pants. As soon as he spied Erik Tamen, he walked over with his hand extended in greeting. "Hello, my friend! I am Traynor and that young lady over there is my daughter, Roisin. We might have taken a wrong turn somewhere because this doesn't look like the town I was aiming for. Can you tell me where we might be, my friend?"

Erik Tamen shook his head. "This is not much of a town, sir. More of a village, and a small one at that. We've been known as the Valley's Edge for so long, the name stuck. We sit at the end of the valley before you climb to those mountains beyond us. Turn around and go back the way you came, for there will be no roads through those mountains fit for a wagon like yours."

The man called Traynor rubbed his hand across his forehead and gazed toward the mountains. "I see what you mean. The mountains look unpassable from here. Can we camp for a few days and rest ourselves and our mule? Perhaps the people of your village would like to see what we have to sell and take advantage of our stop."

"I know of at least one person who will be glad to have you stay. Set up your camp right here on the green but watch out for the sheep droppings; they're everywhere since we use the sheep to keep the grass mowed short."

The man nodded his thanks and stepped back up into the wagon seat, clucking at the mule as he did so. Turning the mule with ease, he drove the wagon to the far end of the green, and there he released him from his traces and picketed him where there was still plenty of good, sweet grass to crop. He patted the animal on the withers and stroked his neck. "I'll turn you loose after we finish setting up camp. The hobbles will keep you from wandering too far away, and you'll be able to eat to your heart's content."

The girl, Roisin, jumped down from the wagon and begin untying and pulling back the heavy tarps. There, she found a stout tent, stakes, and ropes hidden from view. She jumped up into the back of the wagon and threw down the stakes and the ropes. The tent was heavy, and she strained to heave it over the side of the wagon. Once on the ground, she untied it and rolled it out. "Where do you want the tent, Da?"

"Let's put it on the other side of the wagon, Roisin. I don't fancy stepping in old Jasper's piles in the morning when I roll out of the tent." He said that with a smile. Hanging up Jasper's harness and reins, he bent to help her carry the heavy tent of good stout canvas to the other side of the green. Next, they used a small sledgehammer to drive the stakes deep into the ground and tying off the ropes they pulled them tight to raise the tent. Roisin set up short blocks of cut timber, and Traynor placed a long board across them to create a rough table. From the back of the wagon, she brought out an old wooden trunk with leather straps that kept it tightly closed. Undoing the straps, she removed plates and bowls, cups, and assorted small pots. The last thing she brought out was a small iron kettle that she set on the ground.

She walked around the edge of the green towards the stream and found several good-sized rocks. One by one, she carried them back and set them in a circle for a fire. She then set up three pieces of black iron rod, leaning them in towards one another at the top to form a tripod. From this, she hung the blackened kettle over the fire ring. Next, she found some dry sticks and one or two bigger pieces of wood from beyond the stream. Meager as they were, they would get a fire going until she could find more wood. She laid the smaller sticks down inside the circle of rocks and pulled up some of the taller dry grass the sheep had not eaten. Piling that on top of the sticks, she pulled a knife from her belt and a rock from her pocket. Striking the rock against the blade of her knife, she fed sparks to the dry grass until a wisp of smoke rose. Kneeling close to the earth, she blew gently on the grass until a small flame leaped up to reward her for her efforts. The flame she fed with dry sticks until it was big enough to take larger pieces of wood without smothering. Once she had the fire going, she took potatoes and onions from the sacks at the back of the wagon. Using her belt knife, she sliced the vegetables on the rough wooden table until she had a good pile. She brought down a bucket from a hook on the wagon frame and filled it from the nearby stream. With the kettle over the fire, she sat down to wait for the water to boil. When it did, she poured her chopped onions and potatoes in the kettle and gave it all a stir. Finally, she took packets of dried herbs from the trunk, and opening each one smelled deeply of their aromas. Once she decided on the herbs, she sprinkled them across the water. *I'll need him to bring me something besides potatoes and onions if we're to have any kind of stew.*

Satisfied that their dinner was cooking over the fire, she left the camp and strolled through the green. The tavern held no interest for her, but the smithy drew her. She looked at the forge, cold now with no fire and admired the tools leaning against one corner of the shop. *Not poor work. I could do as well if I had a forge, but not bad at all.*

She continued through the village, glancing at the cottages with thatched roofs and stout porches. Her lips curled in disdain. *Imagine living here for the rest of your life. Never seeing the world, seeing nothing at all. Not for me!*

She watched with curiosity as a young girl came strolling down the road towards the green, dressed in a plain brown skirt with sturdy shoes peeking out from the hem. She wore her blond hair braided, falling down her back nearly to her waist. Roisin watched the easy way she walked, swinging her arms, and singing to herself. Roisin ran her fingers through her red hair, smoothing the curls. She tucked one side behind her ear and brushed off her skirt. She regretted not putting her shoes on before she left their camp. Wiggling her toes down in the grass, she waited until the girl drew near.

Tilly looked up in surprise to see the girl with waves of red hair standing at the edge of the green. "Well, hello! I did not know that we had travelers in our village. Are you here with your family? Are you traveling far?"

"Just my da. He's a peddler, so we travel everywhere. I've seen nearly everything there is to be seen."

Tilly frowned at that but remained pleasant. "Welcome, then. We're glad to have you. My name is Matilda, but everyone calls me Tilly."

Roisin looked Tilly up and down before answering. "Aren't you a little young to be a married woman?" she asked.

Tilly reared back at the question. "Why ever do you think I'm married? Most certainly, I am not!"

Roisin gestured with her hand. "Your hair. It's braided. Anywhere I've ever been, girls don't braid their hair until they are married. You braided your hair; therefore, you must be married."

Tilly snorted at that. "I braid my hair because I like to climb trees and my hair gets caught in the branches. I am not married, thank you."

With that, she turned on her heels and stomped away, leaving Roisin to smile quietly to herself. *Pour out charm like cream from a pitcher, huh? We'll see about that, Da! Just maybe I am tired of being your bait.*

Chapter Three

DOIRANNE

Smoke curled lazily from the lopsided chimney that stood at the far end of the cottage. Chinks of light shone through the walls and the door hung lopsided above the rough steps. Inside, a slight haze filled the room and caused visitors, should there ever be any, to blink and wipe their eyes. Doiranne sat in front of the meager fire, the damp wood she used smoldered and smoked more than it burned. She pulled an old wool shawl around her. *If this is the best I can do for a fire when the weather is good, what will become of me when it turns cold? No one has brought me wood in ages. What if they never do again? How will I live?*

She wiped her eyes with the end of her shawl and stared into the fire. Slowly, she edged her hand into her apron pocket and fingered the tobacco pouch hidden in the depths. She sighed as she felt it in her fingers. *I never thought I would say this, but I miss that little man. Maybe it wasn't so bad after all. He wasn't much of a builder, but at least he tried. I should have helped him more. At lease, I should have given him his tobacco pouch before he left.*

Doiranne heaved herself up from the chair and lumbered across the room to the window. Taking her sleeve in her hand, she scrubbed across the old glass, clearing out a small circle. The outside light poured through the tiny spot as if begging to light the room. Turning from the window, she looked at the cottage. Stacks of greasy dishes stood on the shelf beside the table. There were pots and pans stacked haphazardly on the floor, and the shelves held an assortment of rough canisters, none labeled and many with no lids. A forgotten broom stood in the corner alongside an equally forgotten mop. Doiranne looked at all of this dispassionately as if it belonged to someone else, not her. She reached up and fingered her hair, long and lifeless. Her wrinkled dress had food stains on it from weeks of neglect. She leaned against the wall and crossed her arms across her chest.

She spoke to the room, "Is this the best I can do? Is this what I deserve out of life? This room, this cottage falling down around my ears." She wandered over to the kitchen table, stuck in the far corner of the cottage. Trailing her fingers through the dust, she looked at it curiously, as if she had never seen dust in her house before. A basin of cold water sat on the shelf next to the dirty dishes. Gobs of grease floated on the surface, and she blew on them and watched as they skittered across the water. Everywhere she looked, it was as if she was seeing it for the first time; the grease, the dust, the soot from the fire that coated everything. "How did I end up like this? Sean wasn't much of a husband or a provider, but he was better than nothing. Now I have nothing, and I am likely to have nothing for the rest of my life unless something changes."

Doiranne turned away from the room and opened the door to the bright day outside. She blinked at the sunshine and stood quietly for a moment, looking at the space between her house and the dusty road in front. Thistles and dandelions grew of their own accord, covering the space and trails of ivy, overgrown and woody, hid the rude steps leading up to her front door. Lost in the deep weeds were the stone steps Sean built to make a walkway to their small cottage. Doiranne sighed and scratched her left arm until she left long red welts.

She sighed again and stepped down, being careful not to trip over the ivy. Kicking at the weeds to find the walkway, she made her way to the gate and to the road beyond it.

She walked toward the village until she came to the first cottage. Opening the gate, she noticed the clean, trimmed grass, the wide walkway that led to a comfortable porch. Heaving herself up the steps, she banged on the front door.

The door opened to reveal a tall man with blond hair, brushed smooth and hanging around his shoulders. A look of surprise on his face soon turned to a frown. "Doiranne. What can I do for you? Have you run out of food so soon? If so, bring it up with Erik Tamen." He crossed his arms over his broad chest.

Her eyes on the ground, Doiranne blurted out in a rush of words, "No, Quinn, I have plenty, thank you. I was wondering if you had a bucket I could use. Sean had one, but it is so buried in the weeds that I might not find it. If you will lend me one, I will bring it back, I swear." When she finished, she took a deep breath, and only then did she raise her eyes to look at Quinn.

"A bucket? Yes, I have a bucket you can use. I have an extra one, so you can keep this one as long as you need. But what do you need a bucket for, Doiranne?"

Doiranne sighed and looked off across the village green. "I think I would like to wash my windows, Quinn. It's such a nice day and maybe some sunlight would be nice in the cottage." She fingered her apron as she talked.

"Then let's go find you that bucket. Do you need some rags as well?"

"No, I have some old things I can cut up."

"Here's a good stout bucket, Doiranne. Keep it as long as you need it."

Doiranne took the bucket and turned down the road to her cottage without another word. Once there, she beat a path to the pump and, after priming it, filled the bucket with good, clean water. It took all she had to carry it back to the cottage, spilling a good portion on her shoes along the way. Inside, she found an old shirt and ripped it into smaller pieces. Pouring some soap powder into the bucket, she gave it a good swirl with her hand to mix it. Doiranne set about scrubbing the windows until they sparkled. It took most of the day and several trips to the pump, but at last, light streamed through the windows and filled her tiny cottage with warmth.

She carried a fresh bucket of water and poured it into a big black pot sitting on the hearth. Stirring up the fire, she blew on it to get a better flame. *This will not do. I need better wood if I am to heat this water.*

She climbed down the steps once more and went to the back of the cottage where Sean had built a crude lean-to for wood storage. Kicking the weeds out of the way, Doiranne found some drier wood and an old ax, rusty and dull from weather and neglect. Filling her arms with as much wood as she could carry, she tucked the ax into the belt at her waist.

Throwing the wood down on the hearth, she used the poker to stir the fire and then added the drier wood. Almost immediately, flames shot up and begin eating away at the fuel. For the first time, she smiled to herself. *Now see, you can do something right. And if you can do one thing, you can do one more.*

Grumbling to herself, she grabbed up the broom, opened the cottage door, and began sweeping with long strokes. As she swept the old dirt off the wooden floor, her grumbling softened and soon she was humming a tune. Surprised, she held the broom for a moment and then shrugged. She hummed and swept while the fire heated the water on the hearth. When it was hot enough, she dipped water out to fill her basin. Sprinkling more soap powder in it, she set to scrubbing the dirty dishes on the shelves and the pots and pans scattered on the floor. Before she knew it, the shelves held clean, stacked dishes, and the pots hung from hooks swinging in the light. She took the rest of the soapy water and scrubbed the table until she mopped up the last bit of grease. Filling the pot once more, she waited for the fire to heat the water. While she did, she looked around at her work. For the first time in months, her kitchen was clean, the table free of days' worth of crumbs and bits of food. The floor was as clean as she could get it with the old broom she had. *I'm going to need a new broom and some more rags to make a better mop. This one has seen better days.*

She carefully took down the canisters from the shelf, peering into them to see what stores she had. Some tea, rye flour, and sugar. Putting the canisters back on the shelf, she looked into the baskets which held a few carrots, turnips, onions, and dried apples. *I could use some potatoes and some meat. What do I have to trade?*

Once the water was warm in the pot, she filled the bucket and carried it past the front steps. Going back in the house, she dug around a cupboard next to her bed until she found what she was looking for, a pair of old trousers and a good wool shirt. *Probably much too small for me, but it will have to do.* Shrugging out of her dress and apron, she slipped the wool shirt over her head. Getting her legs into the trousers took some doing, but between tugging and pushing, she managed it. She grabbed up her dress and apron and stuffed them into the bucket of water, sloshing them up and down and around. Doiranne scrubbed the garments until the water turned gray with her efforts. Smiling to herself, she shook out the water and twisted and wrung them as dry as she could. These she laid out on the weeds in the sun to dry. *I will need some posts and some rope to hang out my clothes and linens.* She laughed to herself. *How many linens might you have, Doiranne?*

She emptied the bucket of gray water on the weeds and turned it upside down on the steps to dry. Taking one last look at her cottage, she turned and went out the gate towards the village. Walking as quickly as her legs would allow, she traveled to the far end of the village until she came to a small, neat cottage. A white fence and gate shimmered in the sun, and the yard beyond was full of bright flowers, herbs of all sorts, and twisted vines that curled around the posts that held up the porch roof. A walkway led to the wide porch on which sat two rocking chairs, inviting a person to sit and have tea or gaze at the mountain beyond.

"Hello! Is anyone home?"

A voice answered her from beyond the porch, "Come in, come in. I am just cutting some lavender. I'll be right there. Go on up on the porch and wait for me."

Doiranne did as the voice bade her, sitting in one of the rocking chairs. Leaning against the back, she let out a sigh. *I'm tired. When was the last time I was tired like this? When was the last time I worked this hard?* She chuckled to herself and began humming.

Granny Matilda came around the end of the porch and stopped in surprise. "Well, I can't say I expected to see you, Doiranne. I don't remember the last time I saw you out of your cottage. What brings you to my porch?" Granny climbed up the broad steps, and placing her basket of herbs on the boards, sat in the chair next to Doiranne.

"I want to know about Sean, Granny. Will you tell me what happened to him? I know, Erik Tamen said he threw himself on that witch, but I want to know exactly what happened. Please."

Granny sighed and sat back in her chair. "Not without a cup of tea, Doiranne. Give me a moment to heat the water. Come inside while I do it."

Doiranne looked around Granny's cottage. A small, cushioned bench sat in front of the fire, flanked by two more rocking chairs with thatched seats. Her kitchen held a table of wood polished to a high gleam, and shelves with dishes and cups stacked neatly. From every rafter, herbs tied in bundles hung upside down, making the air sweet yet savory at the same time. Doiranne's nose twitched with delight at all the smells. On the hearth, from a small tripod, hung a black pot giving off smells of meat and vegetables. Granny took a small tea kettle and filled it from a bucket of water she kept in her kitchen. This she placed on the hot bricks closest to the fire. While it heated, she set down cups and lifted a cannister from the shelf from which she shook out tea leaves. She then sprinkled those with chamomile leaves. When the tea kettle sputtered and sang, she poured the hot water over the leaves and let them steep.

"We'll sit outside if you like. I like to watch the mountain while I drink my tea."

Doiranne gratefully accepted the cup of tea and sat looking at the mountain. "I can't see it from my cottage. Doesn't matter, I don't have a porch to sit on or a rocking chair to sit in." She smiled as she said this.

Granny shook her head. "What has come over you, Doiranne? I've never known you to have any sort of humor, much less good humor. Have you been nibbling on those dried mushrooms I brought you?"

"No, it's not the mushrooms, Granny. I've just been thinking, thinking that I want more for myself and maybe the only way to get it is to get it for myself. But first, I want to know what happened to Sean. The entire story, please. I owe it to him to think on it."

"It's been two years since we found the children and brought them out of the cave. It's been two years since you lost Sean. Since *we* lost Sean in that cave, Doiranne. Why now, I would like to know?"

Doiranne ducked her head and studied her boots as if they were the most interesting thing she had seen all day. Finally, she shook her head and brushed her hair back. "I know I am to blame for what happened to Sean. I drove him out of this village and into those mountains. Into that cave. I nagged at him and hounded him until he had no choice but to go. Go where he had no business going. It's a hard thing to live with that. I can't take it back, and I can't make it up to him, but maybe if I own up to it, I could find some peace for myself. I don't know more than that, Granny."

Granny sipped her tea and considered Doiranne. "There's not too much more to tell, Doiranne. You know we found the Mountain Folk. They've been visiting with us, and Ronan has been here on and off, studying herbs and healing with me. You know that we all traveled to the cave at the top of that mountain." Granny tilted her head towards the towering mountain in the distance. "We all, Mountain Folk and villagers, made a plan to bring the children out. Erik Tamen was to distract Mara and Jebez while Ronan and I woke the children. It was Tilly's task, after we woke her, to take them out of the cave and let Conor and Sean lead them down the path to the clearing we camped in the night before. I counted on those two to take the children away and not come into the cave, but I counted wrong. Conor and Sean came in, and Conor saw Mara and Jebez, but it was Sean who recognized them immediately. He knew them for the people who had stolen his mother from him."

Granny paused and looked off toward the mountain, studying the black clouds that swirled endlessly around the peak. She looked back at Doiranne and continued, "Mara was screaming, calling up Ceobhran, and we were desperate to get away before that happened. There was Erik and Conor to think of. I was holding Jebez and Mara back, but I was tired, Doiranne, and my strength was not what I needed it to be. I was losing the fight, and I knew it. If that had happened, make no mistake, Ceobhran would have swallowed us all up and none of us would be here today. Instead, Sean threw himself at Mara and when he did, the fog covered them completely." Granny sat back in her chair and took a sip of tea to calm herself.

"He saved you, didn't he? In a manner of speaking, he saved you all."

"Yes, Doiranne. He saved us; Conor, Erik, and me. He saved us indeed."

Doiranne sipped at her tea and stared at the mountains. "The black clouds are still there. Does that mean the evil is still there?"

"I believe so, yes."

"Where do you think Sean is?"

"I imagine he sleeps, much as our children did, in the cave."

"Do you think they use him to do bad things? Like the children?"

"I don't know, Doiranne. I simply don't know. As far as I know, Mara sleeps now, caught in Ceobhran the same as Sean. About Jebez, I cannot say. I fled. I left Sean there, and I ran."

"Oh, I don't blame you for that, Granny. If my legs had let me, I would have run too. Your job was to get the children to safety, not look after Sean. I was the one who nagged and goaded him into leaving. I thought I would be happier with him gone. Funny, but I'm not. I'm not at all. But I will be. Thank you for the tea and the honesty."

Doiranne struggled up from the rocking chair and handed her teacup to Granny. "Come and see me sometime, Granny Matilda. I have no fine teacups, but I will give you what I have, with pleasure."

Doiranne stepped down from the porch and walked through the yard. As she walked, she trailed her fingers over the flowers and herbs, pulling off a leaf and rubbing it between her fingers, holding it to her nose to smell deeply of the smell released from the crushed leaf. When she reached the gate, she turned for one last look at the mass of green and vibrant colors, the butterflies flitting from one vibrant flower to the next. She put her fingers to her nose once more and smelled deeply of the fresh scent. Smiling to herself, she opened the gate and walked away.

Not far into the village, she stopped outside a garden. Surrounded by a stout fence to keep out rabbits and the village sheep, rows of bean plants, peas, cabbage plants, and potatoes filled the interior of the garden. Doiranne opened the gate and wandered up and down the rows. Spotting what she searched for, she crouched down and began digging in the dirt with her fingers.

"Who's there?"

Doiranne stood up with a grunt. "It's just me, Quinn."

"This is the second time I've seen you today, Doiranne. I asked you if you had enough food and you said you did. So why are you here now?"

"I thought I might try to be useful, Quinn. There are some weeds here among the potatoes, and I thought I might pull them out. Maybe haul some water if I'm able."

Quinn reached up and scratched the back of his head. "Doiranne, first you want a bucket and now you want to dig weeds. What's come over you? Have you been eating too many of Granny's mushrooms?"

"No, but she asked me the same thing. I will tell you what I told her. I want something different for myself, Quinn. And I think the only way I'm going to get it is if I do it myself. Let me just work here a little while. The potatoes won't be ready until fall, but if I work a bit, maybe you and Molly could spare me a potato or two for my stew."

Quinn narrowed his eyes as he stared at Doiranne. "We could do that, I think. Yes, we could. Let's get this row of potatoes cleaned up. A rake and a hoe would go a long way towards helping us."

Chapter Four

A Way Back

Doiranne and Quinn worked through the afternoon, hoeing weeds and raking them into a pile. Doiranne's face was bright red, as much from exhaustion as from the warm sun that made the borrowed wool shirt wet with her sweat. She paused and wiped her face with her sleeve. Looking down the rows of potatoes, she felt a moment of pride at seeing the rich, freshly turned soil that held no weeds. She leaned on the rake and tried to remember a time in her life when she felt proud of the work she had done.

"Doiranne, I think we've done enough for the day. The men are going to be surprised when they come to work here in the morning. I don't think we've left them a single weed. Let's walk over to my cottage, and we'll put the tools away and see if I can put together some potatoes for your stew."

Doiranne gratefully followed on shaky legs. Still humming to herself, she waved at a couple of women minding the village children on the green. Surprised at Doiranne's greeting, the women reluctantly lifted a hand in answer. "We don't leave the children alone still, Quinn?"

"No, I don't know if we ever will. After losing them as we did, we guard them more than we should, but we really can't help it. Once lost, forever shy."

Doiranne nodded as she followed Quinn to his cottage. Quinn stepped up on his porch and, with his hand on the door latch, turned to Doiranne. "Come in, Doiranne."

Doiranne shook her head. "No, I don't think I will. Another time perhaps, but for now, I am covered with dirt and garden smells, and I don't think Molly would thank me for bringing it in to the house. I'll wait here in the sun."

Quinn shrugged, but he knew Doiranne was probably right. Molly kept a strict house. She never allowed Conor's pup in for thinking of the fleas that he might drag along with him. Before long, he emerged with a cloth sack tied at the top. His wife, Molly, came to the doorway and leaned against it, scowling down at Doiranne. Doiranne turned her back and pretended not to notice. There had never been good feelings between her and Molly, and the gift of a couple of potatoes would not make it any better.

"I found some potatoes and there's a bit of dried meat you can put in your stew. I wish I had some fresh to give you, but I haven't checked my traps yet today. If I can catch an extra rabbit, I'll bring it by your cottage. I thank you for the work you did today, Doiranne. I've had no one work harder in the garden than you did today. You should be proud of yourself."

Doiranne ducked her head and muttered a 'thank you'. Taking the sack, she headed across the green toward the blacksmith's shop.

Set far back, the shop was out of the afternoon sun, and with the forge quiet, it was cool and still inside. Doiranne wandered around the forge past the workbench nearby, fingering the tools that hung from the walls, touching the surface of the worn anvil that stood next to the forge. She pulled once or twice on the bellows that hung above the forge, feeling the rush of air as she did.

"Hello, did you need something?" a gruff voice brought Doiranne out of her reverie and she turned with a guilty look on her face.

"Please pardon me. I was just looking around, but I need something, please. I have this ax and I need to chop some firewood, but it's dull." She pulled the small hatchet from her belt and held it out to the blacksmith.

Taking it in his hands, he grunted. "Looks like you haven't taken very good care of this tool."

Doiranne blushed in shame. "It's true, I have not, but if you would sharpen it for me, I promise to take better care of it. I'll leave it in the woodshed instead of on the ground."

"I usually charge for sharpening tools, you know. But from the looks of you, I'd say you might need this one for free. Let's go to the back of the shop, and I'll see if I can put an edge on this old thing."

Doiranne followed the blacksmith as he made his way to the back. There, a large grindstone with a seat and pedals stood in the dark. The man sat his bulk, substantial as it was, down on the seat, and using the pedals, began turning the grindstone. As it turned, he held the hatchet against the top of the stone at an angle. Sparks flew off of the grindstone, and Doiranne noticed a slight burning smell in the air. She watched as he turned the hatchet to the other side and repeated his actions. He would stop now and again and run his thumb up and down the blade, until at last, he grunted in satisfaction. Heaving himself off of the seat, he handed the hatchet back to Doiranne.

"I'm grateful," she said. "I noticed that you have some tools out in your shop. The ones hanging on the walls. Did you make them?"

"No, those are mostly old tools that people have cast off. I fix them up the best that I can, sharpen them, and keep them around in the chance someone needs a tool. Are you looking for something?"

Doiranne ducked her head and studied the ground at her feet as if it held the most interesting story. "I could use a hoe, but I have nothing to pay you with. If you would let me have it, once I grew a garden, I would repay you with the vegetables I grew."

The blacksmith stood silently and stared at Doiranne. *What do I need with more vegetables? I have enough as it is and more than I can eat.* He stared for a while longer while Doiranne fidgeted and scratched a hole in the dirt with her toe. "I could use some vegetables if you were to want to pay for the hoe. Let's pick out a good one for you, not too heavy, but one that will break up the dirt. We will check the balance of it and make sure it fits you."

Doiranne put the hatchet back in the belt at her waist, and picking up the sack at her feet, followed the blacksmith out to the front of his shop. He lifted a hoe from the wall and felt the balance in his hand. He nodded and held it out to Doiranne. "I thank you." Doiranne put the hoe on her shoulder and turned away.

"You're Doiranne, right? Your husband was Sean?"

"Yes. He didn't come home from the mountain with the rest of them." She said this softly, looking off into the distance. "I have to look after myself now, I think."

Once home, Doiranne gathered up her dress and apron from the weeds where they lay drying in the late sun. Wrinkled as they were, at least they were clean. She held them to her nose and breathed deeply. *It smells so good. How did I not notice that clean laundry smells so good? Like Granny's herbs smell good. Like the blacksmith shop smells good, but in a different way.* She walked to the back of her cottage and carefully placed the hatchet under the lean-to roof out of the weather. Then she leaned her new hoe in the corner next to the wood, keeping it dry.

Once in the cottage, she slipped out of the dirty trousers and wool shirt. She blushed at the thought of what the ladies in the green must have thought of her, walking around dressed like a man, dirty as she could be. *Well, there's no hope for it now. I guess they'll think what they think.* She pulled on the clean dress and tied the apron around her waist, smoothing the wrinkles from the skirt with her hands. *I'll need something to press out the wrinkles. I wonder if the blacksmith will have an iron I could heat on my hearth.*

Stirring up the coals in the fireplace, she laid a bit of the dried wood she had brought in earlier and lit the fire once again. Filling the pot with water, she sat down to open the sack from Quinn. A smile lit her face when she saw potatoes, mustard greens freshly picked, bundles of thyme and marjoram, and the packet of dried meat at the bottom. *Doiranne, you are going to feast tonight!*

Her fire crackled, and the stew hanging over the fire filled the cottage with its rich smell. Doiranne sat back and closed her eyes, a small smile on her lips. It had been a very long time since she had felt this good. Tired from a good day's work, sitting in her clean cottage, and wearing a dress that smelled like laundry soap and sunshine, there was no other place she would rather be. *Sean, I wish you could see me now. I don't think you would believe your eyes.*

Tomorrow I will dig up some weeds and see if I can get some seeds from Granny. It won't be much of a garden at first, but if I keep working at it, maybe I can grow enough to feed myself. The villagers don't need to be looking after me, though I would appreciate a bit of meat now and again. How can I get some chickens? Wouldn't a fresh egg be wonderful? Maybe I can trade something for a couple of hens. From now on, it's going to be a hand up, not a handout. I'll talk to Erik Tamen tomorrow or the next day. The Light help me, I'm not sure how, but I'm going to find my way back.

Chapter Five

A Decision

The evening breeze was still warm and the scent of roses hung in the air. Traynor finished grooming his mule and tied a nosebag of oats from his neck. Jasper gratefully stuck his nose down deep in the bag and began munching.

"Dinner's ready, Da!" Roisin finished putting bowls of thick stew on the rough plank table. She used the knife at her belt to cut hunks of bread and laid them on a plate.

"Smells good, Roi," Traynor grinned at the girl. "I have no idea where you learned to cook like this, but I thank the Light you did."

Roisin smiled back at her Traynor. "Don't you think it's time to move on? There's nothing much here for us. The folks haven't got a lot of money, and I've had to take things in trade for our goods. It's nice to have fresh meat and vegetables, but that will not help us replenish our goods for trading later." Roisin shoved a spoonful of stew into her mouth.

Traynor looked up towards the mountains. The highest peak was not visible from the village green, but he knew the direction to look. He chewed his stew silently, imagining the dark clouds swirling around the peak, always moving but never blowing away. "No, Roi, we stay right here for now. I told you there's something here that I need. We'll worry about the villagers paying us for our goods later. This is far more important."

"More important than making a living? Humph... I don't see how..."

"Enough! It is enough that I say we stay here."

Roisin looked down at her bowl of stew. Traynor reached over to pat her hand. "It's not for you to worry about, Roi. We will make a living, we always have. But there is something I need you to do for me. There are two people in the village I need you to get to know. A young girl with a long blond braid and a boy with dark hair pulled back and tied with a piece of leather. Have you seen either of them? I think you might find them together."

"The girl. I talked to her a few days ago. Her name is Matilda, but she said she is called Tilly. The boy I don't know."

"Let's see if we can bring them out. I think a fire and a little music might do the trick. You know what to do when I play. I want as many of the villagers to come out as we can coax from their stingy cottages. I need to get a sense of who is here and what they can do. The mayor is an agreeable man; I don't think he will object to a little evening fire and music."

Roisin carried the dishes to the basin near the fire while Traynor gathered more wood and brought it to the middle of the green. Piling it high, he scooped coals from their smaller fire in a shovel from his wagon. Soon, flames leaped high towards the night sky. Climbing aboard the wagon, he moved crates and barrels of goods until he found what he was looking for; an old worn, leather fiddle case. Sitting by the fire, he tuned the instrument until the bow he dragged across the strings made sounds pleasing to his ears.

The fire drew the villagers who ventured from their cottages for an evening stroll after supper. Calling out to them from his seat, Traynor bade them to come sit by his fire and listen to the music. The sounds of his fiddle echoed across the green and drew still more villagers, until they were sitting on the grass in small groups or standing under the trees, listening. One young man, made brave by the lively music, grabbed his sweetheart's hand, and soon had her swinging off her feet.

Erik Tamen, as was his usual habit, walked through the village checking on gates to see that they were shut and everything was safe. He smiled when he heard the music and smiled even more when he saw the villagers gathered in the green to listen and dance. He backtracked to his own home and called out to Guin to join him. "Let's go see what all the fuss is about," he said as he took her hand in his.

Together, they joined Quinn and Molly as they walked towards the green. Guin and Molly walked on ahead, murmuring together. Quinn asked, "Have you seen Doiranne lately, Erik?"

"Doiranne? No, I can't say that I have. What is she up to now? What fresh trouble is she causing?"

"No trouble, Erik. She asked me for a bucket this morning. Said she wanted to wash her windows. I lent her an old one I no longer use. But that's not all. Later I found her in the village garden?"

"Stealing?"

"No, weeding!"

"Weeding what?" Erik Tamen looked puzzled.

"Erik, the woman was weeding the potato rows. She worked for the better part of the afternoon, and the rows of potatoes have never looked better. Later, she walked back to my cottage with me, and I gave her some potatoes and some herbs, a little dried meat. She wouldn't come in; said she was too dirty. She had man's trousers and shirt on. Probably Sean's, I'd guess. Never thought they would fit her, though." Quinn said this last more to himself than to Erik Tamen.

"Will wonders never cease? I don't know what caused this, but I hope it continues. That woman has been a thorn in my side since the first day I met her. Always whining about something, always finding fault. Poor Sean, I wonder he wasn't happy to go off to the mountains." Erik Tamen stopped at the look Quinn gave him. "You're right, Quinn, that was not generous. He didn't deserve what happened to him, and I guess neither did Doiranne. I'll look in on her in the next day or two, I promise. Let's go listen to some music!"

Tilly joined the group and sat with Quinn and Molly. She turned her neck back and forth, searching for Conor to no avail. "Da, have you seen Conor today?"

Quinn shook his head. "Have you not been seeing him, Tilly?"

"Not so much. He keeps to himself more than he ever did if that's possible."

Molly snorted, "That boy always liked his own company better than anyone's, except maybe that mangy dog of his and you, Tilly. If he's not seeing you, then he's not seeing anyone."

"I know he thinks he bears responsibility for what happened to the children, but I've told him that isn't true. Not one villager would hold him responsible for actions taken by someone he doesn't even know." Tilly sighed and laid her head on her father's shoulder.

"Tilly, I'll talk with him if you like. But for now, let's enjoy the music and the dancing."

Tilly turned her face towards the fire. Traynor was standing now, playing his fiddle with abandonment, his long hair untied and hanging loose around his shoulders, his face held an almost dazed look on it. In the fire's light, Tilly could see a girl with dark red hair halfway down her back, twirling and stomping her feet in time to the music. She threw her head back and laughed as she danced, as if nothing else mattered but the music and the movement. Tilly frowned.

When the song ended, Traynor begged time off to rest and drink something cold. Roisin threw herself down on the ground next to Tilly. "Hello again. We seem to run into each other a lot."

Tilly's frown deepened. "I wouldn't call this 'running into each other.' I think you came over here to sit next to me. Why, I can't think."

"Oh Tilly, I'm afraid we got off on the wrong foot. I didn't mean any harm; it was an honest mistake. Can't you look past it and try to be friends with me? I'm a long way from home, and lonely as I can be. I could use a friend or two."

Tilly smiled. "Yes, I can look past it. We'll try to be friends."

Roisin rewarded her with a smile that lit up her face. "Thank you, I mean it. And do you have a friend? A boy? Not meaning anything by that, Tilly, just a boy."

Tilly looked puzzled for a moment. "You mean Conor? We've been friends since we were young. He's my best friend, always has been."

"Good, then we'll all be friends, the three of us. I'm off, but I will find you tomorrow, Tilly. My friend." Roisin left with a flip of her skirt and a toss of her long, red hair.

The young boy with long brown hair tied back with a piece of leather sat beneath a tree at the far end of the green. As he sat, he listened to the music and watched the dancing from a distance. Absentmindedly, he ran his hand down the back of the small, wiry dog next to him. He watched with curiosity as the red-haired girl made her way to Tilly's side. The girl threw back her head and laughed and Tilly frowned at her. Even from a distance he could feel the heat of that frown, having felt it a time or two himself. He smiled to himself knowing that whatever the girl was up, she wouldn't get far with her unless it was Tilly's idea.

Conor had gone back to his old habit of spending more time alone than with anyone, even his best friend, Tilly. There was a time, not so long ago, that if the villagers saw one of them, they saw the other close behind. Now, as he had done before when his parents left him to fend for himself, Conor spent most of his time alone walking in the nearby woods, setting his traps, or digging in the garden behind his cottage. He could not seem to remember how to be part of the village again, not after what he had seen in the mountain cave. He shook his head to clear the tears from his eyes at the memory of Mara screaming words that made no sense to him then or now. *Who was she? What was she? What made her leave me behind like she did?*

Conor leaned his head against the tree, feeling the rough bark. "Wolf, what do you think is the matter with me? Why can't my own parents care for me?" He laid his hand on the dog's back, feeling the wiry coat beneath his fingers. It brought him a measure of comfort just to touch Wolf. "Come on, boy. It's getting late, and the music is sounding the same. Let's call it a night, what do you say?"

Conor and Wolf were up before the sun had brought out the birds the next morning. After stirring up his fire, he heated water for tea. He poured a little leftover stew into a bowl for Wolf and sat down with bread and cheese for his morning meal. Sipping his tea, he looked through his open door to the fields beyond. His cottage lay on the outskirts of the village, chosen for its remoteness and the fact that no one else in the village wanted it. Conor was alone here, and he liked it that way.

"Wolf, I've been thinking for a while now. We should leave. I haven't talked to Tilly about it, but I don't think she can change my mind. It doesn't feel right here. It's like I don't fit here anymore if I ever did. You'll come with me, you know, so don't look so worried." Wolf raised his head from the bowl and gave his best worried impression. Conor laughed.

Wolf heard the approaching steps on the porch before Conor heard the knock at the opened door. Tilly stood in the doorway, smiling at both of them.

"Good morning. I have someone who wants to meet you, Conor." A figure with dark red hair stepped from around the corner. Wolf lifted his head and growled softly. His hackles raised, he took one soft step forward, his eyes on the girl.

"Wolf, back! Mind your manners!" Conor stood, still holding his cup of tea.

"This is Roisin, Conor. Her father, Traynor, is the peddler who has been here the last few days. She's a long way from home and could use some company."

Roisin came forward, holding out her hand. Conor took it and smiled. *What a beautiful girl. I've never seen hair like that before.* He stammered an awkward 'hello' and stood staring, not knowing what to do with his empty teacup.

"Well, for goodness' sakes, offer us some tea, Conor. Either that, or let's take Wolf for a walk. Roisin, that's Wolf, the dog with no manners."

Roisin bent down to pet Wolf, who eyed her cautiously. His growl was soft but sounded dangerous still.

"I would, Tilly, but I need to talk with you. About something important. Roisin, I'm glad to meet you, but I need to talk with Tilly, please."

Roisin looked from Conor to Tilly. She shrugged and shook her head. "I'll find you two later. I need to make Traynor his morning meal before he bellows." With one hand, she flipped her skirt on the way out the door.

"Conor, I've never known you to be rude, you or Wolf. What's gotten into you?"

"Tilly, sit down, please. I need to talk with you. I'll fix you some tea, the water's still hot."

Conor fussed over the tea, pouring the steaming water, and stirring the tea leaves until Tilly fidgeted. Handing her the cup, he sat down on the only other chair in the cottage. "How are your lessons with Granny coming, Tilly? Are you learning to travel? Is she teaching you how to help folks with her herbs and poultices?"

Tilly sighed, "I am learning a lot from Granny. I know how to feel for broken bones without hurting a person further, search out injuries on the inside of folks, and I'm quite good at bandaging wounds. I can fix a poultice nearly as good as Granny can, and my teas seem to help people with colds and coughs. What I can't do is travel, not one step from where I sit! It seems I might not have the gift that Granny has. Oh Conor, it's a terrible disappointment. I wanted to be just like her so badly. She says I'm not to worry. There might be other gifts I have that she hasn't found yet, but we've been working since we brought the children home, and there's no sign of any gift. It appears I am just ordinary."

"The last thing you are is ordinary, Tilly Mathuin! Maybe you're a healer like Ronan. Maybe that's your gift, Tilly. Not a poor gift, if you ask me."

"You are kind, Conor, but you said you had something to tell me. What is it? Have you decided to join life again and be part of the village? You have kept to yourself since we came off the mountain. I hope you think you've paid enough penance for whatever you think you have done."

"Tilly, I'm not paying penance exactly. But sheep's dip, Tilly, the people who call themselves my parents did this to the village and to you. They stole you out from under your own roof and put you in a never-ending sleep. Never ending, that is until they needed you to do their dirty work!" Conor jumped up from his chair and turned towards the wall. "If it hadn't been for Granny and Erik Tamen, you would still be in that cave, asleep forever. She had her hands on you, Tilly. That despicable woman had her hands on you. I can't just forget that. I can't just pretend it didn't happen. And yet, she's my mother. How do I reckon with that?" Conor sank back down into the chair and put his head in his hands. "You don't understand. I know I am not responsible for what she did, but she did it. And she's — my mother. The woman who gave birth to me. How do I make any sense out of that, Tilly? Just tell me, please."

Tilly knelt in front of Conor and took both his hands from his face. "I don't know how this feels, Conor. I can't know, but what I know is that you are my friend, and you're hurting, and I want to help. How can I?"

Conor sat up straight and took her hands firmly in his. "I want to go away for a while, Tilly, and find out who I am, your friend or the son of a monster. Seeing the children every day, the same children she stole and feeling responsible, is tearing out my heart. There is no way for me to make amends, but maybe, just maybe, I can find some answers to who I am or, more important, what I am."

Tears slipped down Tilly's face, and she pulled her hands away from Conor to wipe them. "Where will you go? When will you come back?"

"I want to go to the Mountain Folk and spend some time with Cormac. Erik Tamen has tried to talk to me. Light, even your father has tried. I think I need to spend some time with Cormac. He sees things differently than most of us, and he might help me."

Tilly sat back on the floor and hugged her knees to her chest. Resting her chin on her knees, she looked thoughtfully at Conor. "I don't want you to go, Conor, you know that. I want things to be as they were, us being friends forever telling each other everything, but what I want and what I have are two different things right now. If this will get me what I want and what you need, then I think you should go to the Mountain Folk. If there is anyone who can help you see things clearly, it just might be Cormac. You have my blessing if that's what you are asking."

Conor bent his head and rested it atop Tilly's. "Yes, that's what I was asking."

Chapter Six

A Discovery

Tilly lifted her head and smiled at Conor. "When will you leave?"

"Today. Now, I guess. I didn't want to go without talking it over with you. But you have been the same generous friend you've always been, Tilly. I knew you would. There's no reason to stay any longer."

"Will you stop and see Granny Matilda before you go?"

"Yes. I need to talk with her. She knows more about Mara and Jebez than anyone else. I'm not sure why I need to know, but I do."

"Travel safe, Concobhar." Tilly gave him one last quick squeeze before she left. She tried her best to flip her skirt as she walked out, but it caught between her legs, and she stumbled through the doorway. Conor could hear her cursing all the way down his steps. He smiled and rubbed Wolf's head. "Let's pack up, boy."

Conor and Wolf stopped outside Granny's gate and called to her from the safety of the road. Even Conor would have gotten the rough side of Granny's tongue if he had come in her yard uninvited.

At her invitation, they climbed the steps to her wide front porch. "I've been waiting for you two," she said with a smile. "You took your own time packing, didn't you?"

"How did you know? Did Tilly come by? Or is this another of your foretelling you are so good at doing?""

"Yes, I did have a notion you were leaving. I know you're going back to the Mountain Folk to sit with Cormac for a while. You need some answers, and you think he might have them. Even if he doesn't, Conor, spending some time with

Cormac will be good for you. Let's have some tea before you go. And I want to look in that pack of yours and see if I need to add anything; herbs or some such."

Conor and Wolf followed Granny into her small cottage. Small as it was, it was neat and comfortable. Her herbs were still hanging from the rafters, making his nose tingle and twitch. Her hearth had a good fire going, despite the warmth of the day. "I banked up the fire so we could have tea. It's a good thing you got here when you did, or this little house would have been so hot I would have to fan myself."

Granny set out cups and shook tea into the bottom of them before lifting the steaming kettle off the hearth. Just as she lifted it, she cried out, and the kettle slipped from her hands. It crashed towards the floor, but in a blink of the eye, it stopped its downward movement and hovered for a few seconds before gently coming to a rest. "Granny, are you hurt? Did you burn yourself?" Conor leaped from the chair to grab her hands.

Granny turned her hands front and back. "No, I'm not hurt. How long have you been doing that?"

"Doing what? I don't know what you're talking about."

"Conor, you stopped that kettle before it hit the floor. You stopped it, and then you let it down as gently as if it were a newborn lamb. All along I thought it would be Tilly, but it isn't, it's you. You who have the gift. How long have you known?"

Conor lowered himself into the chair and stared into the fire. "A while now. It started when we came back from the mountain. I would reach for something and before I touched it, it would be there—in my hand. At first it just happened; but rarely. Then I started trying to make it happen. At first it was just fun, but soon it scared me. What if I'm like them? What if this comes from them?" The last Conor cried out and looked at Granny with eyes wide.

"Oh Concobhar, I'm not sure how it is you have the gift. My mother before me does not, and Tilly might not. I don't know where it comes from, Conor, but I know it is a gift. A gift that can benefit others. Mara used the gift to her benefit and hers alone. We all make choices, Conor. What we do with our talents and our gifts is up to us. We can use them to benefit others or we can use them to grasp as much as we can and hold tight in the fear that someone will take it away, but you are not like that, Conor. You have loved Tilly since the moment you two met. Your heart is so big and so full of love that you couldn't be like Mara, even if you tried. Can you travel as well?"

"I haven't tried yet, but I think I can. I don't know what makes me say that, but sometimes I feel as if I am in two places at the same time. And I can see both of them clearly. I can't control it, but I think I could learn."

Granny handed Conor a cup of tea. "Let's sit out on the porch. I like to look at the mountain when I need to think."

They settled into her rocking chairs and sipped their tea. Conor watched the black clouds swirling around the highest peak of the mountain. Their movement was constant, as if they strained to break free and race across the sky, far from the mountain that seemed to tether them to it.

"You're going to spend some time with Cormac? You think he can help you sift through all of this?"

"Yes, I hope he can. My head feels like it's going to burst some days, I think about this so much. But first, I want you to tell me what you know about Mara and Jebez. I understand now why you didn't want me to know, but you had to think I was going to find out some day. How did you think you could keep it from me, Granny?"

"Oh Conor, forgive an old woman. I couldn't think past the moment. The moment of getting Tilly and the other children out and you far away from Mara and Jebez. I didn't have a plan for the future, just for the moment. I will tell you what I know." She stopped and rocked softly, sipping her tea, and gazing towards the mountain.

Granny spoke pensively, "They came to the village years ago, before you were born, even. We thought they were gypsies; they traveled like them. A cart, a small donkey, as I recall. They put up a tent next to Nedra's cottage. Nedra was a widow with one small boy. You know him, Conor, Sean. We didn't think too much about it, but they stayed far longer than any of us thought they would. The next thing we knew, the tent was down, but they were still here. Somehow, they talked Nedra into letting them in to her cottage. We should have known better, but we were busy and they did nothing that raised an alarm. What we didn't know was what was going on inside the cottage." Granny paused and stared at the mountain until Conor thought she had drifted off to sleep.

"What was going on?"

"I can't be sure exactly, although I have my suspicions. I think Mara took control of Nedra somehow. Sean mentioned that his mother was drinking a lot of very dark tea. There are teas that will rob you of your ambitions, keep you in a stupor. Conor, I'm uncertain what gifts Mara has. If she has the ability to keep our children in a deep sleep, she could have done almost anything to Nedra. All I know is that over time, we saw less and less of both Nedra and Sean. Until one day, Sean told us that his mother had died. I examined her, but there was nothing for me to see, just a woman old before her time. I spoke with Erik Tamen, but with no proof, he had nothing to go on."

Conor kept his eyes on the mountain as he listened to Granny. "When did I come into the story?"

"Soon after Nedra died, you were born. I was not called to the birthing, which I thought was strange, but it was clear Mara did not trust or like me. The two of them stayed on in Nedra's house. Sean, by this time, was ready to marry. He found Doiranne, and I believe he thought he should have his mother's cottage, but Mara and Jebez refused to budge, and it wasn't like Sean to argue. It seems they took all the fight out of that young man."

"When did they leave our village?"

"You were almost six years old when they left. The funny thing is, no one knew they were gone for the longest time. I think there must have been food left in the cottage, and you survived on your own. By this time, the cottage was falling down around you. Jebez never was much for work. The roof leaked, windows were cracked, and even broken in some places, and the chimney was so stopped up with birds' nests, you couldn't have built a fire in the fireplace if you wanted to." Granny shook her head.

"One or two of the villagers tried to take you in but you kept running away, back to that old rundown cottage. Why, Erik Tamen and Guin tried more than all of them. I think Guin would have liked you to take the place of her Matthew. Finally, Erik Tamen told them to leave you alone. The villagers dropped off food and clothing, kept an eye on you, but other than that, we did as he said. You know the rest. You stayed in that old shack until you found your own cottage at the far end of the village." Granny chuckled, "To our amusement, you hauled wood from the old place to lay your porch. We saw you drag chairs and tables down the road, and we watched you clean up the weeds and plant a garden. Conor, you couldn't have been much more than eight years old, yet you were taking care of yourself. After a while, we stopped dropping off food, you left it out on your porch so long. You raised yourself, and then you met Tilly. I was worried about you until then. She didn't look after you so much as be a friend, but you had someone in your life, and she let me know you were all right. And then we became friends."

"Yes, we did, Granny. Is there anything else you can tell me? What sort of powers do Mara and Jebez have? What can they do besides call up Ceobhran?"

"Conor, I don't call them powers, I call them gifts. But I see what you mean. It's not much of a gift the way Mara wields it. As far as I know, Mara is the only one with any gift. Jebez does her bidding and I'm not sure how willing he is. Mara has the gift of sight. She knew I was coming before I ever found the cave. I don't know if she can travel, but I suspect not. I don't know what else she can do besides call up that creature she controls."

Conor sighed and put his teacup on the porch. He stood up and leaned over to kiss Granny on the top of her head. "Yes, we are friends, Granny Matilda. And I think we will become much more than that. When I come back, maybe you will teach me to travel."

Conor stepped off Granny's porch and whistled up Wolf. Together they slipped through her gate and headed out of the village toward the mountains.

Chapter Seven

BETRAYAL

Traynor strode through the village, raising his hand in greeting to the villagers, stopping now and again to admire a garden or pass the time with one of the men. He reached into his pocket and brought out a handful of sweets to give to the children he met along the way. When he arrived at Erik Tamen's house, he climbed the steps to the great wide porch and knocked on the heavy oak door.

Erik Tamen's wife, Guin, answered his knock. A woman of medium height, her face boasted bright pink cheeks and startling blue eyes that crinkled at the corners with laughter. She smiled as soon as she saw the peddler standing on her doorstep, and he bowed deeply in greeting. "My dear woman, please allow me to introduce myself. I am Traynor, a traveling peddler. Your husband has graciously invited me to camp in the green for a few days. In the back of my wagon, I have a fine collection of fabrics and ribbon I have yet to unpack. If you would do me the honor of coming by to view them, I would make you an excellent offer on whatever you choose."

Guin sighed and put her hand on her breast. "I have seen you in the green, sir, and enjoyed your fiddle music. New fabric and ribbons, you say? I have not seen the like of that for some time now, but coin is hard to come by here at the Edge of the Valley, and I have none to pay you. So, thank you, but no thank you." And she reached to close the door.

Traynor stopped the door with his hand and smiled. "Perhaps you don't have coin, but you have quite the herb garden, almost the best I've seen in town. If you would pick and dry bundles of, say, thyme, some rosemary, sage, and tarragon, I could sell them down the road and recoup my losses for the fabric. I could use some garlic and onions too if you grow them. What do you say to a little trade?"

"I would say that would be more than generous. I hardly think herbs make a good trade for fabric, but if that pleases you, it pleases me as well."

"Good, then it's a bargain. Come by this evening and I will lay out the things I have."

Whistling a tune, Traynor stepped off Guin's porch and turned toward the green. He stopped at the tavern, and ducking his head, went through the low doorway. He stood for a moment, giving his eyes time to adjust to the gloom. A single shaft of sunlight came in through a small, dirty window set nearly to the ceiling that did little to cut through the gloom. Dust motes danced in the weak light stirred up by the breeze from the open door. Across from the door was a crude bar made of unfinished wood, with rickety stools lined up in front of it. Another long bar behind that one held bottles and glasses of different shapes and sizes, the bottles nearly empty and the glasses in need of a good dusting. Nearby, a small cask, tapped, sat on a table. He walked over to it and bent low to smell its contents.

"Hello, can I help you?" The tavern owner came from the back kitchen to stand behind the bar. A tall man, he was broad shouldered with an enormous head that looked as if it had been placed directly on his shoulders with no benefit of a neck to hold it up. His apron, surely white at one time, was smeared with so many stains, it was difficult to imagine it ever being clean. He used the last remaining clean spot on it to wipe his hands, dropping it when he finished the task. For all of that, his smile was welcoming, and the small frown between his eyes only showed his curiosity at finding a visitor in the middle of the afternoon.

"I hope I can help you, friend. I am Traynor, the peddler, and I am camped on the green for a few days. The villagers tell me you brew beer now and again. I was hoping for a tall glass with a bit of foam on top."

The tavern owner looked Traynor over carefully. "Aye, I brew beer when I can, but only when I have the makings. Hops have been scarce these days, so there is no beer. Now ale, I can make. It don't take hops, you know, just some yeast. And I have some apple brandy there in the barrel if it pleases you."

"No beer, you say. Beer was the one thing I had my heart set on. I'll tell you what, friend. You need hops to brew beer, and it happens that I have hops in my wagon. I'd be happy to trade with you."

"What would you want?" Now the tavern owner squinted suspiciously at Traynor.

"How about this—I give you the hops and you give me a fine glass of your apple brandy whenever I stop in? It wouldn't be every night, but now and again, if there's a chill in the night air, apple brandy would hit the spot."

"That is as good a deal as I've ever heard. How much hops do you have?"

"A barrel, sir. A whole barrel full."

The tavern owner's eyes bulged, and a smile lit his face. Wordlessly, he held out his hand and Traynor shook it with a small smile.

Traynor left the tavern, whistling his tune. Crossing the green, he stepped into the blacksmith's forge. The heavy smell of smoke and hot metal made his nose twitch and his eyes water. He watched as the giant man stood before his forge and beat on hot metal to form a scythe, raising his hammer over and over again. He laid the glowing metal against the anvil and beat it until it was nearly flat on one side. Plunging it into the bucket of water at his feet, he watched as the metal hissed and steam rose to surround his head. He looked up and nodded to Traynor. "I can stop while the metal cools. What can I do for you?"

Traynor leaned against the doorway and crossed his arms across his chest. He was silent for just a moment. "I have a mule who needs new shoes. Can you work on him for me?"

The blacksmith looked embarrassed. "I don't do much farrier work, there's not much call for it. And even if there was, I haven't had horseshoes in my shop for a long time. I'm sorry, but I can't help you." He bent down to pull the metal out of the bucket of water with his tongs.

"Oh, I have the shoes myself. In fact, I have buckets of them. I'd be happy to trade one bucket of horseshoes if you would shape them and fix them on old Jasper."

"You have horseshoes? Then why don't you just put them on yourself?" The smith frowned in his direction as he plunged the length of metal into the glowing coals once more.

"I don't have the talent for shaping shoes. It would take your forge and anvil to do the job. I'd trade you all the shoes in one bucket for the job done."

The blacksmith stopped pumping the bellows and stared at Traynor for a few minutes. Horseshoes would be a great thing for a blacksmith to have. He could work on tools all day long, but shoeing horses, now that's what blacksmiths did. "Your horseshoes for new shoes on... What did you say his name was?"

"Jasper."

"We have a bargain. You bring the shoes and Jasper, and I'll get him fixed up."

Traynor turned to leave, whistling as he did. When he returned to his camp on the green, Roisin was working in the makeshift kitchen, a pile of potatoes, carrots, and parsnips on the board beside her. Using her belt knife, she was scraping the skins from the carrots and chopping the vegetables into small chunks. Traynor sat down on a stump and, crossing his leg over the other, pulled a pipe and a pouch of tobacco from his pocket.

"You've been gone a while." Roisin looked at him from beneath her lashes.

"Yes, I have been meeting with all manner of the villagers. A most prosperous venture, I'd say. The mayor's wife will be by later to pick out some fabric and ribbons, and the tavern owner will take that barrel of hops off my hands in exchange for some apple brandy on a cold evening. Oh, and the blacksmith will shoe Jasper for that bucket of old horseshoes I have in the back of the wagon. Yes, not a bad afternoon's work."

"And what, pray tell, did you take for the fabric? You know that's hard to come by these days. "

"Bundles of dried herbs."

"Traynor, I have enough dried herbs to last me the rest of my life. What kind of trade is that?"

"The kind, my dear, that gives more goodwill than goods. Something I need right now to get what I came for. Speaking of that, have you seen the girl and the boy lately?"

"I saw Tilly this morning. She was on her way to Granny's. We didn't talk long, just long enough for her to tell me that Conor has left."

Traynor was quiet for a moment. He set his pipe down on the stump and crossed the green to stand next to Roisin. "What do you mean, he's left? When? Where did he go?" This he said in a quiet voice.

"He's gone to the mountains, I think. There are folks who live up there, Mountain Folk, they call them. He has gone to stay with them for a bit." Roisin continued to cut potatoes into small bits, but her hands were shaking now.

Traynor took the knife from her hand and flung it across the green. He gripped her arm with fingers like iron. "I told you I needed you to get close to them. Both of them!"

"You're hurting my arm. Stop!" Roisin tried to pull away from him, but he gripped her arm harder still and slapped her across the face with his other hand.

Reeling, she stepped back as far as he would allow her to go. "Stop, please! He left before I even knew he was going. It's not my fault!"

Traynor turned her and held her by both shoulders. Shaking her until her hair flew in masses of red curls, he yelled through gritted teeth, "You will find out exactly when he left. And you will not leave that girl's side until I tell you, do you understand?"

"I understand, I understand." She gasped. Traynor released her and stepped back. "I don't know why you make me lose my temper with you, girl. If you would do as I say, things would be so much easier for you. Now, dry your eyes and finish dinner. I'm starving after the hard day's work I've done."

Roisin picked up the corner of her apron to scrub away her tears, and as she did, she saw a figure halfway across the green, standing stock still, watching the scene unfold. She blinked away the tears and looked again, but the figure was gone.

Doiranne walked back across the green to her small cottage, thinking of the scene she had witnessed. It was clear Traynor did not see her across the green, watching. He would not thank her for witnessing his cruelty to Roisin. *I had hoped he had a rake or a small shovel that I could trade for. Never mind. I don't think he's the sort I want to trade with. He certainly has everyone in this village fooled.*

Doiranne lifted the latch on her gate and stopped to view the space in front of her cottage. There was still no wide porch to sit on, but she had hammered old nails she found into the steps and straightened them out a bit. They were sturdier, and she was proud of that. She finished clearing the yard of weeds and now rows of tiny, green sprouts grew out of the clean dirt. Doiranne stood for a moment and admired the straight rows; beans, peas, and squash plants already up and growing like weeds. The herbs were behind, but she thought a little extra water might help them catch up. She grabbed the bucket that Quinn had given her weeks ago and started towards the pump behind the cottage. As she did, she heard a voice.

"Doiranne? It is Doiranne, right?"

She turned to see the hefty man at her gate, a leather apron tied around his enormous girth, sleeves rolled up to expose muscled arms, only slightly dirty. "Yes. I am Doiranne. You're the blacksmith?"

"I am. I came by to see how the hoe was working for you, but I don't think I even need to ask. You have worked some wonders here, Doiranne, by the Light, you have!"

Doiranne ducked her head and turned to look at her garden. "It won't be long before I can repay the hoe with some vegetables and herbs. I'm sorry you have to wait."

"That's not why I'm here. When you can, I know you will pay. I came by to see if you needed a shovel or maybe a rake. A farmer gave me a couple in trade the other day. The shovel has some nicks out of its blade, but I put a new handle on it, so it ought to last for a while. The rake is missing a couple of teeth, but it will still gather up the bigger weeds and sticks. If you can use them, I will bring them by after a while."

Doiranne looked thoughtfully at the blacksmith. "What is your name?"

The blacksmith looked at the sky. "I guess you must think I'm pretty backward, not even saying my name. I don't know where my head is. My name is Tomas, Tomas Givvens. I am pleased to meet you, Doiranne."

"Pleased to meet you. And yes, a shovel and a rake would be a fine thing to have. I could get so much more done, maybe even plant a tree. Don't you think a tree beside the cottage would be nice? And someday, I'm going to build a regular porch, a wide one. Why I think I could..." Doiranne stopped and looked at the ground, red rising from her neck to the top of her head.

Tomas smiled. "I think a tree would be grand, and every cottage needs a good porch. I tell you what. When I get back to my shop, I'll look behind the smithy. There are stacks of old timbers there. Maybe I can find enough to help you with that porch. I have a man bringing a mule to shoe so I better get back to my forge, Doiranne. Will I see you later around the fire? They have one nearly every night now on the green. I'd be glad if you'd let me walk you over after evening meal."

"No, I don't think I will go tonight. I have chores yet to do. Thank you, Tomas." Doiranne picked up her bucket and walked towards the back of her cottage.

Quinn was waiting by her gate when she returned, lugging her bucket, sloshing water over the top. "Let me help you with that, Doiranne."

"No, but thank you, Quinn. I can do this. I have many a bucket of water to haul before my evening meal."

"Doiranne, you have worked the Light's own miracle here. Where there were weeds, you have sprouts poking their heads out of dirt in rows so neat, I don't think I've seen better. And it looks to me like you might have a suiter, Doiranne." Quinn smiled as he said this, raising his eyebrows.

"A suiter? Who? The blacksmith?" Doiranne sputtered. "I don't know what you're talking about, Quinn Mathuin. The blacksmith and I have business. I'm buying my tools from him. He lets me pay him in garden goods and on time."

She dumped her bucket of water at the top of a row and stomped off, mumbling to herself as she went.

Quinn laughed. *You think what you think, Doiranne, but I have never seen Tomas Givvens walk down the road to ask someone about rakes and shovels before. And I've surely never heard him ask to sit by the fire with anyone. Wouldn't that be the thing, Doiranne with a suiter?*

The villagers drifted from their cottages towards the green after evening meal, a habit they had developed in the last weeks. The fire and the music from the peddler's fiddle drew them like moths to the light. Erik Tamen and Guin greeted folks as they made their way to a bench close to the fire.

Roisin craned her neck, looking for Tilly and was rewarded with the sight of her and Granny Matilda walking arm in arm towards the fire, their heads together talking quietly to one another. She stood and waved to Tilly, who looked puzzled, but lifted her hand in return. "Come sit by the fire with me. I have a place for you." She swept her skirt aside to show the space she had saved.

"Thank you, my dear. Have I met you?"

"I am Roisin. I travel with the peddler, Granny. May I call you Granny? I don't have one of my own. I would like to be friends with Tilly, but she's hard to get to know. Can you help me?"

Granny chuckled. "Forthright, aren't you? My dear, Tilly is her own person. She will like you or she won't and nothing I could say will change that. Slow down, get to know her, and it might just work out. And yes, you may call me Granny, dear. Everyone does."

Tilly rolled her eyes and pretended that she was anywhere but there.

Traynor took up the fiddle, and his music swelled and filled the air, first with notes that flew around the green, inviting everyone to join him and then becoming softer, more melancholy. The villagers leaned against one another or lolled on blankets on the ground. Voices hushed and mothers rocked babies to the sounds of the fiddle. Husbands draped their arms over wives, and wives leaned against their husbands' shoulders, closing their eyes, and swaying slightly to the music.

Roisin spoke up, "Tilly, I was looking for Conor, but one of the villager said they saw him leaving. I didn't get a chance to get to know him. When did he go?"

"The morning after you met him, Roisin. You remember he said he needed to talk with me about something. That was the something. He went back to the Mountain Folk; a friend of his is there in the village, someone Conor trusts.."

"Will he be gone long?"

Tilly looked quizzically at Roisin. "I do not know. Why do you ask? What does it matter to you how long he's gone?"

Roisin shook her head. "I just thought it would be so nice to spend time with both of you. I have no brothers or sisters, or cousins that I know of, at least. Nothing special, just that."

"I can tell you, that might not happen, my dear." Granny spoke up, looking at Roisin out of the corner of her eye. "Conor is not one to spend time with many people. He keeps to himself more than he keeps company with our villagers. Tilly is the only one I've known him to want to be around. And Cormac, from the Mountain Folk. He gets along well with Cormac. Now, let's listen to the music, shall we?"

Roisin nodded and sat back. Granny reached out a finger and lightly stroked the bruise on her forearm. "If you need some liniment for that bruise, come by my cottage and I will mix some up for you. That is a terrible bruise, my dear."

Roisin stared straight ahead and did not acknowledge her offer.

Doiranne finished her evening meal and washed and dried her dishes. She liked the look of the dishes stacked neatly on her shelves. Reaching up to the top shelf, she brought down an old, worn tobacco pouch. She fingered it thoughtfully and sighed. *Had I ever loved Sean? I must have loved him enough to marry him. Oh Light, the many arguments we had; the fights about the broken-down cottage he built, the lack of fine dresses, and curtains at the windows. I grumbled constantly about the poor food we ate. But mostly, it was the lack of respect he received from the villagers that bothered me. I was never proud of him. A wife should be proud of her husband. Am I proud of him now that he risked his life to save Granny and Conor? Yes, I am proud of his memory, but do I love him? Probably not, not then and maybe not now. But I should be sure of that. I shouldn't just wonder. How can I be sure if he is in that cave in the mountain and I am here?*

She placed the tobacco pouch back on the shelf and, picking up a shawl, opened her front door. The stars were strewn across the sky like fireflies racing after each other, blinking and shining. She stepped down and walked across to her gate. She hesitated, her hand on the latch. *Should I go sit by the fire? What will the villagers say if I do? I haven't talked to many of them, only Quinn and now Tomas. Wouldn't be nice to just sit quietly and be part of the village? I've never felt like I was.*

She straightened her shoulders and reached up to pat her hair. It was clean, brushed, and tied back with a small piece of ribbon she had found. She looked down at her dress. It was worn but clean, with no stains. She smiled to herself. I don't look good, but I don't look that bad. She raised her head, straightened her shoulders and walked toward the green.

The fire was dying down to embers by the time Doiranne arrived. Most of the villagers had picked up their sleeping children and were carrying them home. One or two of them smiled at her as she walked past. She ducked her head but smiled to herself. *I need to smile and answer them! No more ducking my head every time someone looks at me.*

"Doiranne! Over here!" Tomas Givvens stood up and waved to her. "I thought you weren't coming out tonight. You had chores to do."

"I finished them early and thought I should come and see the fire, but I see I'm too late. It's nearly out. And the music? Has he stopped playing?"

"I'm afraid so. The peddler seemed to have spotted someone he knew in the crowd. He put his fiddle away and said he needed to go. By the Light, he was acting strange, but I think he might not have all of his turnips in one basket. He offered me a bucket of horseshoes if I would shoe his old mule for him. And I heard he offered Ayden over at the tavern a whole barrel of hops for a drink of apple brandy now and then. And we all know his apple brandy tastes like it would take paint off the side of your barn if you let it set on there too long. I'm not sure he's a very good peddler." Tomas laughed a big, deep laugh that sounded like it came from the bottom of a well.

Doiranne smiled at him. "Well then, I think I will walk on back home. The work in the garden has me tired out. Good night, Tomas."

"You won't let me walk you home, Doiranne?"

"Another time, Tomas. I have some thinking to do tonight. Another time, please."

Tomas stood and watched thoughtfully as Doiranne walked off. She crossed the green and stood for a moment looking at the blacksmith shop. It was sturdy and well-built, with stout timbers and a shingled roof, the pieces laid out in a perfect pattern. No thatch for this roof, so close to the forge fires. Tomas had hewn the shingles by hand and nailed them himself in neat rows, each one overlapping the next to keep out the rain. *He is a hardworking man. He builds things to last a lifetime.*

She crossed the green and headed toward her cottage. Just as she did, a dark figure flitted across the corner of the green in the moonlight and disappeared behind the tavern. She stood for a moment, tilting her head to one side. Backing up slowly so that she stood beneath the low-hanging branches of a fir tree, she waited. Sure enough, a second figure followed the first, ducking behind the tavern. She stepped slowly out from under the tree and, being careful not to make a sound, followed the two shapes.

Breathing slowly, she stopped at the corner of the building and pressed against the rock wall. Here, she could hear voices but could see nothing from her position.

"I told you not to let any of these people see you, Liam! What makes you think you can disobey me?"

"Traynor, I wouldn't have come if I didn't think it was important. I've been combing the mountains looking for Mara and Jebez, and I've found them! Both of them, and with them, we can get the boy, Concobhar, if he is the one you need. Mara is under Ceobhran's hold and Jebez is tending her. It seemed best not to wake her. Better to wait for you, I thought, but Traynor, we could use them to bring the boy to us. I thought you would want to know."

Traynor regarded the man he called Liam, thoughtfully. The moon was out and there was enough light for him to see the anxious look on the man's face. He leaned against the tavern wall and kept him waiting.

Liam spoke again. "Traynor? Didn't you want to know?"

"Yes, this is good news, but you still disobeyed me by coming to the village. You could have sent a message. I have creatures at my disposal, and you know that. You should not have come, Liam."

"I'm sorry, Traynor, it won't happen again. Next time, I will send a messenger." Liam wiped his forehead with his sleeve as he stepped back. "Do you know which one you need yet? The girl or Concobhar?"

"I haven't had enough time to judge them. Roisin was supposed to keep them in sight, but she failed me. She let Concobhar leave with no effort to stop him. I have been close enough to the girl, Tilly, but I feel nothing that interests me. I think she has some power, but it is as weak as water right now. Her grandmother is very gifted, powerful. I can feel her power from across the green. It has been a very long time since I've felt anyone that strong." Traynor spoke softly, with a faraway sound to his voice.

"There is a little talk in the village, not much, but enough for me to know the old woman has the gift of travel and the gift of sight. I suspect she has a lot more, but she keeps it to herself. Now her granddaughter, I have stood as close to her as I dare, and I can't feel much. She has something, but it is weak and undeveloped. She goes into Granny's cottage almost every day, and I wonder if the old woman isn't trying to teach her. If she is, it isn't working, not yet anyway. Now the boy, Conor, they call him. I haven't gotten close to him, but there is another person in this village that pulls me with a power so strong I can feel it in my sleep. It can only be him. I have every Light forsaken villager around my fire at night, and there is not another glimmer of power except for that old woman. I thought maybe she was so strong she was blocking everyone, but the times she didn't come, I still feel nothing. Concobhar won't come to my fire. He waits behind the trees and watches. He thinks I don't know, but I can feel him. I know it has to be him!" Traynor looked off in the distance and his voice grew softer. "Go back to the mountain, Liam. Stay there until I come. Do not let Mara and Jebez out of your sight. Do not lose them, but do not let them know you are there. Stay back from them. Do you have a place to keep out of sight?"

"Yes lord, there is a long tunnel, large enough for me to walk through. It opens up to so many chambers, I have lost count. I need some supplies though, Traynor. I've been living off what I brought with me, but there's nothing left. That's another reason I came down. You know I'm not much of a hunter. If I am to stay in that cave, I need food from you."

"I'll see that you get it, enough to keep you for a few days. Then, if I haven't come, I will leave you bundles of food on the trail I showed you earlier. Do you remember?"

"Yes, it's the same one I came down."

"Good. Go now and don't let me see you in this village again, or it will cost you. Do you understand, Liam?"

"I do. I do."

Doiranne melted back into the night before the men came around the corner of the tavern. Just in time, she slipped beneath the low-hanging branches of the fir tree once again. She watched as Liam left first and Traynor came around the corner. He stopped and stood perfectly still, as though listening for something. He took a deep breath and appeared to hold it. Cocking his head, he stared at the fir tree and took one step in that direction. Doiranne squeezed her eyes shut and held her breath.

"Traynor, are you there?" Roisin came into view, calling as she did.

"I'm here, Roi. Just out for some night air. No need to worry yourself." He flung his arm over her shoulder and they started across the green. Just once, he turned and looked at the fir tree before he went back to his camp with Roisin.

Doiranne let her breath out so slowly, it didn't make a sound. She moved one booted foot forward and then the other, peering out from behind the branches. Without another thought, she pushed the branches aside and ran as fast as she could to the warmth and safety of her cottage.

Chapter Eight

A Journey

Conor put his back against the rock warmed by the sun, stretching his legs out in front of him. Leaning his head back, he lifted his face to the sun as his hand absently stroked Wolf's warm fur. He opened his eyes when he felt a nudge against his leg. Cormac was standing over him, having come so quietly that Conor never knew he was there. Squinting up at him, he smiled and took the cup of tea Cormac offered. Awkwardly balancing the cup, and being careful not to step on Wolf, he rose from the ground, and took a seat next to Cormac on the bench the man had carved years before. Worn smooth now from a combination of hand planing and scores of people taking their ease on them, the wood felt almost soft to the touch.

"Are you planning on telling me what you're doing here, Conor, or am I to guess that this is just a social call to make sure that I am well and happy? If so, let me assure you I am. We will wed, Ronan and I, at next winter's end. I never thought it would happen to me." Cormac said the last softly with a shake of his head.

Conor reached over and slapped Cormac on the back. "That is wonderful news, Cormac. You finally got the nerve to ask her, did you? I am happy for you both. There are not two people better suited unless it's Aelf and Shaen. Tilly and Granny will be glad to hear about it unless Granny already knows. That old woman knows things about us before we know them ourselves, I think."

"You might be right, Conor. Granny schools Ronan now in her arts; the art of healing, the making of poultices and medicines from herbs, and even traveling.

I'm afraid for Ronan to learn too much from Granny; I'll never be able to keep a secret from her!" Cormac laughed as he said this, but he shook his head ruefully. "Still, you are doing a good job of not answering me, Conor. What brings you back to the Mountain Folk village and to my door?"

Conor looked off toward the highest mountain peak. The ominous, dark clouds still swirled endlessly in a circle around the peak, moving constantly but never blowing away, blocking any sunlight from illuminating the highest point. He frowned as he watched the clouds. "I'm not sure what I'm doing, Cormac. When we brought the children back home, I thought everything would go back to the way it was. I would live in my cottage, spend time with Tilly and Granny, explore the forests and mountains with Wolf, and grow my garden. But the thing is, everything feels like it's for nothing. I remember somebody once saying that it felt as though the food he tasted were like ashes in his mouth. That's the way I feel, Cormac, like everything is just ashes. I can't seem to find joy in anything, not even Tilly's company." Conor drank the last of his tea and sat still with the cup dangling from his finger. Tears gathered in his eyes and he brushed them away with a sleeve.

"Ah, Conor. I can guess it is one of two things you feel: guilt for what Mara and Jebez did to your village or perhaps you are wondering how you could have come from such people. Let us not call them your parents. They lost the privilege years ago when they left you to fend for yourself. But that doesn't mean that they aren't and you must have questions that need answers. Have you spoken to Granny about them?"

"I did. She told me the story of how they came to the village, how they killed Sean's mother, and stole his cottage. How they left in the middle of the night, leaving me behind. Cormac, what manner of people would leave a small child alone like that? What would make them do that? Was I such a terrible child? Was I evil?" Conor held his head in his hands as he spoke.

"No! I cannot believe that you had anything to do with their choices, Conor. Look what they did. They are not good, kind people, they are monsters. But you need to know, if they are monsters, are you one as well? Is that what you need?"

"It seems I have a gift, Cormac. I don't know if I can travel like Granny, but I have some gifts. These gifts could only have come from Mara or Jebez, and I want nothing that comes from them, but how do I get rid of it? Granny thinks we should work together, and part of me knows she's right, but I'm afraid to find out what I can do. There is so much that I'm afraid of right now, Cormac. I need answers, and the only place I know to get them is that mountain and that Light forsaken cave. And I fear what I will find there."

Cormac looked off into the distance without answering. *How do you tell someone that the things he is looking for are not worth finding? How do you say that the people he thinks have answers have none, at least not for him?* Cormac blew out a long breath and turned to Conor. "For the life of me, I cannot think what it would be like to have the thoughts and feelings that you have. The Light blessed me with wonderful parents and a great brother. I grew up happy, knowing exactly what I wanted in my life. So, I can't think what it would be like to be you. But Conor, you have the things that I have, just in a unique form. You have Tilly who loves you like mad, you have Granny, a better friend you'll never find, and you have us, the Mountain Folk. I've seen the admiration that Erik Tamen has for you. And you have Wolf. What if the things you are looking for don't exist? What if that man and woman have nothing to tell you, nothing to offer you? Will you put yourself in harm's way to go chasing things that might not be? If you are asking my opinion, and you can tell me you are not, but if you are, then my advice is to stay here, go back to your village, go for a long walk across this valley, climb as many mountains as you can, and see as many towns and villages as you need to see, but do not go to that cave in the mountain. Do not seek answers from those people, Conor. Find the answers within yourself. You have them, I know you do. You know who you are and what you can do. If your gifts scare you, then sit with Granny or Ronan, and they can help you learn how to control them so that they need not frighten you. That is all I have to say on the matter." With that, Cormac reached out gently to take the cup from Conor's hand and walk back into his cave.

As Conor watched him walk away, tears gathered in his eyes, and he brushed them away with the sleeve of his shirt. "Wolf, maybe that's what we need, a nice long walk, a good climb in the mountains." He stood and stretched his back, considering the mountaintop the whole time.

The warm, afternoon sun felt good on Conor's back as he climbed the mountain. Halfway up the steep slope, he stopped and stood for a moment, looking down into the valley. *Will I see the village again? And Tilly? Will I ever see her again? I wonder if she can understand why I have to do this thing. Why I have to look Mara in the eyes and ask her why she left me behind? Why I have to know how much of her is in me?*

Conor reached the mountain's peak by late afternoon. The sun's rays were slanted and cool now as they struggled to reach the ground outside the cave. Some distance from the cave, he found a small grove of stunted pines trees in the mountain's shadow, kept from reaching their full height by the lack of sunshine. Leaning his back against the largest of the trees, he patted the ground for Wolf to sit near him. He reached out his hand and laid it gently on Wolf's back and the feeling of the small wiry dog comforted him as it always did. *How long have I sought comfort from this small brown dog?* He smiled to himself and closed his eyes.

Conor did not seek the respite of sleep, but sought the flow of the river, the lapping of the water against the rocks, and the sound of waves running across the pebbles in the shallows. He held the water in his mind, closing off everything but the sound. Gradually, his mind drifted, and as it did, he pulled it towards the cave entrance. From where he sat, he saw himself standing at the dark opening, felt the cold damp air that drifted from the cave on his face. He heard the water dripping down the cave walls and the small scurrying noises made by mice and insects. Taking a deep breath to steady his nerves, he kept himself focused on the opening.

Slowly, in his mind, he took one step toward the blackness before him. He stopped and gathered in the sounds and smells, breathing deeply and slowly. Another step, and he halted once again to allow the sensation of traveling to sweep over him. There were so many feelings; the cave and its ominous, inky depths, the odd sensation of leaving his body behind. The sense of freedom he felt traveling in his mind alone was thrilling, yet terrifying.

Another deep slow breath and another step so that now he was fully inside the cave. Once again, he stopped to listen and probe the cave with his mind. He expected to hear voices or see a light perhaps, but only the darkness embraced him and the sounds of the creatures of the cave met his ears. A moment of panic overtook him. How would he return to his body? Who would pull him back? He doubted Wolf would be much help, but even so, he concentrated on the small wiry dog lying beside him in the grove of pines. As he pictured Wolf in his mind, he once again felt the dog's coat beneath his hand. He could be here in the cave and still be next to Wolf.

Reassured he could find his way back, Conor took another step into the cave. After every step, he stopped to listen for voices, strained to see any bit of light that would indicate another person inhabited this space. Anyone in the cave with him, but there was nothing but stale air and the sound of dripping water.

Gradually, his eyes adjusted to the dark, and he could make out the shapes of the stone platforms. He took a deep breath and pictured Tilly and so many of their children lying on those platforms, covered head to toe with cloth. The anger built in him as he thought about the harm the children suffered, the things it made them to do against their will. He wondered at the hold Mara cast on them using the thing she called Ceobhran. His mouth twisted with the name of that thing she used to bind and control Tilly, as if he had bitten into something bitter. He stopped and spat on the cave floor. Astonished, he looked at the mark his spittle left.

How could my body be out there under the trees with Wolf and yet, in my mind alone, I left a mark on the stone floor? How was that possible? Conor shook his head.

I have a lot to learn from Granny. I might be able to travel, but I can't control what I do. Or can I?

He reached out his hand to touch a stone platform, his fingers traced the grooves and ridges in the rock. He could feel them! The sound of the cave water trickling down the walls pulled him. Again, he reached out his hand and drew it back, fingers wet with the water that streamed down the walls of the cave. Holding his fingers up to his nose, he inhaled deeply and smelled the rock smell, earthy and rich with minerals. His explorations took Conor deeper and deeper into the cave without his realizing it. This was an adventure that he hadn't expected. *I thought I would be an observer, watching but not being able to feel anything. Does this mean that I could change things when I travel?*

Conor took another deep breath and smiled at the wonder of it.

"I knew you would come, boy! Sooner or later, I knew you would have to come." The voice sounded behind Conor, making him jump and spin around to see who joined him in the cave. The man was tall, dressed in black breeches with a white shirt trimmed with lace at the cuffs. Tall boots fitted his legs, and his face was clean shaven except for the small beard that covered just his chin. His hair was long and pulled back, tied with a ribbon. He leaned against the wall of the cave; his arms folded across his chest. His face was almost handsome except for eyes set too close together and the sneer spread across his lips. "I've been waiting for you and I am not the only one, boy."

"Who are you? How did you know I would come here?" Conor stood as still as he could, ignoring the beating of his heart and the drumming in his ears.

"Never mind who I am, boy. I am not the one you seek. You were bound to come once you knew who was here. The woman draws you like a dying man to water. There is no help for you but come to her." The man chuckled softly and took a step toward Conor.

Conor resisted the temptation to back up, instead, standing his ground as firmly as he could. He pretended ignorance. "I don't know who you are talking about. I don't know anyone here. I've been traveling through the mountains and found this cave. Thought it might be a good place to spend the evening, but I see it's damp and cold, and occupied. I'll be on my way." He turned to leave, but the man reached out and grabbed his arm. Conor shook it off and continued to walk away.

"Don't worry. You'll be back and when you come, she will be waiting for you. She has so much to tell you and so much to teach you. You will be back, boy, mark my words." The man turned on his heels and strode toward the tunnel at the back of the cave.

Conor shook himself and looked down at Wolf, still lying next to him. "What have I done? I didn't think that anyone would be there. I didn't think anyone would know I was there. Oh Wolf, what have I done?" Conor shook his head and leaned back against the tree. He stared up at the darkening sky, the sun already hidden by the tall mountains. He shivered slightly from the cool wind that came up as the night crept in.

"Let's find a place to sleep, somewhere away from this Light forsaken cave." He stood up, realizing that his muscles were stiff. *How long was I in that cave? How long have I been sitting out here?* He shook his head once again in bewilderment and started down the mountain.

"There's a good clearing near to here, Wolf. You'll remember it. It's where we took the children after Granny woke them and Tilly brought them out. There's a fair-sized stream and a rock outcropping that will give us shelter for the night." He headed down the side of the mountain with Wolf close on his heels.

Once in the clearing, he gathered enough dry sticks for a fire. Reaching into his pocket, he brought out his flint and, striking it against a rock, soon had a wisp of smoke rising from the dried leaves and sticks. He blew softly on the pile, and the small flame that leaped up was his reward. He sat back against the rocks and fed the fire until it crackled and gave off a good measure of warmth. Here there was little wind where the rocks sheltered them.

Wolf looked at Conor with a steady gaze, expecting something. Conor dug around in his pockets until he found a small piece of dried meat. He bit off half and held the other half out to Wolf. "Sorry, boy. That's all I have. I didn't plan for an overnight stay. To be truthful, I'm not sure what I planned for. I think I ought to make better plans and think things through a little more." Conor stretched out next to the fire with Wolf at his back. Between the warmth from the flames and the comfort of Wolf's body against his back, he soon fell into a troubled sleep.

The woman came to him in the dark, her long black hair flowing behind her in the night breeze. She whispered his name while he slept. "Concobhar! Awake, awake my son! I need you, my son. There is someone that you must meet. He is strong, Concobhar, stronger than anyone I've ever known, but he thinks you might be stronger still. If you are, you could lead us. You could be our lodestone, bringing us everything we need. Your strength would attract all manner of creatures that we could control. Ceobhran is the least of those we seek, and they will come to you, Concobhar, they will all come to you! Wake up and come back with me."

The woman bent down, her dress sweeping the surrounding dirt, raven's hair falling over Conor as he slept. She brushed his forehead, smoothing the hair that fell over his eyes. She stroked his head and crooned. Wolf crouched nearby, his low, rumbling growl starting deep in his chest. She waved her hand towards him and he was silent. "Come back to me, my son, my dear one. Come back to me!"

Conor sat up straight, gasping for breath, his heart leaping out of his chest with each beat. Wolf was beside him in a flash, the hair on the back of his neck raised, the growl that started deep in his chest rumbling softly. Conor looked around wildly. There was no one in his camp, no woman, no voice, nothing. The fire had died down to coals, and the night air was cold and quiet. No sounds of nightbirds or insects broke the dark. He reached out to touch Wolf, anything to bring him back to his own reality. Slowly, his breath returned to normal and his heart quieted. He felt his face, wet with tears. He reached for the last of the sticks that he had piled near the fire, but they were scattered and nowhere near his reach. Puzzled, he gathered them up again, and fed the fire until the flames lit the rocks around him and warmed him.

"Wolf, we need to go down the mountain in the morning. I need to talk with Ronan. I need some answers."

Conor leaned against the rocks, keeping his hand on Wolf's back until the sky grew light, a rose-colored sunrise greeting the day. He kicked dirt over his fire, and stumbling out of his makeshift camp, made his way towards the hidden home of the Mountain Folk.

Cormac stood in the doorway of his cave and watched as Conor sat on his carved bench with Wolf close by. "You were gone in the night. Let me guess—up the mountain to the cave? Am I right? Did you find what you were looking for, my friend?"

"Make me a cup of your tea, and I will tell you, Cormac."

Cormac stared at the boy but said nothing. A moment later, he handed Conor a steaming cup and sat down on a nearby bench. Leaning his back against the rock wall, he stretched his legs out to the sun and still said nothing. Conor blew on his tea and waited for it to cool before he drank it gratefully.

Setting the cup on the ground, he turned to Cormac. "Yes, I went to the mountain, to the cave. Cormac, please try to understand. I have so many questions, and the truth is, I think I'm hoping that I am wrong about Mara and Jebez. Please believe me, I want to be wrong. I want them to be someone I could love, someone who could love me. Is that so hard to understand? Is it so wrong to want that?"

"Of course not, Conor, but let's talk about the reality for a minute, shall we? Because the facts as I see them show me you have proof against all those wishes. You know what they did, you know how they stole Tilly and others. No, I can understand you wanting things to be different, but what I can't understand is you not seeing things for what they are. When there is so much evidence of their wrong doing staring you in the face. You are a smart boy, Conor, smart enough to know there is a difference between what we want and what is. But let's leave that for now. Tell me what happened, please. Or do you need Ronan to be here as well?"

"Yes. I need Ronan, Cormac. Please."

Cormac sighed. "I figured as much. Let's go see if she is at home."

Cormac and Conor rounded the last bend in the path that led to Ronan's dwelling at the far edge of the Mountain Folk village. She liked her peace and solitude, and her gift for healing meant that she could insist on it whenever she had patients. Now it had just become her habit and the Mountain Folks' custom to honor her needs. Ronan sat on a bench with a high back carved with bears and eagles soaring over the mountain tops. Conor recognized the loving hand of Cormac in the work. On the bench across from hers was a plate of her cakes made rich with berries, groundnuts, and bear fat.

Cormac raised his eyebrows when he saw the cakes. "Are you expecting company, love of my life?"

"Yes, and you are right on time." The twinkle in her eye and the smile playing around her lips told the story of her gift of foretelling.

Conor sat down and immediately reached for a cake. Stuffing it into his mouth, he mumbled a thank you. Ronan laughed, "You look like you haven't eaten in a while, Conor."

"He hasn't. He wasn't at my fire last night so, unless he packed food, he went without." Cormac reached for a cake and broke off a small piece to chew on.

They sat in silence enjoying the morning sun while Conor finished the pile of cakes. Finally, wiping his mouth with the sleeve of his shirt, he sat back and rubbed his belly. "A proper 'thank you' now, Ronan. You were right, I was hungry. So, you knew we were coming?"

"Yes, Granny has taught me well. Now let's hear of your adventure. What did you find in the cave?"

"First, let me tell you, Ronan, that I traveled into the cave while my body sat outside with Wolf. Granny described how she emptied her mind and when it was empty, she pictured a river flowing slowly over shallow rocks. This I did, and the next thing I knew, I was in the cave.

Conor paused and looked toward the mountain peak. "Ronan, it was wonderful. I thought I could only watch and maybe hear things, but I could touch and taste things as well. It was so much more than I thought it would be. I got lost in it. It was so much more, and I loved I could do it. At any rate, I wasn't paying attention, and I wandered too far back into the cave. A man found me, a stranger I did not know, but he knew who I was. I pretended he was wrong, that I was just a traveler, lost in the mountains, but I could tell he didn't believe me. He told me my mother was there. Not in so many words, but it was clear she was waiting for me. That was the message he was bringing me." Conor sat back and wiped the sweat that had gathered on his forehead.

"I ran back to my body as fast as my mind could take me, and Wolf and I found a place away from the cave to camp where I built a fire and ate a small piece of dried meat I found in my pocket. During the night, she came to me. As I slept, she knelt next to me. She stroked my hair and face, and she told me I had powerful gifts, powers she called them. But that there was someone I needed to meet. Someone who knew me and knew I had gifts. I thought it was just a dream, but when I woke, my pile of wood was strewn around as if someone had walked through them or kicked them out of the way. Wolf's hackles were up and I think it was his growl that woke me."

Ronan stared at Conor with knitted brow and a frown on her face. "Concobhar! You traveled without training? Without knowing how to get back? You traveled alone, with no one there to guide you?" Ronan shook her head. "The stupidity of youth! The Light save me from stupid people! I'll start with that first and then we'll talk about what happened. Conor, there are so many ways to get lost when you travel without knowing what you're doing. I understand the pull, the temptation, but please promise me you won't do it again without some guidance."

Conor looked shocked at her vehement tone. He glanced at Cormac, hoping for some support, but Cormac shrugged his shoulders and shook his head. "You are on your own, my boy."

Ronan continued, "Now we'll talk about what happened. First, that the man found you so soon means someone had the gift of knowing you were nearby. I can't say if it was him or Mara, but someone knew. I believe some people can set themselves for knowing when certain people are close by. It sounds strange, but it is as if they set themselves so intently on knowing when that person is close, they can feel it above all else. I believe they have set such an intention on you.

"Second, you found it was possible to touch and feel things when you travel. I cannot do that, Conor. It takes a much stronger gift than I possess to change the world around you. Granny can do it by her touch but also with just her thoughts. I suspect you can do it as well, but Conor, learn how to control these things so they don't start controlling you! You say you felt Mara touch you in your sleep. That means one of two things. She can touch as she travels, or she was well and truly there next to you as you slept. Which one do you choose? Mara beside you as you slept, or Mara finding you in her travels. Either can only mean one thing; trouble for you."

Ronan sat back in silence, giving Conor time to absorb her words. Cormac looked off into the distance, avoiding either of them for the time being. Conor studied the space between his feet, moving the dirt into small piles and then smoothing it out again. "I understand what you are saying, Ronan. I do. You mean to protect me as if I were still a child. But I am not a child any longer. If time alone didn't help me grow, the things that have happened made sure I did. Sometimes, the things that happen to you force you into leaving your boyhood behind sooner than you might wish, but that's the way it is, Ronan. I don't feel like a boy anymore, and there are things I must know if I am to become the man I want to be."

Conor chewed on his lip as he watched Ronan's face. "Believe me, I have to know the rest of me, the people who brought me into this world and left me behind to fend for myself. There are answers I need, and as much as I care for so many of you; Granny, Tilly, and you, I have to find these answers for myself. Now, I will let you help me learn to travel safely, Ronan. I will stay here for that, but mark my words, I am going back to the mountain, and I will find the answers I need." With that, Conor stood up and smiled down at Ronan, trying to show her that there were no ill feelings, just strong ones. He whistled for Wolf and set out down the path toward the main part of the Mountain Folk village.

Ronan looked pleadingly at Cormac. "I know how much you care for him, my heart. Can't you please talk some sense into him? Please try to convince him to stay away from that mountain. I fear for him! I do not have the sense that Granny has for the future, but my common sense tells me there is nothing but evil on that mountain. He doesn't know what he is doing, traveling without a teacher, someone to guide him. Granny explained it to me. When you are traveling, you are between your space and the space you want to go to. These spaces are not always connected, Cormac. There is something between them, and a person who does not know what he is doing could get lost in that space."

Cormac looked at Ronan thoughtfully, "I will talk with him, Ronan, but he is stubborn and the best way to make him dig in his heels and show you that side of him is to insist that he do this or that. Let me just talk about things with him. I think you agree that allowing you to show him the traveling way was giving up a large argument on his part. He would have liked to have ignored your offer, but he cares too much for you to do that. My dearest, walk softly around Conor right now. He is a mass of porcupine quills, waiting for any opportunity to throw them at anyone who crosses him."

Ronan nodded in agreement. Rising to gather up the cups and dishes, she leaned briefly against Cormac. "You do what you can, please. I have to look in on Shaen's youngest. The rascal has been trying to climb trees bigger than most mountains. He took quite a fall down, scraping off most of the front of him on the bark. Now, I'm not sure which one has more of his skin, the tree or Neall. I promised Aelf and Shaen I would look in on him and bring them some salve. Perhaps the best thing would be to let him suffer, teach him not to climb trees, but that is not my job!" The last she said with a sigh and a smile.

Chapter Nine

Doiranne Seeks Help

Doiranne slammed the cottage door behind, leaning against it, gasping for air. She felt her heart beating wildly beneath the hand she held to her chest. Her eyes were squeezed shut, and she listened with every thread of her being for boots walking up the steps to her door. Satisfied that she was alone, she crept to her fireplace and bent down to stir the ashes. Rewarded with a modest glow from the coals, she searched her hearth for more wood. Finding none stacked, she turned once more to the door.

Dare I go out for more wood? What if he's out there? What if he knows it was me? With her hand on the doorknob, she hesitated, listening for any sound that would cause her to lock the door once more and sit beside her cold fire. Hearing nothing, she opened her door the barest of cracks and peered cautiously out. Nothing. No one was there. Cursing herself for a foolish woman, she opened the door and stepped out on the steps. Gathering her skirt in one hand, she scurried to the back of her cottage and grabbed up a few pieces of dried wood. Stacking them in her arms, she turned toward the front of her cottage. As she rounded the corner, she stopped, frozen as if a winter storm had caught her in its grip. A dark form stood outside her gate, one hand on the gate latch. Doiranne could not move, neither forward nor backward. Just as surely as an animal in a steel trap, she was caught.

The figure stepped back from her gate, lifted a hand as if in greeting, and melted into the darkness. Straining with all of her might, she could hear the sounds of his boots against the dirt as he moved away from her cottage. Still, she stood, unable to move. Gradually aware that the wood was scraping her arms she held it so tightly, Doiranne took one step and then another until, without realizing it, she stood once more in her cottage. Calmly, she walked to the hearth and dropped her bundle of firewood. Only then did Doiranne collapse in her chair and, burying her head in her hands, allowed the sobs to shake her shoulders.

Drying her eyes and face with the hem of her skirt, she returned to the door, opened it a small crack and peered into the darkness. Nothing. Closing it firmly, she dropped the lock into place and stirred up her fire once again. *He was real, I know he was real. His boots made sounds on the road like scraping across rocks which means he was real, not my imagination. The Light help me, he was real.*

Watching the flames lick at the wood and grow, she considered her choices. *I will see Granny Matilda first thing in the morning. She will know what to do. What if she doesn't believe me? That man has made a place for himself here in the village. Perhaps Granny will think I am making this all up? What if she marches right up to his camp and tells him what I've said? No, I can trust her. She will listen and know exactly what to do. I have to warn her that the man wants Conor for something. Something about powers. I wonder, does Conor have gifts like Granny Matilda? How could that be? If anyone in this village has a gift, it would have to be Tilly, related as she is to Granny. Oh, this is too much for me to sort out this late at night. I will look at it more clearly in the morning.*

Doiranne fed the fire, checked the door once more, and sought vainly for sleep in her small bed.

The crow of her rooster woke Doiranne at first light. With her eyes closed tightly, she let the memory of the night creep back into her mind. Not a dream, but a genuine threat. A threat to Conor and to her, she believed. Throwing back her quilt, she poured water into her basin and washed. She thought about a morning meal but considered Granny might offer her tea and something to break her fast. The thought of the comforting aroma of herbs, and the sound of Granny's tea kettle whistling with its heat, made her mind up for her. Finding a clean dress and apron, she stepped into her boots and opened the front door, half expecting to see a tall man, dressed all in black, standing by her gate. Nothing.

Taking a deep, shaky breath, she stepped out into the morning sun. *Why does everything look so much better in the sun than in the dark?*

Doiranne stopped outside of Granny Matilda's gate. Very aware that no one could enter without permission from the inhabitant, Doiranne hesitated. "Granny! Granny Matilda, are you within? It's Doiranne. I am here on a matter of importance. Granny, can you hear me?"

Doiranne waited, but her only reward was silence from the cottage. Grimly, she considered her options. Stay at the gate and yell at the cottage porch or take matters into her hands and step into Granny's space, risking her wrath? *There is a boy's safety to be considered. There can be nothing more important than that.*

Doiranne lifted the latch and stepped onto the path. Climbing the steps, she knocked loudly on the front door. "Granny! Granny Matilda. It's Doiranne. I must speak with you." No sound came from behind the cottage door. Shaking her head, Doiranne stepped off the porch and walked to the back of the cottage. There, Granny's sheep fold stood empty, gate ajar. No sign of Granny Matilda anywhere.

Now what do I do? I didn't think of what to do if I didn't find Granny. Perhaps she's at someone's bedside, nursing them. I have only to find out where, and my problems are over. Maybe Quinn will know something.

Doiranne hurried to the garden space in the village where she spent long hours weeding and hoeing in exchange for fresh vegetables. Knowing that Quinn worked most days in the morning's cool, she was certain she would find him bent over a row of potatoes or turnips. Opening the gate, she searched up and down the rows, to no avail. No Quinn.

Now what? I could ask Quinn's wife, but she refuses to talk to me, so that might not help. Who can I go to? Doiranne thought of the blacksmith, Tomas, who had showed her such kindness. Shrugging her shoulders, she headed toward his shop.

Doiranne was relieved to hear Tomas's hammer shaping metal as she stepped into the dark forge. Waiting for her eyes to find him in the gloom, she called out, "Tomas! It's Doiranne. Can you spare me a moment, please?"

Tomas looked up from his work and squinted through the smoke from his forge. "Why, Doiranne, I never expected to see you in my shop this morning. After refusing my offer to sit with you last night, I thought you were done with me."

"Sit with you? What are you talking about, man? Sit with you where?"

"At the fire. In the village square. The one the tinker and his daughter build every night while he plays the fiddle and she dances. Remember?"

Doiranne hesitated, "Yes, I am sorry. I remember, but so much has happened since then, I had forgotten. That's not why I'm here. I'm sorry, Tomas, but I'm looking for Granny Matilda or Quinn. Have you seen them this morning?" "No, not this morning, but I saw Quinn yesterday evening. He said he was going to drive some sheep to market across the valley. Won't be back for a day or two, I think he said. Why do you need Quinn, may I ask?"

"It's not really Quinn I need, it's Granny Matilda, but she's not at her cottage and I thought I could ask Quinn. He's been nice to me." Doiranne's words poured out like spring water.

Tomas looked at her, pondering her words. "That's good that you need Granny. I was worried for a moment."

"Worried about what? Tomas, you make no sense. I need to find Granny. It's important."

"Then I suggest we go find Erik Tamen. He's the man who knows all the comings and goings in this little village. I'll walk with you."

Together, they made their way to Erik Tamen's large stone cottage. As the pair climbed the steps leading to the porch, the door opened and Guin stepped out, catching them both off guard. "Oh, you caught me by surprise. I thought it was Erik coming home when I heard the footsteps on the porch. What can I do for you, Tomas? Doiranne?"

Doiranne frowned. Would no one stay home where they belonged? "Guin, I am looking for Granny Matilda. Erik would do, but it's really Granny I need to see. Have you an idea where she might be?"

"Yes, she and Erik were called out in the night. A farmer in the next village caught a wolf after his sheep. He chased the creature, and somehow he managed to fall down and break his leg, I'm told. Granny Matilda went to set the leg and Erik went along to catch the wolf. I expect they will be gone a day or two. I'm not sure why I thought you were Erik when I heard you. Just hopeful, I imagine. I'm sorry, Doiranne. You look quite desperate. Is there anything I can do to help?"

Doiranne shook her head. "No, but thank you, Guin. You've been most kind. I will figure out what to do myself."

Doiranne stepped off the porch and sat on the last step. Propping her elbows on her knees, she cupped her face between her hands and stared at the range of mountains in the distance. She couldn't see the tallest peak, but she knew it was there. Tomas sat beside her, picking up small pebbles at his feet and tossing them towards the gate. "Are you going to tell me what this is all about, Doiranne, or am I to guess what troubles you?"

Doiranne sighed. "I have one more person to talk with, Tomas. You don't need to come with me. I can find my way."

"Oh no, you don't! You do not come bursting into my smithy, dragging me over to Erik Tamen's home, and then expect me to walk away shaking my head. No, Doiranne, you involved me in this, even if you won't tell me what 'this' is and I am committed. Besides, I see that something is troubling you, and that worries me. You are normally so confident and obviously able to take care of yourself. It is hard to find a way to get close to you besides selling tools, and I'm sure you have enough of those by now."

Doiranne turned to look Tomas in the face. "Tomas, you are a man who makes no sense most of the time. I am the last person anyone would describe as confident. I am scared most of the time and then spend the rest of the time worrying about what else I should fear. And what is this about getting close to me? You make no sense, no sense at all, Tomas!"

"Doiranne, I am trying to court you, woman! You sure don't make it easy for a man to do that, but I'm trying."

"Court me? Me? Oh, Tomas! Court me, he says!" Tears gathered in Doiranne's eyes, but she blinked them back before they could run down her cheeks. Placing her hands on her knees, she rose to feet and turned to look at Tomas. "I am a married woman, sir. I know my husband isn't around, and the Light knows if you had been there when I was a younger girl, I would gladly have answered you. But that's not how it is, Tomas. You are my friend, but nothing more. I owe Sean a great debt, and I mean to pay it back. I'll take my leave now and find the last person who can help me. Go back to your fires, Tomas, and let us just be friends."

Doiranne closed the gate behind her and walked towards the village green without looking back. There, she found the tinker's camp, the wagon beneath the trees, and the mule cropping grass at the end of a long tether. She stood back under a small grove of nut trees and watched the camp. *What am I doing here? What if Traynor sees me? Think, Doiranne, think! What is your plan?*

She watched from her vantage point as Roisin untied the mule and moved him to a place with thick, green grass. There, she pounded a stake into the ground and tied him off. Briefly, she leaned her head against his shoulder and ran her hand down the length of his neck. Patting him, she walked back to camp and began pulling boxes out of the back of the wagon. Doiranne watched as the girl unpacked dishes and food, carrying them to the makeshift table in the center of the camp. Still, Doiranne hesitated to walk forward. She watched as Roisin cut some vegetables with her belt knife and built up the small fire. Handfuls of meat and vegetables went into the black iron pot hanging over the fire. Dipping water from a nearby barrel, she filled the pot and stirred it all together. Before long, Doiranne could smell the rich stew as it bubbled over the fire. Still, she hesitated. Finally, Roisin dipped out some of the stew and sat on a rough bench near the fire to eat.

Doiranne waited still. When it was clear the girl was eating alone, Doiranne approached her. "I was wondering if you were ever going to come into my camp." Roisin's voice held laughter as she squinted up to look at Doiranne. "You're the one who keeps company with the blacksmith, right? Good choice of men, I'd say. Hold on tight to that one." She laughed and wiped the stew from her mouth with the hem of her skirt.

"I do not keep company with anyone, thank you. Can I talk with you for a minute, please? I saw what your father did to you that night. I need to ask you about him. Will you talk with me?"

Roisin stared across the green without answering. "I don't know what you are talking about. He did nothing to me, then or ever. I will talk to you about a lot of things, but not him."

Doiranne sighed. *What did she expect from Traynor's daughter? Help? The truth? Not likely.*

She sat down on a bench across from Roisin and looked at her. "I know you have no reason to believe me, but I think you will. I think you know things you would rather not know. So, I'm going to try. Your father met with a man last night, a man who came down from the mountains, he said. He was not happy to see this man and even threatened him, I think. Even so, they talked about people who used to live in this village. About finding them. That seemed to please your father. The man asked him about finding someone here in the village. He wanted to know if Traynor had found someone special here. Your father talked about Granny Matilda and Tilly. But I don't think it's them he wants. I think it's Conor. He says Conor is strong somehow, and that strength seems to be what he wants from him. Now this doesn't make much sense to me, but I thought it might make sense to you. I needed to tell someone; I can't just keep quiet about this." Doiranne sighed and leaned back from the table.

Roisin tapped her spoon against the side of the bowl. "It makes sense now," she muttered. "That hateful man. I thought he had given up, but it's clear he has not. And now he has found what he's been looking for all these years. The darkness take his soul!" She stood abruptly and turned to look at Doiranne. "You won't find him here. He's gone off. He does that sometimes, just leaves. There's no telling when he'll be back. I'll tell him you were here and he will come and find you. You can ask him all the questions you dare ask him when that happens. In the meantime, I think you should go home, bolt your door, and hide under the covers of your bed. You are no match for Traynor Gill."

Doiranne looked up from her seat on the bench and considered Roisin. "What can he do that any other man couldn't do?" she asked.

Roisin shrugged her shoulders. "It's not for me to say. I'm just warning you, but you take it or leave it as you wish. Just don't come back and say that I didn't warn you." She flipped her skirt and walk towards the wagon.

Doiranne considered pressing the girl, but it was clear Roisin would not give her any answers. At least now she knew Traynor had left the village, and she guessed well enough where he had gone.

She trudged back to her cottage, deep in thought. There was one more person she could ask, but it meant gathering enough courage to knock on Quin's door. If Molly Mathuin answered the door, she wondered if she could hang on to the bit of courage long enough to ask for Tilly. Deep in thought, Doiranne made her way across the village once more. *What am I even going to say to Tilly? What do I really know? That this man Traynor has come to our village looking for someone, maybe her, maybe Conor. But for what? What reason could he have to be interested in either of them?*

Doiranne knocked on Quin's door and stepped back three paces until she stood nearly at the edge of the porch. The door opened and Molly stood, wiping her hands on her apron. "Oh, it's you. Quin is not here. He's gone to the market with some sheep. Won't be back for a couple of days." She backed out of the doorway and began to close the door.

Before the woman closed the door completely, Doiranne held out her hand, "Wait, Molly, please. I'm looking for Tilly. I need to ask her about Conor. It's important, Molly, or I wouldn't be here troubling you."

"Well, first it's my husband you're after and now my daughter, Doiranne. Can't you find anyone for yourself without taking what's mine?"

"I promise, Molly. I just want to ask her about Conor." Doiranne's voice pleaded, and she looked down at the porch.

"Well, ask her whatever you want when you find her. Tilly went off with Granny to set some poor farmer's leg in the night, leaving me here alone to cope with all the household chores. Won't be back for at least a day or more. And as for Conor, he left to go to the Mountain Folk village. He's no better than those folks of his, mark my words. He will come to no good end, that one."

Doiranne's shoulders slumped, and she turned to step off the porch., muttering as she did, "Won't anyone stay home where they are supposed to be?"

Doiranne shut her cottage door behind her and looked at her meager surroundings. It wasn't much, not much at all, but it was hers and she had been making a home out of it. Make no mistake, the chimney still leaked a bit, but she had mixed mud and straw and chinked up the holes until there were nearly none, and she could light a fire and still breathe pleasant air. New curtains covered her windows, clean and pressed with an old cast iron Tomas had found in his smithy. A quilt made of every color she could find covered her small bed, cheerful if somewhat startling to the eye. She scrubbed the kitchen table and shelves until the wood was smooth and shone in the light,, and her dishes were clean and stacked on the shelves in neat piles. There was even a small vase of flowers on the table she cut from her own garden. There were herbs hanging to dry; not as many as Granny, but a good start, and they filled the air with their pungent aroma.

The hooks beside her bed held clean pressed clothes and the small table nearby held a cracked pitcher and bowl for her wash water. She even had some homemade soap that Granny had given her as a gift, a rare treat. All in all, it was a very pleasant cottage, one she was proud of.

Doiranne sighed and went to the shelves. She took down an old sack she used to carry her vegetables from the village garden after she worked. From her shelves, she pulled apples, cheese, and a loaf of bread. Smelling the bread, she thought back to the day she had baked it in the kettle on her hearth. It had been a proud day for her. Shaking her head, she carefully wrapped the cheese in cloth and stowed everything in her sack. Digging around the shelves, she found an old leather bag for water. It smelled of mildew and water gone bad, but she rinsed it until the water ran clear and it smelled somewhat better.

After she stored the food, she packed a few rags and the precious bar of soap for washing. She might have to climb a mountain, but there was no reason she couldn't keep clean. With a sigh, she turned back to the shelves that held her meager dishes. Dragging a chair over, she climbed up and reached behind the baskets stored on the topmost shelf where she pulled out a small leather bag. Stepping off the chair, she held the bag to her nose and breathed deeply. After all this time, the rich smell of Sean's tabac still tickled her nose. She slipped the pouch into her bag, and with one last look at her cottage, she closed the door firmly and stepped down. Without another look back, she turned her face to the mountains and began her journey.

Chapter Ten

SEAN

The journey to the mountains was a quiet one. Doiranne marveled at the beauty around her as she climbed higher and higher, through the aspen groves to the edge of the evergreen forest. She had never been out of the village, not one day of her life. There was so much to see here; wildflowers of every color and size, birds diving and swooping to catch winged insects on the fly, bees and wasps buzzing around her, and maybe even a hawk wheeling far above her, though her eyes were not sharp enough to be certain. Still, it made her smile to think that it might be a hawk.

Doiranne marveled that she could climb so easily. *I think the hours in the garden have helped. I guess all the work I've been doing at the cottage has helped as well.* She couldn't help smiling to herself and even tried whistling a little as she walked. *All right, Doiranne, what is the plan? You seem to bumble around a lot lately with no good plan in mind. I think it's about time you had one. You are about to walk into a hornet's nest that you might not get out of. Roisin is right, I am no match for Traynor Gill. Especially without a good plan.*

The sun was warm on her back as she continued to climb, using the switch back trail she found. When the sun was high enough in the sky, she looked for a comfortable place to eat her midday meal. With her back against a tree and her legs stretched out in front of her, she opened her bag and took out an apple, some cheese, and bread. Chewing thoughtfully, she weighed her options. There was a certainty that she would not go into the cave. *I would be a fool to walk willingly into that hornet's nest. I'm not sure what's going on in that cave, but I'm certain that the man who talked to Traynor came from there. He said he found the two people Traynor was looking for, Mara and Jebez. I know they are Conor's da and ma, but how this all came to be, I can't see. Doiranne, think! What do you know for certain? First, that Jebez and Mara are still in that cave. That Sean is most likely still there as well. You know Conor has left the village, either for the Mountain Folk or for that cursed cave. At least that's what Molly said. You know Traynor is gone as well. No Quin, no Erik Tamen, no Granny, not even a slip of a girl like Tilly. You are on your own, Doiranne! So, what do you plan to do now you are halfway up the mountain?*

Doiranne finished her meal and tucked the leftover food into her bag. She clamored to her feet, thinking as she did that she should have taken off her boots to rest her feet while she ate. Shaking her head, she found the trail and began climbing again. *So, if you don't plan on going into the cave, what good are you going to do? Sit outside and watch? Yes, that's an idea. I could watch for Conor and warn him not to go in the cave. If I could get there before he does, I could tell him what I know. If he went to the Mountain Folk, maybe he doesn't plan to go to the cave for a few days. Oh Doiranne, you goose. You don't have enough food to sit outside the cave for days waiting for Conor to come. So, I'll go to the cave and make certain he's not there, and then I could try to find the Mountain Folk village. They might not mind me coming if they know my intention is to warn Conor. Good. I have a plan. Go first to the cave and make sure Conor isn't there and then try to find the Mountain Folk village.*

Doiranne knew it wasn't the best plan, but it was the best plan she could make by herself. The sun slipped behind the mountains and the purple shadows grew longer when she found a small stream with a rock abutment beside it. She drank from her water bag and refilled it from the stream. *I think I will wait and eat the cheese and bread for morning meal. Perhaps I should have brought more food. Then again, I should have packed food for Sean to eat. I wonder what he ate while he wandered around the mountains until they found him. Serves me right if I go hungry myself.*

With that thought in her head, she closed her eyes and slipped into sleep. Doiranne's head jerked and her eyes flew open. *How long have I been asleep? Hours from the feel of my poor back against the rock.* She sat still, listening for the night noises and giving her eyes time to adjust to the dark.

As the moon came out from behind a cloud, Doiranne drew a sharp breath. Standing casually against a nearby tree, his arms crossed over his chest, a man dressed in black cocked his head to one side and then the other. There was no need to see his face, hidden in the shadows. There was no doubt in her mind who watched her. She held her breath and made no movement, save for the small flicker of her eyelids. The rock felt so hard against her back and her legs longed to stretch and ease the cramps that grabbed at them after the long climb up the mountain. Still, she sat, her hands gripping her skirt tightly, her breath coming in small, ragged gulps. She stared at him, not daring to close her eyes. *I cannot show it. I cannot show that I'm afraid. Just be still Doiranne. If he was going to hurt you, he could have done it while you slept. He just wants to frighten you. Well, he's doing a good job of it, Light knows. A very good job!*

The man uncrossed his arms and kicked at the dirt around his feet. He hummed a tune as he stared at her; a tune she recognized from the fiddle music he played around the fire. Still, he stayed by the tree, leaning against it again, humming louder now. Doiranne tried to swallow but there was nothing to work with. Not a drop of moisture in her poor mouth, her tongue stuck to the roof of her mouth. She wanted nothing more than to close her eyes and open them to sunlight, but she dared not close them. Staring at him was the only thing that kept him from coming any closer, this she knew for a certainty without know how.

Oh, Light, I want to go home! I just want to go home! Doiranne gripped her skirt even harder, feeling her fingernails dig into the palms of hands through the stout wool. *Would he not say something? Would that be worse? Will he not go?*

The man reached up casually and pulled a handful of leaves from the tree. Crumpling them in his hand, he shook his fist at Doiranne. Suddenly, opening his fist, he dropped a handful of red flower petals to the ground. These he kicked lightly toward her, and then brushing his hands together, he turned on his heels and melted into the dark.

Doiranne breathed again for the first time, drawing in one long ragged breath after another. She struggled to her feet, stomping to rid herself of the leg cramps that bit into her muscles, causing her to wince. She hobbled over to the tree and looked down at the ground. What should have been a pile of crushed leaves was instead a mass of blood red rose petals, the like of which Doiranne had seen only in the best tended gardens in the village. She sank to the ground and gathered up the petals, and holding them to her face, breathed in the sweet rose smell. *They are really rose petals. They smell so good.* Doiranne sprinkled them across her lap and wondered at their beauty. They were not bruised but looked as if they were just plucked from the flower. *You are right, Roisin; I am no match for Traynor Gil!*

The warm morning sun woke Doiranne where she leaned against the rock abutment. Afraid to open her eyes, she strained to hear any sound that did not belong to the forest. *Goose, the man doesn't make any noise unless he's humming that Light forsaken tune he loves so much.*

Opening first one eye and then the other, Doiranne faced a glorious sight. Down by the stream that poured out of the rocks, three deer browsed on sweet grass growing at the water's edge. Two doe and a small fawn, so new she still wore her spots, stepped across the stream, and continued their morning meal. Doiranne was loath to disturb them, but her back ached and once more, cramps gripped her legs despite stretching them as far as she could. Quietly she reached for her boots and slipped them on her feet. The larger of the two doe threw up her head at the slight sound, her white tail flicking wildly. At the signal, all three leaped as one and disappeared into the cool forest, making no sound on the leaf strewn floor.

Doiranne smiled to herself. Never had she seen deer so close to her. *What a way to wake! If I could live in the middle of this forest, I think it might not be a bad place to be.*

She knelt by the stream, and with her small bar of soap, washed her face and hands in the icy mountain water. Running her fingers through her hair to untangle it as best she could, she sat down to eat the last of her bread and cheese. *Teach me to come out here with such little food!* She licked every crumb off her fingers when she was done and packed her soap and wash rag away in her bag. As she did, she fingered the tabac pouch that lay at the bottom of her sack. Sighing, she took it out and put it in the pocket of her skirt. *I let him go off without his pouch because I was angry and just plain mean. I have a lot to make up for.*

Before she left her small rude camp, Doiranne wandered over to where the man had dropped the petals the night before. The morning breeze had scattered them, but they were still there and looked as fresh as they did the night before. She bent to gather them up and walking to the stream, let them drift from her fingers to be carried away by the water. *It's a cheap magician's trick. I don't know how he did it, but it's just a cheap trick meant to scare me. It did last night, but not this morning. Not now!*

Midday found Doiranne at the base of the largest mountain in the range. Squinting against the sun, she shaded her eyes with her hands and stared at the peak. Sure enough, the same black clouds swirled across and around the peak, constantly moving but never blowing away. *What could it mean? Does something evil hold those clouds in place or do they stay to warn us away from the cave? If so, they do a good job. I'd like nothing better than to turn around and go home.*

She started the climb upward, using the switchback trail that Granny and the others used so long ago to bring the children out of the cave and back home. *Too bad they couldn't have brought Sean as well, but he made his choice and maybe it helped save the children or at least Conor.* Doiranne shook her head and kept climbing.

Her legs ached and her back longed for a good night's sleep in her own bed, but Doiranne kept climbing until, finally she came to the last turn in the trail. Beyond she could see the black hole that was the entrance to the cave, but it was not the cave that caught her attention. It was the sight of a young man who sat cross legged with his back against a tree. Perfectly still, yet with his hand resting on a small brown dog by his leg. Doiranne drew in a sharp breath. Conor. *I was not soon enough.*

She called out his name softly so as not to alert anyone in the cave, but there was no response from Conor. He sat so still; she wondered if he had fallen asleep.

She tried again, louder this time. Wolf raised his head and looked curiously at Doiranne. A small growl started deep in his chest and rumbled its way out, but the dog did not move from Conor's side.

Doiranne picked up a handful of small rocks and threw them one at a time at Conor. Most missed, but one or two bounced off his leg. Wolf continued the low growl but still did not leave Conor's side. *What in all the Light is he doing? He can't be sleeping so soundly. There's something I don't know going on here.*

Doiranne crouched down behind a leather leaf tree to watch and wait. Moments passed and nothing changed. Conor continued to sit motionless while Wolf rumbled his low growl but did not move from under Conor's hand. *He's in the cave! He's gone in the cave like Granny can do. I had no idea he could do that. It's little wonder I didn't know. I don't know half of what goes on in the village. Light, it's too late to warn him. Doiranne, think! What do I do now?*

At the end of the great chamber filled with silent stone platforms, a tunnel formed by the carving out of rock in ages past opened to a cluster of small naturally formed rooms, all facing a larger circular area. Beautiful tapestries covered the rock walls in places, and candles burned in every nook and cranny to light the space. Outside the glow of candlelight, the dark swallowed the remainder of the room, leaving nothing for eyes to see.

In one room, brightly colored pillows lay scattered across the floor, with small low tables carved from dark wood placed around them. Traynor and the man he called Liam sat on pillows and held silver bowls from which they spooned up a greasy mixture of vegetables and broth, old carrots and wizened turnips floating across the surface. Taking up a round loaf from the middle of the table, Traynor tore off a hunk of the stale bread and used it to wipe up every drop of broth in his bowl.

Tossing the bowl onto the table, he called, "Jebez! We are finished. Come and clean this up. If there's any left, you may have it." He was about to speak again when he suddenly cocked his head to one side. "We have company, Liam. I believe the boy has come, just as I knew he would. But there's someone else. Someone outside the cave. That Light forsaken woman, that nosy old brood hen, has come on to the cave. She has more in her than I ever gave her credit for having. Either that, or she is so blindly stupid she doesn't know her head from good sense. I mean to deal with her once and for all."e was about to speak again, whHH`

He rose in one smooth motion, kicking aside a pillow as he did. "Jebez, I want that man. What's his name? That one you've had doing your bidding?"

"It's Sean, Lord. He's from the village. He was caught up with Ceobhran at the same time Mara was. You told us to keep him quiet, so we never woke him unless we needed him to fetch and carry." Jebez mumbled all this while he cleaned up the bowls and cups from the table.

"Wake him now and bring him to me," demanded Traynor. "We will see what happens to nosy old women who come sneaking around here."

Jebez nodded and scurried to do his bidding. Some moments later, he returned with Sean behind him. Sean's eyes were open, and they burned with a feverish light.

"Did you wake him to where he could take commands?"

"Mara did, Lord. I don't have the words to wake people or control Ceobhran. Only you and Mara have those words, Lord."

Traynor nodded. "Sean, look at me."

Sean turned his head in Traynor's direction. No sign of acknowledgement drifted across his face, but his eyes burned with an urgency as if something unseen called to him.

"There is a woman outside the cave who does not belong here. She does not belong in our world. I want you to get rid of her. You will know her because she has something that belongs to you. You are to take her to the cliff and throw her over the edge. Do you understand?"

Sean nodded his head, "Woman. Cliff. She does not belong here."

"That's right and when you are done, you will come back here and I will reward you. Would you like that? A reward?"

Sean nodded his head, but there was little recognition of the words Traynor spoke.

"Jebez, take him to the cave entrance. He will find this woman. She will draw him to her because she has something that once belonged to him before he belonged to me. It will pull him to her. Come back immediately. If you see anyone else, know that I will deal with him. Do you understand me?"

Jebez bowed his head, "Yes, Lord. I understand." Jebez grabbed Sean's arm and pulled him toward the cave entrance. Once there, he shoved him out toward the sunlight and turned on his heels. He wanted no part of what was to happen next, not even to know who the woman outside was. The less he knew, the safer he was, he thought.

Doiranne looked up to see a figure standing in the cave entrance. Thinking it was the man, Traynor again, she shrank back against the tree, making herself as small as she could. She watched as the man hesitated in the sunlight, blinking his eyes as if he had not been in the light for a very long time. Slowly his eyes adjusted and he turned to scan the area. He looked briefly at Conor, still sitting motionless with Wolf against his leg, but he paid the boy no mind. His eyes moved across the trees and rocks until they rested on the place where Doiranne crouched. He nodded to himself and stepped out into the light.

The man's hair was longer now and hung in ragged clumps around his neck, his face drawn and gaunt, but he was still recognizable to Doiranne. She stood up and walked toward him, calling out to him, "Oh thank the Light! Sean. It's me. It's Doiranne."

The man stared at her with eyes that burned bright in his face, skin drawn so tight until it seemed the bones themselves might poke through. He held out a hand to her as if asking for something. Not understanding what he wanted, Doiranne held out her hand to take his. The grip on her wrist swept a moment of doubt through Doiranne. "Sean, it's me. Your wife."

Sean continued to stare at her, eyes burning into hers, his fingers tightening on her wrist. "Please, Sean. You're hurting me. Please let go." Doiranne tried to pull her arm away, but his grip only intensified. Sean turned away, dragging her along with him.

"Where are we going? Sean, why won't you answer me?"

The only response was a tighter grip on her wrist as he pulled her across the clearing.

Doiranne called out, "Conor! Conor! Help me, please. Conor, wake up. Conor, I need you to help me." The wind carried her pleas off as it carried the dry autumn leaves in front of it.

Sean continued to pull her along with him, never speaking, never loosening his grip. Doiranne dug in her heels until he was dragging her, creating deep furrows in the ground.

"Sean! Stop!" Despite her strength, Doiranne was no match for Sean. Slight of build he might be, but every muscle was corded in the effort to drag her toward the edge of the clearing.

Doiranne used her other hand to pry his fingers loose, but the grip he had was of iron and her fingers were useless. "Please, Sean. Wake up. You have to wake up and remember me. Look. See this? I brought this to you." She reached into her pocket and brought out the worn leather tobacco pouch. Holding it out to him, she entreated him to see her, really see and remember her.

He turned and stared with wild eyes at the pouch she proffered. Grimacing, his face stretched into what might have seemed like a smile if it were not for the wild look in his eyes, he snatched the pouch from her fingers and held it between his teeth. He grabbed at her again with his free hand.

"No, Sean, please. I'm sorry. I'm sorry for everything, but you have to wake up. Stop. You know me, Sean. You know me," The wind snatched Doiranne's sobs from her throat.

With one last burst of strength, Doiranne threw herself to the ground, pulling Sean on top of her. Thrusting him aside, she kicked out wildly with her boots, trying desperately to gain some leverage, some distance from this man she no longer recognized as her husband. Sean rose on his hands and knees, still staring at her with eyes that burned with hate. She kicked out again, catching him squarely on his chin. He laughed and wiped the blood away with his hand and kept coming toward her.

Doiranne jumped to her feet and whirled to run, but Sean was quicker. He caught the back of her skirt and pulled her toward him. Turning, she beat at him with her hands, catching him on his arms and face and chest. He dropped her skirt and grabbed at her arms, pulling her toward him. With of all her might, she pushed against his chest with both hands. She felt him give, and she pushed again, harder. This time he staggered backwards, but quickly regained his balance and came toward her again. All she could see were his eyes shining with a feverish need.

Again, she steadied herself and pushed against his chest. Again and again she shoved him, pushing with all of her might, unaware that she was screaming at him. Everything was lost to Doiranne except the need to escape, to get away from the man with the eyes that burned in his face. Closer they came to the edge of the clearing, until with one last shove, Sean toppled over and out of her sight.

Collapsing on the dirt, Doiranne drew a sobbing breath. On hands and knees, she crept across the dirt to the edge of the clearing and looked down. Sean lay below, arms and legs splayed out at odd angles, his head twisted to one side as if he were sleeping. Doiranne threw herself down on the ground and sobbed, grabbing handfuls of grass, ripping them from the earth. Her sobs echoed through the valley and across the clearing, but still the young man sat motionless, his hand resting on the small brown dog.

After a time, Doiranne's sobs subsided, and she pulled in long deep breaths that calmed her. She sat up, wiping her face with her skirt, making mud out of the tears and dirt smeared across her face. She looked once more over the edge of the clearing, hoping she wouldn't find Sean down below, hoping she would find him gone. The body that had once been her husband still rested across the rocks below. Doiranne stared for long minutes, hoping she would see a twitch, a slight rise and fall of his chest that might show life, but there was none, not the slightest movement in any part of him.

She rose slowly to her feet. *I have got to figure out how to get Conor back. I cannot lose him as well.*

She made her way slowly toward the cave, moving stiffly, her muscles screaming in pain as if they were torn in two. Doiranne stopped at the sight of another man coming out of the cave entrance and stepped behind the nearest tree, hoping to make herself as small as possible. The man called Liam came out of the cave, stopping to blink in the sudden light. He looked around the clearing, and finding Conor, nodded his head and smiled to himself. The man more sauntered than walked the distance between them as if he had not a care in the world. Standing over the boy, he looked down at him and the small wiry dog who still sat patiently under Conor's hand. With one swift kick, he sent the dog rolling and tumbling away from Conor. Laughing now, he bent and scooped up the boy as if he weighed nothing. Wolf came charging at the man, but another kick sent the poor dog halfway across the clearing to land in a quiet heap. With a sneer on his face, the man carried Conor into the cave and disappeared from Doiranne's view.

Hastily she ran to Wolf, bending down to feel for his heartbeat. Under her hand, the dog opened his eyes and whined softly. She sat beside him, pulling his head into her lap, and stroking his fur ever so softly. "It will be all right, little one, it will be all right. I will think of something, I promise."

Chapter Eleven

TRAPPED

Conor stood quietly against the rock wall, not moving despite the trickle of cold water that ran down the wall and across his back, soaking his shirt. His body felt odd, not like his anymore. His arms felt weighed down, too heavy to lift, and his feet were stuck to the cave floor, mired in a thick dark fog that gripped his ankles and held him fast. He looked around at the cave, saw the stone platforms, each with a cloth neatly folded across the ends of them, saw the water running in rivulets down the walls, and heard the drip, drip, drip as it splashed to the floor, but everything was clouded as if he looked through a fogged window. The sound of the water was muffled, as if he had stuffed lambs' wool in his ears. He blinked his eyes, thinking to clear away the fog, but nothing changed. He refused to panic, letting his mind travel around the area as much as he could without moving his body. *This is different from before, but I don't know everything there is about traveling. Maybe this is what Ronan was warning me about when she said I needed to learn. Well, the sheep is out of the pen now, no sense crying about it.*

Conor heard sounds coming from the cave entrance. Turning his head slightly, he could make out the thickset man in black breeches and tall boots carrying something in his arms. He recognized the man from his earlier visit to the cave when the man laughed at him and told him he would be back. *He was right, here I am.*

The man carried something in his arms, but Conor could not see what it was from his position, that is, until he turned to lay the burden on one of the stone platforms. He stared at the still form the man placed on the platform, taking two or three deep breaths to steady his nerves as he watched the man unfold a cloth to cover the body. *Oh Light, it's me. He is carrying my body into the cave. Where's Wolf? Why isn't he here too?* Conor watched helplessly as the man pulled the cloth from the end of the platform and covered his body completely.

Don't panic. No yet, anyway. If I'm there, I should be able to get back to my body. With the thought firmly in his mind, Conor closed his eyes and pictured his body lying on the stone platform covered with the thin, white cloth. He concentrated with all his might, squeezing his eyes shut and thinking himself into his body, but he stayed stubbornly against the wet rock wall, unable to move any part of himself. He strained until the muscles stood out in his neck, and sweat ran down his face, despite the cold air. Nothing. No movement in the slightest from the wall.

Conor opened his eyes to stare at the form he knew was his body, still more curious than afraid. *I hate to admit I was wrong, even to Ronan, but I was. Here I am, stuck like a fly in amber, unable to reach my body no more than twenty feet from me.* Conor chuckled to himself. *What would Granny Matilda say? Oh, I think I know. She would start with a few 'sheep-dip' curses and end with my ears burning from midday to eventide while she lectured me on being a Light forsaken fool.* Conor sighed and slumped against the wall.

Across the rows of stone platforms, toward the back of the cave, he saw a faint light. Again, he shook his head and blinked his eyes, trying desperately to clear his vision. Everything remained as it was, murky and vague in his sight. He saw dimly that the light was coming closer, held up by the very man who had carried his body into the cave. Behind the man came more figures; the tinker who had camped in the village green, followed closely by a tall woman with raven black hair that fell in waves down her back.

The woman he knew from his dreams, the black hair that shone in the torch's light, the hem of her dress sweeping the cave floor, rustling as she walked. She was so familiar to Conor, he could almost feel the touch of her hand on his forehead, brushing aside the hair that fell across it. An unkept man who lumbered along, mumbling and muttering to himself, followed those two. The man seemed familiar and reminded Conor of someone he knew long ago. His dark hair was long and greasy, falling in tangled locks to his shoulders. With a beard as black as the woman's hair and so thick it covered half of his face as if someone had painted it on, his look bordered on dangerous. His brows were heavy and came together in a frown over his eyes, narrow and darting suspiciously around the cave as if he expected the shadows to yield something unfavorable. The clothes he wore were slovenly, badly patched, and much in need of a washing.

But it was the tinker that Conor watched closely. He was obviously the man to whom they all looked and waited for. Traynor stopped, quietly looking down at the figure on the platform. His hand, long and narrow, reached out to the cloth. Taking it up, he pulled it back just far enough to see Conor's face. "It is as if he sleeps, Mara. See, I told you no harm would come to the boy." The woman he called Mara rushed past him to look at the boy. She snatched the cloth from Traynor's hand and covered him once more.

Traynor held out a hand toward Mara. "Do not try my patience, Mara. I have held onto it as long as I can, but do not push me, woman. You will not dissuade me. I will have my way and nothing you and that idiot husband of yours, Jebez, can do will stop me. Do you understand?"

Mara took a quick step backwards and held out one hand. "Traynor, don't, please. Pease don't. I just wanted to see Concobhar; I just wanted to make sure he was only sleeping."

Traynor dropped his hand and Mara grabbed at her wrist, rubbing it with her free hand, grimacing as she did. Her wrist appeared red, as if she had run it through a patch of nettles.

All of this Conor watched from his place against the wall, listening to the muffled exchange between the man and his mother. His eyes narrowed as he strained to listen. *The man has plans for me. She warned me about that. At least, I think she was trying to warn me. Maybe not. Maybe she was trying to lure me in. By the Light, if that was her intention, she did a good job of it.*

Traynor turned from the stone platform and crossed to where Conor stood, pinned to the wall like a butterfly mounted on a board. He stood and stared thoughtfully for a moment, his arms crossed over his chest, his eyes measuring the boy before him. After a moment, he closed his eyes, standing perfectly still as if he waited to hear something. After what seemed like minutes, he smiled and opened his eyes to look fully at Conor. "Never have I felt such strength as I am feeling right now, boy. Even through this." He waved his hand across the air in front of Conor. "You are the strongest one I have encountered in my lifetime, and I have lived an endless life." Traynor chuckled to himself. "I have waited for this, boy, a very long time. But here you are now, and here you will stay until you and I can come to some kind of agreement."

Conor struggled to answer the man, but the words stuck in his throat. He shook his head from side to side, and tried again, but still the words stayed stubbornly in his throat.

"Stop struggling, boy. It only makes it worse. I have you for as long as I want to have you. We'll talk later, but for now, know this. You are mine as surely as if I chained you to me. The sooner you recognize and accept that, the sooner I can let you go and we can begin our work together. In the meantime, you think on this, think long and hard."

Traynor turned on his heels and with a hand signal the others followed him out of the great space and into the tunnel leading deeper into the cave. Conor sighed and slid down to sit on the floor with his back against the wall. At least he could do that. *So, his coming to our village was not by chance. And Roisin trying to get to know Tilly and me, not an accident either, I'd reckon. I've been in trouble before, but I guess this time must be the best I've ever done. I hope Wolf is not hurt. If that man hurt my dog, he'll wish he had met someone else besides me.*

Conor's head dropped to his chest, and he closed his eyes and breathed deeply. A scuffling sound of footsteps across rocks and dirt brought his head up. Before him stood the disheveled man, holding a small torch. His skin was sallow and looked greasy in the light of his fire. Despite the chill air, a small sheen of sweat stood out on his forehead, catching the light. He licked his lips once or twice and brushed back his hair with his free hand. Still, he did not speak, only stared at Conor.

Conor looked up from under his eyelashes, not raising his head to look the man over. *Not someone I'd want to meet by myself.*

The man cleared his throat with a guttural sound. "Are you awake, boy? Can you hear me? I know you can't speak but nod your head if you can hear me." He licked his lips again and looked over his shoulder toward the tunnel.

Conor raised his head at the man's words and nodded, slowly.

"I came to warn you, boy. Traynor is a man to be taken seriously. He wants something from you, but I don't know what, and it's not for me to know. I just know he needs you for something he has planned. He and Liam talk about you. Whatever he wants from you, just do it, boy. That's my advice. It will go a lot easier for you if you do. If you try to fight him, he can do terrible things to you. Painful things. I know. If he knew I was here, my skin wouldn't be worth making into boots. Just do what he wants, boy." The man stared at Conor. "I don't know why I'm risking my life for you. I don't owe you anything. Whatever happened back in that village, it was Mara's idea, not mine." He shook his head again and, for just a moment, looked sadly at Conor.

Conor stared at the man until he dropped his eyes and shuffled his feet. Shrugging his shoulders, he shook his hair out of his eyes and looked once more at Conor before turning away.

Sighing, Conor rested his head against the wet wall. *Now there is a man who has as many problems as I have. He looks familiar, but I don't know why.*

Despite the uncomfortable position he was in, the cave floor rocky and uneven under him, the wall behind him constantly dripping water down the back of his neck, Conor felt the familiar heaviness that comes before sleep. His eyelids fell softly down, and his head nodded to his chest. Through the veil of sleep darkness, he heard the rustling sound that Mara's skirt made as she crossed the cave floor. He sighed to himself. *They like to pester a fellow.*

He raised his head but kept his eyes closed, probing the air before him with his mind and his senses. Even behind the wall of air that kept him prisoner, he could smell the soap she washed with, he could hear her impatient sighs, and the rustle of her dress. *I have never heard Tilly's dress sound like that. Come to think of it, I have never heard Tilly's skirt make any sound. Why does to make it sound like that, I wonder?*

"Concobhar! Concobhar! I think you can hear me. Wake up! I'm going to release your body so that you can talk with me. You won't be able to leave, but you will move and talk. Now wake up, Concobhar, wake up!" Mara's voice came out as a whispered hiss, impatient and demanding.

Conor opened his eyes a bit and leaned his head against the wall to see her from his position on the ground. He coughed to clear his throat then croaked, "I knew you would come, Mara. It is Mara, right?"

"You can call me that."

"I won't call you mother or ma!" The words came out clipped and harsh. Conor sighed to himself. *I cannot let her get to me. I cannot let any of them get to me. My anger makes me weak.*

"I don't expect you to call me anything, but I expect you to listen with respect, Concobhar. I am your mother, like it or not. And I might just be able to help you."

"I'm listening, Mara, but I don't see what you could say to help me. It seems to me you are in thick with that man. Traynor, right? The tinker. He seems to want something of me, what it is, I have no idea. I have never said two words to the man. What could he want with me, I wonder?" Conor smiled as he spoke, hoping to put Mara at ease with him.

"I am not here to tell you anything about Traynor, but I will say this much, he is much more than an ordinary tinker. I'm here to explain what is happening to you. You traveled into our place, this cave, without knowing what you were walking into. He set traps for you, knowing you would come. Knowing you had to come. And knowing that you didn't know what you were doing. Oh, you foolish boy! You should have stayed away."

Conor stood up in one smooth motion, biting off his words harshly. "You wanted me to come here. You came to me when I was sleeping and you told me to come. Now you blame me for coming? You blame me for this? Mara, it seems you blame everything on someone else. Do you ever accept responsibility for anything?"

Mara sighed. "I'm not here to argue with you nor am I here to explain myself. What I am here to do is to help you understand what is happening. Maybe if you understood this thing happening to you, you could do something about it. Now, stop being a petulant child, and listen to me!"

Conor stood still and stared at her. "All right. Say what you came to say and then leave me in peace."

"Traveling is an ancient art, an ancient expression of our powers, our gifts. It is rare and special, but it is also dangerous. You need something strong, something that holds you to the real world when you travel. It can be a place or a person you love, but it needs to be something more important to you than anything else. You traveled in here with your dog by your side. That was a good thought, Concobhar, but as much as you love him, he was not strong enough to keep you tethered. I know you thought he would be. I know you love him more than you love most, but he was not strong enough to bring you back. When Liam hurt him, any strength he had left his little body. So Traynor watched you come into the cave, and it took just a matter of moments to wrap you in his web of air and keep you here. When Liam brought your body in, you left a small piece of yourself out there. Outside the cave without even knowing it. Now you are caught in this space as a fly in a spider's web until Traynor lets you go.

Mara took a step toward Conor, her hands held out to him. "You cannot reunite yourself with your body until he allows it, but if you learn to surrender, Concobhar, really learn to let yourself go from this space, you might still travel. What good it would do you I cannot say, but it might help you. The ancient ones say it is possible, but I could never do it. I am not strong enough. But Traynor says you are the strongest he has ever met, and he has been searching for your strength for more years than you can comprehend." Mara's voice drifted off with those last words, and her look was pensive.

"Why are you telling me all of this? And why did you leave me all alone? And why do you care?" Conor's voice rose with each question.

Mara stared at him without blinking, her dark eyes glimmered with unshed tears. "I do this because I left you, Concobhar. I say this because I didn't keep you to say the things that I should have said. You think about what I've said, please. I have to go back before I am missed." With that, she whirled and slipped away on silent feet, the rustling of her heavy black skirt on the floor moving across his senses.

Conor sank back down on the cave floor, leaned his back against the wall, feeling the cold water once more slip down his neck and slide across his back. He closed his eyes and concentrated as hard as he could on the river flowing across the rocks; the sun shining on the ripples as it flowed. Now he squeezed his eyes and made himself shut out the cold wall against his back, the stone floor beneath him. Clenching his fists, he thought only of the river; the water flowing across the rocks. Nothing! He opened his eyes in frustration. *Why can't I do it? Why can't I concentrate? I did it before and it was so easy. So simple to leave this body and travel. What am I doing wrong? 'Let myself go', she said. 'Surrender', she said.*

Conor opened his eyes and unclenched his fists. He let his gaze wander across the cave, noting but not worrying about the stone platforms or his body stretched out before him. He softened his gaze and watched the water trickling down the walls; the lichen forming in drier spaces; the sand strewn across the floor. These things he looked at with acceptance, not fighting where he was and what was happening to him. His body relaxed against the wall, even the floor beneath him felt more yielding.

Softly, he closed his eyes and pictured the river flowing once more across the rocks in the shallow beds. He witnessed sunlight dance across the water, and he felt himself being carried on the current, bobbing and drifting with the flow. The water deepened under him, and he felt it pick up speed and now bounce him along. Still, he kept his eyes shut softly and allowed the river to carry him. He felt, more than saw, things bump against him. Even as he felt these things, he kept his eyes closed and let the river carry him where it would. The feeling of weightlessness in the water delighted him; his arms spread out from his body, his legs light. Up and down, the current carried him with no fighting, no resistance from him. Complete surrender to the water, to the river that carried him on its own path.

Suddenly, he realized he was standing next to the platform that held his own body. Surprised, he looked back to see where he had been sitting against the wall. Still there, sitting against the wall with eyes closed, his head nodding to his chest. And yet, here with himself. Not able to put himself within him yet, but still able to be there. He reached out to touch the sleeping form on the rock platform, but his hand felt nothing. He tried to grab the cloth that covered his body, but he could not feel it nor make his hand grasp it. As if he were a dream, he was here, but not really.

I have so much to learn! He smiled down at his sleeping self and began walking toward the tunnel that led to the blackest depths of the cave.

Chapter Twelve

The Mountain Folk

Doiranne felt more than saw the dark clouds gathering around the mountain and the valley below it. She felt the electricity in the air and the wind pick up, blowing her hair into her face as she bent over the small, wiry dog. "Little One, we need to get off this mountain before the storm breaks. The Light save me; I will not go into that cave, not by myself, so we need to find some kind of shelter."

She stood up awkwardly, feeling every torn muscle in her body. Wolf got up on all four feet and gave himself a mighty shake. He looked longingly toward the entrance to the cave, but Doiranne's sharp voice caught his attention. "No! We will not go in there, not without help, Little One. Now let's get off this mountain before we cannot."

She stumbled toward the path that only hours before had brought her to the place where she had unwittingly caused Sean's death. Shaking the thought out of her head, she tried whistling for Wolf. Not much came out of her lips except a sad little squeak. Still, the dog perked up his ears and followed her. "Good boy. I can't leave you here, not matter that you want to stay near him."

Together they made their way down the steep path, Doiranne slipping and sliding in the loose gravel and rock. The storm clouds rushed in now, and thunder rumbled in the distance, signaling rain. Lightning lit up the sky and the trees bent under the wind, their branches nearly touching the ground in places. Doiranne gasped and cried out when a branch broke free of a leather leaf tree and fell directly in her path. "We have got to find shelter," she cried.

Wolf darted past her on the path and trotted ahead a few steps. Stopping, he looked back at her and waited. Hesitantly, she followed him. He would go a distance and wait until finally he was assured she would follow him. The pace he set was more than Doiranne's tired body wanted to do, but she felt she had no choice but to stay up with the dog as best she could. Down the mountain, she clamored until they stopped going down and began winding their way through the forest across the mountains. Again, Wolf stopped to allow her to catch up to him, and then once more, he climbed.

At last, they reached what looked to Doiranne as a dead end of solid rock. "Little One, you are lost; we are lost. Now what?"

With one last backward look, Wolf slipped between the rocks and made his way to the great clearing on the other side. The storm finally broke. Lightning raised the hairs on Doiranne's arms, and thunder deafened her. She cried out to Wolf, but the wind carried her voice away. Through the sheets of icy rain that poured down on her, she could see where one wall ended, there was a space before the next wall began. *Well, the Light save me, there's a way in. He knows this place; the little fellow knows it.*

Doiranne squeezed through the narrow passage to find Wolf waiting patiently in the clearing. "Go on. I'm coming. Show me what you know."

Even through the downpour, Doiranne could see the warren of caves above her. No sign of anyone in the deluge, but she realized Wolf had led her to the Mountain Folk's village. *How will they greet me? I have heard they turn people from the valley away.*

She continued to follow Wolf as he led her directly to a cave set high up the steep path. Even in the drowning downpour, she could see that there was a fire within and even the rain could not wash away the smell of something cooking.

"Da! Look, it's Wolf!" A young boy with long hair and deerskin breeches bounded out to greet Wolf. He skidded to a stop when he saw the bedraggled woman standing just outside the cave, her soaking wet dress clinging to her body, her hair streaming with water. "Da! Wolf has brought us someone. Come quick!"

Aelf stood behind his youngest son and viewed the woman before him. Doiranne stood quietly, her hands beside her, open to show that she carried no weapon. Aelf shook his head and turned, "Shaen, you'd better come. This is woman's work, I think."

Shaen looked up from the fire where she was cooking the evening meal. Pursing her lips in an impatient frown, she motioned to another boy to turn the meat. "Don't let it dry out," she demanded and handed the turning stick to him.

Making her way to the cave entrance, she stopped in astonishment. "Aelf, what in the Light are you thinking, leaving this poor woman out in the rain? Get out of the way, man. Make yourself useful and bring me a blanket, the blue one will do just fine. You, come into this cave. Get out of the storm!"

Gratefully Doiranne obeyed the woman's voice, stopping just inside the cave. Water streamed from her dress, her hair, and her body making puddles on the floor of the cave. "I won't come further," she mumbled. "I'm bringing in more water than the storm itself."

Shaen wrapped her in the wool blanket. It was rough but warm and the roughness swept away the water from Doiranne's body. She shivered now she was inside, great bursts of shivers that shook her from her head to her boots. "Bring tea!" demanded Shaen. "You, come here and sit. Let's get you out of those wet clothes. Keven, hand that turning stick to Brian and fetch me the wool dress off the shelf."

"But Ma, that's your only other dress!"

"Do as I say, Keven. Never mind that, just do as I say. This woman is freezing to death. Would you have her freeze to death so that my dress stays dry? Now hurry, boy!"

With dress in hand, Shean held the blanket high so Doiranne could pull her soaked garments over her head and slip into the warm wool dress. She sat down to pull off her boots and wet socks. Once dressed, Shaen draped the blanket over her shoulders and thrust a cup of steaming tea into her hands. Sweetened with honey, the tea gave off a scent of lavender and chamomile. Doiranne smiled as she sipped it, knowing that before long the warmth of the fire and the herb tea would have her eyes closing and her head nodding to her chest. Determined not to fall asleep before she told them her story, Doiranne set the cup down on the rock shelf next to her.

"I thank you for the tea, the blanket, and the warm clothes and I will drink the tea, but I know it will put me to sleep and I must tell you what I know before that happens."

Aelf handed her a plate filled with hot cakes of grains and dried berries fried over the fire in bear fat. Tender slices of meat seasoned with wild onions and herbs filled the plate, giving off an aroma that made Doiranne's mouth water. "We will talk soon enough, but first, eat. You are freezing and you look like you have eaten little in the last few days. Eat, and then we will talk." With that, Aelf signaled for his three boys to eat the food that Shaen piled onto their plates. Grinning at their father, they fell to meat and cakes, slurping tea and wiping their mouths on their sleeves.

Shaen offered a plate to Aelf, who took it with a smile. "Did we forget to teach these boys manners, love of my life? Did we forget to teach them how to eat when guests come to our home?"

Shaen sat beside Aelf with her own plate and looked up at him. "That is your job, my husband. The raising of the boys falls to the man of the house, as you well know. I raise the girls, but since there are none, I raise nothing and you raise the boys. It's our tradition, dearest, one of the many you uphold." She said this slyly, looking at Aelf sideways.

Aelf sighed, "Boys, slow down before you fall down choking on this good meal your ma has made. Take time to taste the food; the meat she flavors with onions and herbs, the cakes only she is able to make this delicious. Slow down, or by the Light, you will eat grass with the sheep next meal!" The last came out as a growl the boys heeded.

Looking chagrinned, they stopped shoveling meat and cakes into their mouths. They straightened up on their bench and chewed slowly and carefully, keeping a close eye on their father.

Turning to Doiranne, Aelf set his plate down and picked up his cup of tea. "Let's start from the beginning. Who are you and why have you come here with Wolf?"

"So that's his name?" asked Doiranne. "I knew he was Conor's pup, but I never knew his name. My name is Doiranne and I live in the same village as Conor and Granny Matilda live. I call Granny my friend and I think she would call me the same. At least, I hope she would. I don't know Conor at all, but I know who he is, and I have good reason to believe he is in danger. That's what brings me to the mountain." Slowly, Doiranne told the story of the tinker and his daughter, the fires in the square at night, the winning over of the hearts and minds of the villagers. She told them of seeing Traynor hurt his daughter, which aroused her suspicions and the conversation she overheard late at night with the man he called Liam.

"I didn't know what to do. Granny and Erik Tamen were both gone across the valley to another village, and Tilly's mother said she had gone as well. There was no one I could ask for help, no one I felt I could put in danger if there was danger. So, I climbed to the mountain. I found Conor and Wolf outside the cave. He was sitting so still. At first, I thought he was asleep, but I realized there was something else happening. And then my husband, Sean came out of the cave." Doiranne bent her head at this, and tears gathered in her eyes.

Aelf looked at Shaen with a puzzled look. He knew Sean was sleeping under the spell of Ceobhran. "Sean is your husband? And he is awake? What good news! He has been in the cave for so long, we all despaired ever seeing him again."

Doiranne shook her head. "Let me finish, please, while I have the courage to say it. I was so happy to see Sean, though he looked different, pale, and thin beyond words. His face was drawn, skin over bones, but it was his eyes that struck me. They were on fire, burning with a light I didn't understand at first. I was so very happy to see that he was alive, you see."

Doiranne sat back against the wall and closed her eyes as if watching the scene once more. "I held out my hand to him, but he grabbed my wrist instead and began pulling me toward the edge of the clearing."

Aelf nodded his head, "I know the clearing. It falls to the valley below, some distance down to the rocks."

Doiranne shook her head, "I did not understand what Sean was doing. He kept pulling me and pulling me. I called out to Conor, but it was as if he was asleep. He never opened his eyes. I fell to the ground and pulled Sean down on top of me. I thought I could jar him out of whatever held him, but his eyes couldn't see me. They burned, oh how they burned with hatred. I kicked at him and got to my feet, and I just started pushing him and pushing him without thinking, without know where I was going. He kept coming at me, and I wanted him away from me. I remember I was screaming at him, trying to wake him up. I couldn't wake him, I couldn't stop him, so I just kept pushing him, and the Light save me, he fell. My Sean fell over the edge." Doiranne opened her eyes and looked at Aelf, tears running unheeded down her face.

Aelf sat still, looking at Doiranne with quiet eyes. His heart felt heavy for this woman that he did not know, understanding the burden of guilt she carried. He looked down at his hands folded in his lap, giving her time to catch her breath and wipe her face with the hem of the blanket. "You mentioned Conor was in danger. Finish the story Doiranne."

Doiranne took a deep breath, "Traynor said he needed a boy or a girl from our village. I know now that he meant Tilly or Conor. I don't know what he wants with them, but he thinks they have some power, some gift he wants. The man Traynor called Liam came out of the cave. I hid behind some bushes and watched him pick up Conor's body. He kicked Wolf across the clearing and picked Conor up and carried him into the cave. The boy never woke, never stirred. I don't know what to make of it, but I think some part of him was in the cave and now the rest of him is there as well. Whatever it means, I can tell you Traynor is not a good man and whatever he wants of Conor is not a good thing."

Aelf looked sharply at Shaen. "Kevin, go now and bring Ronan and your uncle here. Go quickly, son. It is most important."

Keven opened his mouth to remind his da of the storm that raged without, but one look at his father's drawn face left him speechless. He ducked his head at the entrance of the cave and ran through the slippery mud as if chased.

Ronan and Cormac slipped inside the cave, rainwater running off the tanned deer hide cloaks they had thrown over their heads and shoulders. Dropping his cloak to ground, Cormac shook his head, spraying water off his hair like a shaggy dog. Ronan smiled at him and wiped the drips of water that ran from the end of his nose. "Almost husband, you are making it rain in this dry cave with that wet hair of yours." He smiled at her, but quickly turned to his brother, Aelf. "What in all the light is so important that you send your eldest son out in this storm, Brother?"

Aelf shook his head and indicated the woman sitting quietly under the wool blanket, sipping her cup of tea. "Look what the storm brought in. She has a story, Cormac. Ronan, I think you need to hear this. It has to do with Conor."

Ronan reached out to take Cormac's hand. Together they walked to a stone bench facing Doiranne. "Tell us what is going on with Conor. Aelf, we thought we had convinced him not to go back to the cave, but we were wrong. Now, tell us, what is happening."

Quietly, looking down at the floor, Doiranne repeated her story. When she finished, she looked pleadingly at Cormac. "I did not want to leave him, but there is something going on in that cave I don't understand. Something with Conor I don't know about. And I am so sorry, but I would not put myself within reach of that man, Traynor." She dropped her gaze and sat quietly, as if waiting for condemnation.

Cormac shook his head at Doiranne. "Thank you for coming here. I don't know how you found your way to us, but I thank you for it. No, I am glad you did not go into that cave. More than likely, it would have just meant one more person lost in there." He turned to Ronan. "Is this what you were talking about, my heart? The danger of traveling when you don't know what you are doing? Has he got himself in trouble, do you think?"

"Oh, yes, I don't think, I know. If he was traveling in the cave and the man carried him from his spot, he cannot find his way back to himself. Even if he sees himself in the cave, it is not enough. He has left part of himself outside without even knowing it, an anchor almost. Without that anchor, I know I cannot find my way back. We both know Conor is strong, much stronger than I will ever be, but there are rules to this game, and if you break them, I'm not sure how much your strength will count." Ronan shook her head in disbelief.

Aelf listened silently from across the space. "It looks like Conor has gotten himself into more trouble than he might get out if, is that what you are saying, Ronan?"

"Yes, Aelf. I think he is in more trouble than I can get him out of for that matter."

Aelf shook his head. "I know how you feel about the boy, Cormac, but the rules are plain. He is not of us. He is not a Mountain Folk. We can send for help when the storm is over, but we cannot go to him. Our laws are simple, but they are in place for a good reason. We could help with the children because they were our children, Mountain Folk children, but Conor is not one of us, and the law is clear that we will not go."

Cormac stood up abruptly and faced his brother. "The Darkness take the laws. Where were the laws when you brought Erik Tamen to our village? Where were the laws when you allowed Ronan to heal him? Where were your all-important laws then, Brother?" Cormac's hands doubled into fists and his body shook with anger.

Aelf shook his head. "You are not thinking clearly, Cormac. You know the laws, you helped write them. Unless Conor is a Mountain Folk, we cannot interfere except to call for help."

Cormac turned to Ronan; despair written across his face. She stood quietly and walked to stand in front of the brothers. "Almost husband, you should have told your brother our plans. I realize you wanted it to be a welcome surprise, but I think now might be the time to let him know."

Cormac looked questioningly at Ronan who again smiled and reached out to take his hand. "You see, Aelf, we were going to wait until our marriage in the spring, but now there is good reason to change our plans. You know Conor is nearly an orphan, having been abandoned enough years to make it so by our laws. By my reckoning, he was a small boy when Mara and Jebez left him in the village. No one has made a claim on him, so Cormac and I make that claim. Enough time has passed to make it possible. If you insist we be united first, we will do that or Cormac can do it on his own and I will join the family in the spring. Either way, we will be a family, Cormac, Conor, and me. Make no mistake, Aelf."

Aelf slapped his brother on the back, "I knew you would do the right thing by that boy. Yes, there has been more than enough time by my reckoning for Mara and Jebez to make their claim on him. I will take your word the ceremony will take place as soon as we get Conor back, but for now I will trust this is going to happen and we can act accordingly. Keven, I need you to go down to the valley to take a message to Granny Matilda and Erik Tamen. Tell them Conor is in danger and we need them here."

Doiranne spoke from the corner of the cave, "I tried to get help from Granny and Erik Tamen, but they had gone off to the village at the end of the valley. Something about a wolf and a broken leg. I don't expect them back to our village until the morrow."

Kevin looked anxiously at his father. "Do I still need to go in the storm, Da? Can it wait until the morning light? I will be able to see my way better."

Aelf looked over at Cormac who nodded his head slowly. "Yes, son, you will go after morning meal. I don't think your mother will want to send you down to the valley without her morning meal packed into you."

Chapter Thirteen

JEBEZ

Conor walked down the tunnel that led ever deeper into the cave. He trailed his fingers along the stone wall as he walked but felt nothing. No cracks, no dripping water, no cold stone beneath his fingers, nothing at all. He tried scuffling his feet along the floor as he walked, stirring up sand but again, he heard nothing. There was no scraping, no sound of his heels striking the stone. Silently he walked deeper into the blackness. *This might be the best way to travel, making no sound at all.*

The tunnel was far longer than he imagined it would be, turning and twisting this way and that ever deeper into the belly of the mountain. He was grateful he still maintained his sight while his other senses seemed dulled. After what felt like a much longer walk than he anticipated, he spied a dim light ahead, unsteady and flickering as a fire on a breezy night might do. Rounding the last corner, he saw a group of people clustered around the fire, with their attention riveted on the man standing before them. Conor strained to hear what the man was saying, but it was if he still had lamb's wool stuffed in his ears. There was an echo, but no words that he could discern. *I have to get closer. I have to take the chance that they can't sense me in my present form.*

Conor crept along the dark wall, staying well away from the light cast by the fire. He watched the smoke curling up toward the ceiling of the cave, where it found the smallest airhole and escaped. There was just enough air coming through to cause the flames to dance and twirl in the dark. Conor watched the firelight with fascination until he remembered his task. Blinking his eyes, he shifted them once again to the room and the group of people who occupied the space.

It was a large space, not as large as the one at the entrance that held the stone platforms, but still a good-sized chamber. The woven tapestries that hung on every wall, covering them with elaborate scenes of battles and strange beasts that Conor had never seen before, seemed to dwarf the room. Despite his intentions to watch the people, he stared up at one in particular that portrayed a young man who looked vaguely familiar to him. The man's face was twisted in a grimace of hate, and he held a massive sword clenched in one hand, pointed toward the ground where a creature curled up in front of him, an enormous snake with a monstrous pattern of brilliant colors along its body. The snake lay coiled at the man's feet, its body stacked upon itself, one length on top of the others with its head raised high. Glittering eyes focused on the young man, and even in the dark, Conor could see that the creature tested the air with his bright tongue. *That is something out of a terrible dream.*

He let his eyes rove around the room, noticing the colorfully patterned pillows strewn across the floor, short tables scattered among them that held the remains of food; plates and cups ignored and forgotten. At last, he turned his attention back to the group.

There was the man, Liam, who he remembered carrying the torch to light their way earlier. Now the man lounged on pillows, one leg crossed over the other, and he carelessly flicked dust from his black boots. His shirt was white with lace at the cuffs and his britches were of soft black leather where they met his boots at the knees.

Mara sat upright, one hand on the ground behind her to support her weight. Her raven black hair fell in waves to the pillows behind her, pooling there in soft mounds. The other man, the one who came to warn Conor, sat with his back against the wall, no pillow beneath him. His legs were crossed in front of him, and he stared down at the floor between them, looking sullen.

Conor could just make out the words that Traynor flung around the room. He watched the man glare alternately at Mara and then at the man. Conor stared at the man with the heavy dark beard. *Why does he look so familiar? Why can't I remember him?* He shrugged to himself and turned his attention back to Traynor.

Mara stood now, and held out her hand to Traynor, "Traynor, please. We don't know what you want of us. If we knew what it was, I'm sure we would oblige you. If you want, I can raise Ceobhran again. We can get more children, we could get men and women, if you like. We can send them anywhere to get anything we want. Just let us know what it is you want, Traynor."

Traynor pulled away from Mara's outstretched hand. His voice rose with every word, "You think I want this?" He waved his hand toward the pile of silver dishes and candles sticks piled in the corner of the room. "You think this is what I want, Mara? You and Jebez think too small." Traynor stalked across the room and picked up a silver platter. "You really think this is important to me?" He threw the platter with all his might, where it landed on the stone floor and skittered to a stop at Mara's feet.

With eyes wide, Mara bent to pick the platter from the ground. "Leave it! Leave it where it lies. It is of no use to me or to anyone." Traynor advanced on the pile and began kicking the pieces of silver; the jewelry, the beads, and bright bracelets, kicking them and throwing them across the room. "These are nothing, Mara. Jebez, you're an idiot to allow your wife to waste time on this pile of trash. Its only use in this world is to distract you from what is important. You are idiots, the two of you. Worse than idiots that you allow this to distract you." Once again, Traynor bent to pick up plates and cups, flinging them around to bounce off the walls and the ground until every piece was scattered across the space, dented and dulled.

Mara sank back down to her place on the pillows and clasped her hands in her lap. Jebez scuffed the broken-down heels of his boots against the floor but said nothing. Liam watched Traynor through hooded eyes, appearing bored yet slightly attentive in case Traynor's attention shifted to him.

"Mara, I don't want Ceobhran to help us steal trinkets and worthless baubles. There is so much more that I want; I want to raise an army. An army with me at its head, an army that will follow me and take orders only from me. This is nothing to me." Traynor waved his hand around the room. "I want the world to know who I am. They should be on their knees before me. I want all of you, right now, on your knees to me." The last he bellowed, and the echo of his words bounced around the room.

Liam was the first to rise, knowing full well the fury that could come his way should he be slow to act. Mara too rose unsteadily to her feet. Jebez, however, continued to sit with his legs crossed, staring at the floor between them. He picked up sand and sifted it down to the ground, repeatedly, as if the events playing out in front of him did not concern him.

Traynor walked to where Jebez sat against the wall. His voice was soft and slow, "Jebez, I want you on your knees. Now!"

Jebez looked up from his place on the ground. "Traynor, look around you. We are living in a cave, man. A cave. We don't have money to pay an army or feed one. We are living on the top of a mountain in a Light forsaken cave, man. How do you think we are going to raise an army to follow you, and where do you think you will take this army? I will kneel to you, Traynor, when I think you have more than just empty words to throw around. Until then, let's not talk about kneeling, shall we?"

Mara held her hand out to Jebez and hissed, "Jebez, what are you doing? Get up, right now. Traynor, he didn't mean that. He's just tired and hungry. He didn't mean any of it, did you, Jebez?"

Jebez shook his head and looked sadly at Mara. "You have pulled me and pushed me for years to get what you wanted, Mara. And now you want me to let this man do the same? No. I am tired of being pushed and pulled. I want a say in what happens. Living in a damp, dark cave in the middle of nowhere makes me feel sick, Mara. I want a house, a pleasant house in a town where I can go to the village pub and have a pint of ale and a roasted chicken. A feather bed to sleep on and a fire to prop my feet in front of on a cold night. How is this man going to make that possible for us?"

Mara turned her back on Jebez, shaking her head, her black hair to moving in waves across her back.

Traynor raised his hand high and muttered strange sounding words, but suddenly he stopped and lowered his hand. He stood thoughtfully over Jebez and a small smile played across his lips. "I could crush you where you sit, Jebez. Do you know this about me? Do you trust I could do that, Jebez?"

Jebez shook his head. "Sometimes you are just so tired of living that it doesn't matter anymore what people do to you, Traynor. I am there. I have been eating rats and sleeping on rocks for so long, my life doesn't feel like it's worth anything to me. Yes, I believe you could crush me. Do you believe I don't care anymore? I'm not afraid anymore. I have spent my whole life being afraid, and I just find that I am not afraid anymore." Jebez shook his head and laughed to himself.

Traynor stared thoughtfully down at Jebez who had not moved from his spot. He rubbed his chin and raised his eyes to the ceiling of the cave. Looking back down, he held out a hand to Jebez, "You are exactly what I need, Jebez. You will do just fine. Come, we have work to do."

Chapter Fourteen

TILLY'S DREAM

Granny handed Tilly a cup of tea, the fragrance of lavender and chamomile sweetened with honey wafted up in the steam. Bending over to inhale deeply, Tilly smiled at the scent. Her laughing eyes looked at Granny Matilda. "You think I don't know what you're up to, sly one? You think if I am relaxed, the lessons will go better, perhaps even work?"

Granny hesitated before she answered. "Tilly, my dearest, I know how anxious you are to succeed. To find your own true gift. But sometimes our eagerness gets in the way of our progress. I am only hoping to allow you to relax a little. You might find doors open to you when you stop tugging on them so hard." She smiled at Tilly as she said this, taking any sting out of her words.

Tilly sighed, "Granny, I want this so badly. My dream was to be like you, not like my ma. I kept waiting to feel something, to have some idea I could do special things. That I was special. To be just ordinary. Oh Granny, it makes me so sad. I want to travel the way you do, the way Ronan does. Having the gift of sight is something I am not sure I want. Light knows I've seen the troubles it has brought you over the years; how you are more and more reluctant to share that gift with others, particularly when you know it might bring them sorrow. But, Granny, I want a gift. I want to feel special." Tilly bowed her head and wiped a tear from her cheek.

"Now you listen here, missy. You are special and never think you are not. Gift or no gift, you are the most special creature on this green ground. I won't hear any more about that. You have brought more light into my life than I ever knew existed. Special, indeed! Now do me a friend's favor and finish your tea so that we can get started."

Tilly obediently finished the last of her tea and set the cup on the floor beside her chair. She closed her eyes and leaned her head back, knowing full well what came next and knowing just as well that it was all for nothing. Sure enough, Granny's soothing voice cut through all the noise and clamor in her head.

"Close your eyes and breathe deeply, once... twice... three times. Good, now let your mind drift without forcing it. Let it go softly and gently wherever it wants to go. Let it find a stream of clear, cool water. Look at the water but don't touch it. Listen to the sound it makes as it travels across the rocks. Watch the ripples, how they pick up the sunlight, how the light dances across the surface of the water. Listen to the sound of the water. Hear the small waves as they lap against the bank. Truly hear the water, let the water fill you up. Nothing but the water and the feel of the warm sun on your back. Feel your body in the water. It's warm from the sun, and the waves play against your arms and legs. You feel light, lighter than you have ever felt before. The water picks you up now and holds you in its embrace. You float, feeling as if your body has no weight. Let the water carry you along, feeling the slight bumps from the rocks under the current. Notice the fish swimming along with you. You are light and free, free to allow the water to carry you anywhere you want to go. Now think of that place. Think of your room, the room you have in your cottage. Think of the small bed with the brightly colored quilt, the pictures you have drawn on the walls. Picture yourself there and feel it happen." Granny stopped talking and watched Tilly closely. Something was happening this time. She could feel it; there was something happening to Tilly. It didn't feel exactly like traveling, but she knew the girl was no longer fully sitting in front of her. She was somewhere else. *Please, Light, let her travel. She wants it so badly.* Granny got up from her chair and fixed herself another cup of tea. *This might take a while.*

She sat back in the chair with her cup of tea and watched Tilly closely. She was there, but not there, exactly like you are when you travel. While her body remained in the chair in front of Granny, Tilly's spirit was gone from it. There were still things about traveling that Granny did not entirely understand, the separation of spirit and body felt almost magical.

She knew there was no magic involved, just a gift that you could will to your advantage. Still, it was a wonder, even after so many years of living with her gift. She could understand why Tilly wanted it so badly. It made you feel special that was hard to describe to ordinary people. They could not understand, so she kept it to herself until she met the Mountain Folk, Ronan in particular. It felt so good to talk with someone who had the same gifts. Think what it would be like to talk to Tilly about it without feeling the guilt of having something she did not have. Granny sighed and set her empty cup beside her on the floor. She waited patiently for what she knew could be a good bit of time.

Tilly stirred and a long sigh filled the quiet room. Slowly she opened her eyes and smiled to see Granny sitting patiently across the room, watching her. "Have you been watching me the whole time?"

"No, I made a cup of tea and took a little nap here in my chair. I've got better things to do than stare at you for hours, missy!"

"I had the sweetest dream. It was a dream of you; you and a young man. You were so pretty, Granny, and he was quite handsome. Granny, tell me the story again about the time you met my grandfather. I love hearing that story."

Granny stared at her for a moment before answering, a frown creasing the space between her eyes. "What do you mean, Tilly? I've never told you that story. I've told no one the story of how I met your grandfather."

"Don't be silly, of course you did. How else would I know? You found him in the woods. He had been hunting or trapping, I forget which. Whatever he was doing that day, it was against the law. He was poaching, trying to feed his family. His da had died, and he had a mother and two sisters to feed. But they found him out there, and they took him up and beat him so that he would never come back to poach again. In my dream, you found him under the bushes, covered in blood and dirt. You took him home, and fed him herbs to heal him, covered his bruises and cuts with poultices. I believe you fed him broth, remember? You told me all about it."

Tilly smiled at Granny. "And after you healed him, he went back to where he belonged and you thought you would never see him again. But one day, you heard a knock on your door and when you opened it, there he stood with a handful of flowers. Flowers he picked from your own yard, as I recall. At first you were angry, but then you laughed because you said he looked so earnest with his handful of flowers stolen from your own yard. Remember? You married him and went to live with his mother and sisters. The sisters grew up and married fine men and one day, his beloved mother died. Shortly after that, you had a sweet little girl, my mother."

Tilly frowned at the memory. "But then, something terrible happened, and he died. You tried so hard to keep him alive, but it was no good. He died, and you came back to your cottage in this village, where you raised your daughter by yourself. Such a beautiful, sad story, Granny, but I like it better when you tell it." Tilly sat back in her chair and closed her eyes, waiting for the story to begin.

Granny sat in shocked silence for what seemed like minutes but was only the time it took to calm her breathing. "Tilly, did you just dream this?"

"I don't know. It felt as if I was asleep, and when I woke, I remembered it. You were talking about the water, and then I saw all of this story. It felt like a memory. Isn't it?"

"Yes, Tilly, it's a memory, but it is my memory not yours. I have never told you one word of what you have just related to me. Somehow, you have been able to find the source of my memories and they seem very real to you as if you knew them. My memories have become your memories it seems. What else do you remember?"

Tilly sat up and looked at Granny. "Now I know how it feels when you travel. Sadly, I can't do it, but I know how it feels. It's strange, I don't know how, but Granny, I know it. As surely as I feel this chair beneath me, I know how it feels. And I know more. I know how you choose what herbs to use for what ailment. It's as if there is all this new knowledge in my head. If I start to truly think about it, there is too much knowledge and so many feelings. It's all tangled up in my mind. Oh Granny, what is it?"

"It is one of the rarest gifts I have ever known, my sweet girl. I have read about this in my great grandmother's book, but I have known no one who could do what you can do. You can become another person, with all the feelings and knowledge that person has, memories even, the things that make them unique. This is a rare gift, and I'm not sure how you will control it, but you will learn. My dear, you have found your gift, and it is a wonderful gift indeed." Granny sat back and watched Tilly. The girl's face was serene, calm, and still. No more furrowed brow, no more frown around her lips, just a small smile and a light in her eyes that Granny had never seen before. *And yet, I am frightened for her. This is a gift that is hard to control but control it she must or it threatens to swallow her whole.*

Tilly's face lit up with a smile. "I have a gift? My own gift? I was so sure it had passed me by. You will help me with it, won't you, Granny? Help me learn how to use it without it using me?"

Granny nodded. "Of course. I would never send you out without help, but this is a gift that I am not fully aware of, Tilly. So, we will need to control it together until you learn to control it on your own." Granny raised her finger to make yet another point when a loud knock on the door interrupted her.

With a quizzical look, she rose from her chair to open the door. "Oh Granny, by the Light, I'm glad you are here. I am to bring you to the Mountain Folk as soon as your feet can carry you." Keven stood in her doorway, chest heaving as if he had run all the way down the mountain.

"Light, boy, come in this house and tell me what has you so out of breath and desperate looking." Granny reached out with a hand that was much stronger than it looked and, wrapping it around his forearm, dragged him through her doorway.

"Oh Granny, I am so glad I found you." Keven repeated. "They need you up at our village. My da sent me to fetch you. He says you are to come quickly."

"Why? Is someone hurt? Why can't Ronan take care of it? She is gifted with herbs and such."

"No, Granny. No one is sick. It's Conor. He's gone into the cave, and Ronan thinks he's lost or something. Just come, won't you?"

Chapter Fifteen

TILLY'S GIFT

Granny turned to Tilly, "Looks like we're climbing a mountain, Girl. Keven, tell me everything you know."

Keven sat in the proffered chair while Granny bustled with the teakettle and the fire. "A woman showed up last night in the storm. She had Wolf with her, Granny. We, none of us, knew her, but she is from your village. Doir something, I think she said."

"Doiranne? What on earth would Doiranne be doing up on the mountain?"

"She came because she heard Conor had gone there. There's a man she says is up to no good and might harm Conor. I forgot his name, Granny. I'm sorry."

"It is all right, Keven. I know exactly who you are talking about. It's Traynor, the tinker who has been here for weeks now. I wondered why he didn't move on, and now I know. He is not selling anything, he is searching for something. I should have known. I should have seen this coming. The Light take me for a stupid old woman!" Keven shook his head yes, and then violently whipped it back and forth denying Granny's last words.

"Here, drink this tea. It will revive you." She handed Kevin a cup and turned to cut bread and cheese for him. "Eat all of this, and then you go on back to your folks, Keven. Tell Aelf and everyone that we will be along shortly. I don't want anyone to go near the cave until we get there. Will you make them understand that? Not even Ronan, not even traveling. It is not safe if Traynor is there and he is who I think he is. Now, you eat and then scat, boy!"

Keven gratefully bit into a large hunk of white cheese, stuffing his cheeks full. At Granny's frown, he chewed more slowly, washing it down with tea.

As the door closed behind Keven, Tilly looked questioningly at Granny. "How is that man, Traynor, a threat to Conor? To anyone? He seems harmless if a bit too friendly. And I've gotten to know Roisin a little, now that she is not trying so hard to be a friend."

Granny began pulling things out of her cupboards and laying them out on the table. She shook her head before answering, "Traynor is not anything at all what he seems. I believe he uses the clever guise of a tinker to search from town to village. It's the perfect way to do it because who would question a tinker traveling around so much? It was odd that he didn't move on, but now I know it's because he found what he was looking for here in our little village. We'll need to talk with Roisin before we start for the Mountain Folk village. I'll need more information. As it is, I will not travel to the cave, not yet, anyway. Not without more information." She began stuffing the things she had into her pack, rolling extra clothing into tight rolls to make them fit. "I suppose you are going to want to come?"

"There was no question of that, Granny. I'll pack and meet you in the green."

Roisin sat at her makeshift table, sorting colorful buttons from a large basket, when Tilly walked across the green. She smiled up at Tilly, glad for company. "I haven't spoken to anyone in days. I'm happy to see you, Tilly."

Tilly sat across from her and, with her hands, scooped a pile of the buttons toward her. Without a word, she began sorting them, first by size and then by color. The two worked silently, a comfortable silence that friends sometimes share. Tilly was soon lost in the task; a feeling of weightlessness overtook her as she sat on the hard bench. Her hands paused in their work, as the feeling of floating down the stream overcame her. Roisin searched her friend's face, wondering at her closed eyes and half-parted lips. She didn't speak, didn't want to break whatever reverie Tilly was lost in. She smiled and continued making piles of buttons.

Granny strode across the green as if the hounds of darkness were following her. Her face was grim, her eyes hard as she approached Roisin's camp. She halted and looked searchingly at Tilly. Raising her eyebrows, she turned to Roisin. "She was helping me sort buttons, and I think she fell asleep."

"That is not sleep. It is something else. Do not wake her, she will come back to us in a moment, I hope. Meanwhile, where is your father? I need to speak with him."

"What in the Light does everyone need with Traynor? You are the second person to come into my camp, demanding to know where the man is. He has been gone for days now, Granny. I believe he has gone up to the mountains, but why, I couldn't say. I don't know when he will be back. And honestly, I am not sure I care."

"As I thought. I wanted to know if you would be truthful with me."

"I have no reason not to be, Granny. I am not that man's keeper. He comes and goes as he pleases without my say so, or a single thought for my wellbeing."

"What did he go there for? Do you know?"

"Not for certain, but I think it has something to do with Conor. He was furious that Conor had gone to the Mountain Folk, as you call them. I think he went to their village to find him."

Tilly stirred and shook her head softly, back and forth, as if to clear out a thought. She smiled up at Granny, "When did you get here? Was I gone?"

"Yes, you were gone. I don't want you to do that unless I am here with you to guide you. Tilly, you are playing with fire if you do this on your own. Please?"

"I'm sorry, Granny. But as soon as I sat down with Roisin, I knew I had to go there. There is something that I am called to know about Roisin and Traynor. Let me sort it out, please."

"Good, you sort. Roisin and I will talk, right my girl? I want to know about Traynor. Who he is, what he wants, what he intends to do. I need the truth. Conor's life may depend on it."

Roisin sighed and looked toward the mountains. "I don't know how much I can tell you. He does not confide in me, you know. My job is to cook for him and wash his clothes. I am here to draw people to our fire at night so that he can examine them somehow. There are things I don't know about, but he is clear what my role in all of this. I am the flame to which the moths come. If they come too close, Traynor deals with them, harshly."

Roisin spoke earnestly, "We have been traveling for as long as I can remember. Always a new town or village. We've never stayed in any of them as long as we have stayed here. It was clear to me there is something here in this village he wants or needs. No matter where we've been, there is always a man who comes sneaking around to see him. I don't know if he has come here, but I have seen him in the past. Liam is his name, but this I only know from eavesdropping. I am not supposed to know that he comes around."

"Traynor asked me, no, demanded that I befriend Tilly and Conor. Again, I don't know why. He gives me orders and if I do not obey, it goes badly for me. I've learned to keep my mouth shut and do as I am told. He talks sometimes, mutters really, and I listen. It has something to do with powers. I know Traynor has powers he uses to hurt people without touching them. It's how he punishes me. From across the green, he can strike me or pinch me. I never see it coming. I don't know what else he can do, but I know he sits by the fire and mutters words that have no meaning to me. He says he sees things in the fire, but I see nothing but flames."

At this, Granny frowned at Roisin. "He says he sees things in the fire, you say. Does he do anything after?"

"Yes, he usually leaves for a few hours, sometimes a day or two. When he comes back, he is in a foul mood, and I make myself as small as I can and stay out of his way. This time though, he left for a short time and when he returned, he was quite happy. As if he had finally found what he had been searching for all this time. I'm sorry, I really know only that."

Tilly shook her head. "Tell me about the time he left and came back with two children. You remember, Roisin, the girl and boy?"

Roisin's face paled and her eyes grew large as she looked from Tilly to Granny. "I don't know what you are talking about." She shook her head and looked down at her hands in confusion.

"But you do know, Roisin. And you could not live with yourself, knowing what he did. Knowing what happened to those children. Tell us, or I will tell it."

Granny reached out and gripped Tilly's arm. "You went there, didn't you? You went into Roisin's life! Oh Tilly, you are going to get burnt by this fire you are playing with!"

Roisin looked back and forth between them. "You can see my life? You can see things that have happened to me?"

Tilly nodded and raised her eyebrows. "Start talking, Roisin!"

The girl nodded and wiped at the tears from her face. "Traynor had been sitting by the fire for nights, sometimes all night long, muttering and staring into the flames. After three days and nights, he left without saying a word. It wasn't unusual for him to leave without saying anything, but it was unusual that he spent so much time with the fire. I could see that he was troubled, angry even at what he saw."

"We camped outside a small village some ways away. Very few people came out to our camp; there was no music, no dancing. Everyone in the village was very glum, they wanted nothing to do with us. It fit Traynor's mood, so I was glad there were no villagers coming around."

"Get to it. What about the children?"

"He came back two days later, but not alone this time. This time he had two children with him, a boy and a girl. That had never happened before. You must believe me. He had brought no one back with him before. As soon as he came, he told me to pack up the wagon, we were leaving. I did as I was told. I tried to comfort the children, but it was as if they couldn't see or hear me. As if they were in a trance."

Roisin continued, "We packed up the camp and drove the wagon deeper into the woods, along a trail that was barely there. Our poor mule struggled, but he kept on because Traynor wouldn't have it any other way. He seemed like a man possessed. He muttered and used the whip on the poor beast. I held onto the children in the back of the wagon, afraid it would throw us out. We came to a large clearing, well shaded with trees all around, and there we stopped. He took the children out of my arms and led them back into the trees. Once they left our camp, I followed them, afraid of what he was going to do, but he turned on me so violently I turned back. I set up our camp and made dinner, and still, he and the children did not return. There was enough stew for all of us because I wanted the children to eat." Roisin shook her head and looked across the green towards the distant mountain, anywhere but at Tilly or Granny.

"They were gone until nightfall. When they came back, Traynor was in a worse mood than I had ever seen him in. The children were like sleepwalkers, alive but not aware of us, of anything. He wouldn't let me give them any of the stew. He ate like a starving man, but he wouldn't let them eat. 'They won't touch it,' he said. 'Leave them alone.' I begged him to tell me where they came from, what he wanted with them, what was he going to do. I pleaded with him to take them back to their village wherever they came from. He laughed at me and called me names. He told me I was weak, not worthy of being with him. I must have taken after my mother. Stupid cow she was, he said. I had heard this before, but now there were children involved. While Traynor was occupied, I took them into the back of the wagon and covered them with quilts. I slept with them, hoping to keep them safe from him."

"In the morning, he grabbed them by their hands and began dragging them into the woods again. I called out and ran after them. I tried to pull them away from him, but he lashed out at me in a way that he had never had before. It felt like he was hitting me about the face and neck with a stick or a club. I fell to the ground and let go of the children. It was the last that I ever saw of them. They never woke up, they never spoke, they never even saw me, but I saw them. I saw them then, but never again." Roisin halted then and looked directly at Tilly. "Did you really know this, or did you trick me into telling it? Because I have told no one, not one word."

"I knew it. I saw it, but I thought it might do you good to tell it, Roisin. You have been holding onto that knowledge for a long time, and it has done nothing to serve you. I think it's time to let it go. You could not control Traynor, not then, not now. I think it might just take all of us to control him, if that is even possible." Tilly looked at Granny when she said this.

"Tilly, you saw this from Roisin's past, but can you see what he wanted with those children. Can you see anything that she did not see?"

"No, I can only see what Roisin saw and felt. But my intuition tells me he thought those children had something he wanted, and that he was very disappointed. He is not a man to disappoint, I wager."

"Well, let's see if we can disappoint him a bit more. Roisin, I think he is in the mountain, in the cave that held our children. I have reason to think that Conor is there as well. I don't know what his intentions with Conor are, but you and I both know they can only be evil. We are going to the Mountain Folk and from there, we will see what we see."

Roisin did not answer. She left them and began pulling things out of her wagon and stuffing them into a large pack. "I am coming. I don't know what good I can do, maybe nothing, but I must come. I was a coward. For a very long time, I have been a coward. I know that, but I cannot let Traynor hurt anyone else."

Chapter Sixteen

A Past Life

Granny set a fast pace toward the Mountain Folk village, tucked high in the mountains. Tilly and Roisin attempted conversation but soon lapsed into puzzled looks and a faster pace between themselves, trying their best to keep up with her. "I'm not about to keep them waiting, girls. Keep up or go back home. Your choice." Granny hitched her skirt up around white, bony legs, allowing them to move even faster. The girls followed suit, tucking the hem of their skirts into their belts.

A little past midday, she stopped in a grove of elms, plunked down, and opened her pack. Digging down in the bottom, she brought out bread and cheese wrapped in a linen cloth. Tilly and Roisin more fell onto the ground than sat. Roisin immediately pulled off her boots and socks, allowing her feet to wiggle in the fresh air. Tilly poked around in her pack and found dried apples and cold mutton that she had purloined from her mother's kitchen. *I will pay for taking those, I warrant.* Roisin looked at the feast that was spread out before them and began looking through her pack.

"I have little, but I brought some eggs that I boiled up this morning and I have some carrots and turnips from the village garden."

Granny smiled at her. "Let's leave the mutton and the vegetables for our evening meal. I think the bread and cheese will do nicely with those dried apples for an after meal treat."

The three settled back, leaning against the broad tree trunks, and eating quietly, legs stretched out in front of them, Roisin's bare toes still wiggling back and forth. Tilly brought out a bottle of water and passed it to Roisin who took it gratefully.

"Granny, what exactly does Traynor want with Conor? Do you know?"

Granny shook her head. "Does anyone ever know what another person wants, Tilly? Not even me. No, but I can guess. Traynor is someone much older than he appears, and I believe he comes from a time when powers ruled our world much more than they do now. Over time, and I am talking about a good deal of time, so many of us lost our powers. Thank the Light, I was fortunate to have a grandmother and great grandmother who knew how important it was to nurture your gifts or you would lose them. These gifts are not something that are always with us at the tip of our fingers. They must be practiced and kept alive. That is one reason I have been working with you. It is a mistake to start too soon because most children don't know how to control themselves. They lack the self-control that enables them to use their powers wisely. I never thought to work with Conor, but again, that's my mistake. With Mara as his mother, I should have known he would have gifts. It seems I have missed quite a bit lately. I really am getting older." She shook her head at her last words.

She spoke thoughtfully, "I questioned the idea that Traynor brought those children back to your camp, Roisin, because I thought them too young to be of any use to him. That was his level of desperation, I think. He has been searching for something for a very long time. Now that I look back, I'm glad you did not find your gift until now, Tilly. As strong as you are, he might have set his sights on you instead of Conor."

"You did not know that Conor had gifts?"

"No, I did not. He has kept to himself these last two years since we brought the children back home. I have seen little of him, certainly not spent any time alone and quiet with him."

Roisin looked up from her midday meal. "What is this about bringing children home? I've heard snatches of conversations, but I don't know the story."

Granny began stuffing the leftover food into her pack. "I tell you what, girl. You keep up with me until evening and I will tell you all about it." She winked at Tilly and rose easily to her feet. Roisin laced her boots on and the two girls struggled up, groaning as their legs and backs protested.

Evening found them by a clear mountain stream with a good rock abutment that seemed mercifully clear of smaller rocks. Granny scouted the area around them for larger rocks to build a fire ring. Tilly and Roisin gathered firewood, stacking it in neat piles near the rocks that Granny arranged in a circle. She had flat rocks for heating water and food, and from her skirt pocket, pulled two pieces of flint. Piling dried leaves on top of small sticks, she soon had sparks falling freely to bring a small flame. These she fed with dry kindling until the fire crackled and sent up a plume of clean, white smoke.

Roisin brought out her carrots and turnips, and using her belt knife, soon had them cut in small pieces. Tilly took the small iron kettle that Granny set out and filled it from the stream. Herbs, vegetables, and the leftover mutton all went into the pot; Granny stirring with a stick that Roisin handed her, stripped of bark, and shaved smooth.

Soon bowls were filled with the rich stew and the kettle was cleaned and put back on the fire with water for tea. Roisin ate thoughtfully, looking at Granny and Tilly. "Your story about the children was hard to hear. I can only imagine the grief of the parents when they went missing. And to think that it was Conor's parents who did this. I'm not sure that I understand Ceobhran, but I have heard of worse things, I warrant. Do you think that Mara and Jebez are still in the cave? What about that person, Sean? Would he be under the spell of Ceobhran still? I have so many questions, Granny."

"As I expected, and some of them I cannot answer. I have not traveled to the cave since we brought the children out. I had no reason to do so. As far as I knew, Mara and Sean were both under Ceobhran's power, a fitting end for Mara, I believe. I was happy to think that she would stay powerless forever. Sadly, I guess I didn't consider Jebez. He's always been the sort of person you didn't think about. Sean, too. It's not that what he did wasn't brave, but he didn't do it out of bravery.

He did it out of a need for revenge and without knowing what was happening. I'm not sure you can call stupidity bravery." Granny shrugged and looked off toward the mountain. "Be that as it may, I was never curious enough to go back there. My mistake, apparently. They have been up to no good. And this man, Liam, that you talked about? I suppose he is there as well."

Roisin shook her head. "I don't know, but I can tell you he always showed up, no matter where we camped. He was never far behind us."

"We'll start out early in the morning, girls. Let's get whatever rest we can." Granny wrapped her woolen cloak around her and settled back against the rock wall. Before long, small, soft snores drifted across the small clearing. Tilly smiled and leaned against the rocks, afraid sleep would elude her this night.

She stared up at the night sky as it darkened above her. Roisin was sleeping soundly, used to camping as she was, and except for Granny's soft snores, it was quiet and peaceful in their camp. Tilly watched the night sky as it scattered stars above her head, some shining so brightly it looked as if she could touch them, others faint and barely visible to her eyes. She leaned her head back and watched the sky as an occasional shooting star streaked across her vision, making her smile as she made her wish. Slowly and without thinking, her eyes softly closed as sleep finally overtook her.

Tilly stood in a magnificent house, something not even her imagination could envision, and yet, here she was. Exquisite marble floors swept before a grand staircase, which curved around and up toward balconies of intricately carved ebony colored wood. Tall leaded windows graced the walls from floor to ceiling, draperies of rich silk pulled to the side to let in the bright sun. A fireplace generous enough to roast a small ox filled one wall, and above it hung tapestries artfully woven from threads of beautiful hues.

As soaring as the ceilings were, the tapestries hung nearly from the carved crown molding and cornices to just above the mantel fashioned from half an oak tree. Tilly recognized the black velvet from an ancient scrap of material her mother kept in her sewing basket. Rich velvet it was with vibrant colored threads woven across it that stood out against the black background. Craning her neck to look up at them, she realized the tapestries told a story, one of a young man battling strange creatures Tilly had neither seen nor read about. One portrayed an enormous serpent with jeweled eyes that glittered against the black background, another showed a monstrous cat with fangs that dripped blood from a fresh kill, while the last held a sort of bull with too many heads, steam raging from its nostrils. All were different scenes, save for the young man who appeared in them all. He was tall, even compared to the animals, his straight brown hair falling across his forehead in a way that was familiar to Tilly. She turned around in circles, admiring the wall coverings and the lavish furnishings in the room. *Where am I? This is a dream like no other I have ever had.*

A noise brought her around to stare up at the balcony. A young man leaned against the railing, staring at the wall below him. He seemed unaware she was there. She caught her breath as he brought up a hand to brush the hair from his forehead. *Conor! By the Light, he looks like Conor!*

The young man walked down the wide marble staircase, the heels of his boots sounding against the hard floors. He moved to the fireplace and stood gazing up at the tapestry above. In it, he crouched in front of the snake as if daring it to strike. The snake seemed perfectly willing to oblige the young man, coiled as he was, his head reared back into position, his fangs dripping with poison. The man held a great broadsword in his hand, as if he would strike the head from the serpent. His face twisted in a grimace of hate, lips drawn back from his teeth in a snarl, his arm upraised and steady.

The young man looked up and laughed to himself. "If they only knew how it really happened, they might not be so quick to immortalize it." He chuckled again and sat in one of the matching velvet divans placed in front of the fireplace. Stretching out his legs, he propped one booted foot on top of the other in an obvious position of waiting. Tilly wondered what he was waiting for.

It didn't take long for her patience to be rewarded. A heavy knock sounded on the great oak doors that towered at the end of the long room. The young man smiled and raised his hand. With a flick of his wrist, the doors flew open to reveal a man dressed in black boots with soft leather pants tucked into the tops. A white shirt with lace at the cuffs and neck set off his dark face, a face that should have been handsome but just missed the mark, perhaps because of the constant sneer that played around his lips. The sneer and the small eyes set too close together gave his face a look of cruelty.

"I see you made it, Liam. What does the man want now?"

Tilly shrank back against a wall, half hidden by the draperies that fell beside the window. *Liam? He's the man Roisin said was always coming around. What is he doing here? That man looks like Conor and the way he brushes his hair off his forehead tells me it is him, but that is impossible.*

The man he named Liam walked across the room, his eyes darting back and forth as if he expected to see something other than the man who addressed him. "I've come to beg if that's what you need. Traynor needs you, Concobhar. He says it's time to stop playing around and get to work. He said to tell you he needs his creatures back again." Liam waved his hand at the tapestries on the walls to indicate the creatures woven into the pictures.

Concobhar did not acknowledge his words. He continued to stare at the floor or at his booted foot still propped on the other. Idly, he drummed his fingers on the arm of the divan. Still, he said nothing.

"Are you listening? The Light take you for an impossible fool. You know what Traynor can do, you've seen it. Now work with him, and the two of you can move mountains. Stubbornness will get you nowhere with Traynor, I guarantee that."

Still the man he addressed as Concobhar continued to stare and drum his fingers, without so much as an acknowledgement of Liam's words. Finally, his fingers stopped, and he removed his booted foot from atop the other. He stood up in one fluid motion so quickly that Liam was left blinking his eyes. Tilly held her breath. She had seen Conor move like that, rarely, only when he was angry or was through dealing with someone. She, too, held her breath.

In two long strides, Concobhar crossed the floor to stand over Liam, who craned his neck to look upward. It seemed to him, somehow, the man had grown taller in the space of walking across the room. *My imagination, but he seems taller somehow.*

The words that Concobhar uttered were clipped as if he were biting each word off and spitting them at to Liam. "I have told you this before, but I will tell you again, in the chance that you did not understand me. I will not do his bidding, not now, not ever. He thinks I am weak, but Liam, I am not. He does not want to push this. Go back and tell him no! One more time, no! Now see yourself out. I don't want you in my home." Without waiting to see if Liam would obey, Concobhar turned on his heels and walked across the room to stare out the window, the window at which Tilly shrank behind the curtain. She heard the doors close, but still did not take a breath.

"I cannot see you, but I know you are here. Who are you? What do you want with me?"

Tilly shook her head, but other than that, did not move from her spot. *If I pretend I am not here, he will give up. He'll walk away.*

"So, you cannot answer me. That means you are a dreamer; you are here only in your dreams. I hope you find your way back home; this is a dangerous place to be right now." He turned and walked toward a hallway at the end of the room.

Tilly took a deep, shuddering breath. It was Conor, but not Conor. There was a stillness to him, a shadow across him that Tilly understood was dangerous. *Oh, I am going to have to talk with Granny and she will not be happy that I did this. I wish I could understand how this could be my friend and yet, not my friend.*

Tilly woke with a start, her eyes wide, her breath rapid and shallow. She closed her eyes and slowed her breathing, her mind full of the images she had witnessed. *I don't understand. The man there was so like Conor. Can't be his father, Jebez is that. So, who was that man who looks and acts so much like Conor?* Tilly looked around the small camp. Granny was sleeping peacefully exactly as she had been, her back against the rock wall, her head nodding to her chest. Roisin was still wrapped in her cloak, near to the fire. Tilly stood and stretched, her legs and back aching from the cold ground and the hard climb. She squatted next to the fire, careful to keep her skirt out of the ashes. Using a piece of the wood, she stirred until she found the hot coals hidden beneath the ash. These she spread out before adding small sticks and dried leaves. Soon she had the fire burning brightly, adding warmth to her chilled body. Walking around the camp in ever-widening circles, she gathered up what few sticks she could find. *It will be enough to keep the fire going until first light. We'll be able to make tea to warm us.*

With the fire crackling, she sat with her back against a tree and thought about her dream. It felt almost like traveling might have felt, but it was not quite the same. She thought about the young man, about Liam, and the impossibility of it all.

The sun's rays peaked over the mountains, dappling the trees in light, and still Tilly sat and thought about the scene in her dream. With the sun came the first soft morning sounds; the chittering goldfinch was first to greet the sun followed by the blackbird perched high in a nearby pine. A red squirrel crept close to the camp, nose twitching, searching out discarded and forgotten crumbs. Tilly reached in her pocket for a small piece of bread and breaking it into bits, threw it toward the squirrel. She laughed to see the birds swoop down and grab some of it before the squirrel could make her move. So engaged was she with the morning creatures, she did not hear Granny approach the fire.

"Good morning, Tilly. You are up early. Did you sleep?"

"I did. I slept, and I dreamt. If you fix tea, I will tell you all about it."

Granny raised an eyebrow at Tilly in question, but she shrugged and walked to the stream for water. With Tilly's hot fire, she soon had water boiling for tea. Measuring out the fine leaves of tea into three cups, she covered them with the boiling water and set them aside to steep. Handing one of the cups to Tilly, she carried another to Roisin as she slept and set it down next to her. "She'll have it when she wakes."

With her own cup of tea firmly in hand, Granny sat down easily across the fire from Tilly. "Now, tell me about this dream you had."

As Tilly related her dream, Granny's forehead creased in a frown that grew deeper with each word she spoke. At last, when Tilly ran out of words, she sat quietly staring down into her cup as if the tea leaves at the bottom would provide her with answers to her questions.

Granny drew a long breath and let it out in a whistling sound. "Well, you already know that I am going to be angry at you for doing this without my help, but I suspect your gifts are sneaking up on you without you calling them up. This is not a dream exactly. You might have felt like you were sleeping, but it is my guess that you were doing something before to help set your mind free. Do you remember anything?"

"Granny, why is that important? Isn't it much more important that it could have been Conor that I saw?"

"Yes, and we will get to that, but while it is fresh in your mind, you have got to remember what you were doing right before you started dreaming. It's important, Tilly. I wouldn't ask if it wasn't."

"I'm sorry, I know that. Let me see if I can remember... oh yes, I was watching the night sky, the stars wheeling overhead. I felt like I could lose myself in all the beautiful lights. Like the other day when you asked me to think about the river, it felt as if I was floating."

Granny smiled at Tilly. "First water flowing and now stars across the sky. For most of us, Tilly, there is just one way that we can touch our gifts and bring them forward. For me, it is water, the sound of the river flowing across rocks. I tried that with you, and it worked. But now you say that the stars also worked for you, a rare combination." Granny sighed and smiled to herself. "First the girl has no gifts, and then she has so many I'm not sure what to do about them. We will deal with that later. You think you saw Conor last night, but in a place you didn't recognize. You say the man they call Liam was there, but you have never seen him, so that's hard to say if it is the same man. My instinct tells me it is. That he mentioned Traynor confirms my suspicions about those two. I never thought in my wildest dream that Conor would share their history. This puts a whole new light on the matter."

Granny walked to where Roisin slept on, oblivious to the morning light or their conversation. She shook her shoulder softly and urged the girl to wake. "We need to talk."

Roisin sat up, blinking at the light in her eyes. She picked up the cup of tea that Granny left nearby and began drinking it in loud, happy slurps. At Granny's look, she slowed and sipped it quietly, abashed by her lack of manners. "You both look very serious. Did something happen in the night? Did the wolves come and steal our food?" Roisin smiled as she said this.

"No, no wolves, but something has happened that I hoped I would never see. Tilly had a dream last night that was more than an ordinary dream. It's hard to explain, but it is a combination of dreaming and traveling. That is for another time. The crux is this. She saw Conor as a young man; not in the future, but I suspect in the past. She also saw the man you call Liam, and he spoke about Traynor. He said that Traynor needed Conor, for what he didn't say but it seems it has something to do with creatures of some sort. It seems this has been a pattern for some years. At least, that is my best guess. I want to know from you. Has Traynor ever said anything to lead you to believe that he has lived before this time?"

Roisin sipped her tea quietly and thought about Granny's question. "Not exactly, but there was a time when we met someone in our travels, a woman with long black hair. There was a man with her, greasy black hair and an immense beard. He talked with them for a long time. Mostly her, I think. The man stood by but didn't seem to take part in the conversation. I asked him about her, and he said that he knew her from a time long ago. He did not say he knew her from a long time ago, but from a time long ago. I thought it was an odd way of putting it, but when I questioned what he meant by that, he stopped talking. That's as close as I have come from getting any information from him."

Granny shook her head. "Let's have our morning meal and get as quickly as we can to the Mountain Folk village. I just hope we are not too late."

Chapter Seventeen

CONOR

Conor sat with his back against the rock wall, his legs stretched out in front of him. *How long have I been here? Odd, I don't feel tired or hungry. I do feel like the floor of this cave is hard, but I don't feel uncomfortable. In fact, I don't feel much of anything.*

He stood up and began walking around the chamber. He looked at the tapestries hanging on the walls; tapestries woven from the most beautiful colors. One with a snake, coiled and ready to strike, its fangs dripping with what he imagined being poison. A man, somehow familiar to Conor, stood over the snake, his face in a grimace, his arm upraised, brandishing an enormous sword. Conor moved to the next one which depicted the same man, but this time holding a sword with its point against the throat of a huge cat, blood dripping from its mouth. Still, a third showed a bull with three heads, steam blowing from its nostrils into the face of the same man. Conor stared at the tapestries; memories washing over him. Memories that he could not catch and hold. *He looks so familiar, but it can't be anyone from our village. It must be from a dream.*

Conor turned to see Liam stirring the fire, setting a kettle of water on the coals for tea. Mara sat on a pile of pillows, brushing her long black hair, letting it fall freely to the ground behind her. Jebez brought in more firewood and stacked it next to the fire. Liam acknowledged it with a grunt but said nothing to Jebez. The man shrugged and walked over to Mara. Gently taking the brush from her hand, he ran it through to the very ends, lifting the heavy mass of black hair with his hand as he did so. Over and over, he brushed her hair until at last; she turned and took the brush from him.

Conor watched all of this from across the chamber. *They have no idea I am here. I wonder if my body is still out there, on the platform?*

Liam poured boiling water into cups with tea leaves and handed them to Mara and Jebez. "I don't know what it is, but I have the feeling that someone is watching me. At first, I thought it might be that nosy old woman from the village, but I know Traynor placed defenses at the cave entrance so it can't be her. Must be getting jumpy."

Mara raised her eyebrows at Jebez. He studiously ignored her look, blowing on his tea to cool it. "I don't know, Liam. I feel nothing except the same damp, cold cave I have felt for a long time. When are we leaving this Light forsaken place? When is Traynor going to tell us what it is he wants?"

"When he's ready and not before," growled Liam. "You would be wise not to question him, Jebez. Never mind that he seems to have found favor in you. It might not last."

"You are right, Liam, I will not be questioned." Traynor held out his hand for a cup of tea, fully expecting that Liam would have it ready for him. "And you are right. There is someone here, someone in this chamber as we speak. Someone who has left his body behind for a second time to travel. He is so strong, stronger than he knows, but now I need him to reunite with his body. If he does not, he risks losing himself forever, and that is something I cannot have."

Mara gasped and looked wildly around the chamber. "I didn't think he could it, Traynor. I only told him to calm him down."

"I know. Mara, I will deal with you later. Do not think for a moment that you will go unpunished, but for now, I need to speak with Concobhar."

Traynor turned in a circle slowly, searching all the spaces of the chamber until he was satisfied that he had found Conor. "I know you are there, boy. I can't see you, but I can feel you as if I could touch you with my hand. Let me tell you what is going to happen now. You are going to go back to your body, back to where you sleep on the platform. From there, we will carry your body back outside the cave where you left it. When we do, you will reunite with yourself. If you do not, this part of you that is here now will grow dimmer over time, until there is nothing left of you but a shadow. Already I warrant you do not feel cold or hungry or tired. I guess you can't feel the rocks under your feet or the fire's warmth against your skin. That is your spirit losing itself, becoming thinner until nothing is left of it, just a memory. And a memory is not enough to reunite with your body. This comes from traveling when you don't know what you are doing, Concobhar."

"Your dog is not there to help you find your way, but I think you are strong enough to do it without a guide. I will have Mara sit next to your body where your dog was. She is not nearly as important as that flea-bitten mongrel, but she is the strongest thing I have to pull you back. I hope your need for your mother will be enough to bring you back to us. "

With a signal to Liam and Mara, Traynor strode from the chamber, down the long tunnel toward the front of the cave. Once he reached the platform on which Conor's body slept, he waited quietly, feeling for the one person he needed more than anyone to be in that space. At last, he smiled to himself and motioned for Liam to pick up the body. "He's here. Carry him out. Mara, you go as well and sit next to your son. Close your eyes and think of him as a child, a child you held and rocked and loved, if that is possible."

Conor watched the scene in front of him. He watched Traynor search for him before sending Liam and Mara outside into the bright sun. He walked to the edge of the cave and looked at his body where Liam set him down on the ground next to Mara. She reached out her hand but did not touch him, only just laid her hand close to his body. With her eyes closed, she sat still, barely breathing, and it seemed as if a small tear trickled down her face. From where he stood, he felt the pull of a mother's love, bringing him back to his body, back to where he would be whole again. He closed his eyes and willed himself there next to her.

The ground felt hard beneath him, and he smiled to feel it. The sun was warm on his face, and he wanted to sit quietly and hold on to that moment for as long as he could. He realized how close he had been to losing himself now that he felt the sun's rays and the strength of the ground beneath him. A shadow fell across his face, and he grimaced but opened his eyes. Traynor stood above him, looking down.

"Good. You are back. You will stay with me, boy. I have so much to teach you and you want to learn. I know you do."

Chapter Eighteen

REUNITED

Granny stopped in front of a rock wall that towered far above her head. "And here I thought you knew where you were going, Granny Matilda," Roisin shook her head. "Looks to me like you dead ended us."

Tilly laughed and touched her arm, "It happens all the time. It is the cleverness of the Mountain Folk who years ago hid themselves behind this wall. Watch her, Roisin."

Roisin laughed as she watched Granny disappear behind the wall. Eagerly, she followed, slipping between the two walls to come out into the field that lay beyond. "How clever of them to hide in plain sight." She shook her head in wonderment. "I am ready to meet these folk who have made their homes in the mountain caves. I don't think it would be any worse than living in the back of a wagon all my life."

Granny and the pair were met by the Mountain Folk sentries, whose faces split into huge grins at the sight of Granny and Tilly. "Aelf will be glad to see the shadow you bring, Granny Matilda. May your shadow be long and dark." The tallest of the two threw arms around Granny that swallowed her up in a tight embrace. He turned to smile at Tilly and then frowned at Roisin. "Who have you brought here, Granny? If this keeps up, the entire valley might as well move in with us for all the secret we will be."

"I know, Brenden. Hello, Fergus." Her smile included the shorter man still holding onto Tilly in his own embrace. "Believe me when I say that Roisin will be of help to us. Roisin, this is Brenden and Fergus. We are fortunate that they are on guard duty today. Anyone else and the greeting might not have been so easy."

"Now Granny, are you saying that I'm not doin' my job here?" Brenden's hurt look made Granny laugh.

"Nonsense. I just like the way you greet us, my friend. Now let us get to Aelf before he finds out that we have been passing the time of day while he frets and waits. No good will come of that for either of us."

Roisin followed Granny and Tilly as they wound their way up from the valley floor to the caves above. She stopped and stood with mouth falling open to see the warren of caves nestled in the mountain face. There were children running or playing with blocks of wood and toys carved from antlers or bones. Women stirred fires and the smell of sizzling meat and frying cakes of berries and ground nuts made her mouth water. There was activity everywhere; people laughing and talking, men repairing bows and tying feathers to arrow ends with thin pieces of leather, women hunched over animal skins staked to the ground working their magic with stone scrapers, old women with babies on their laps feeding them bits of soft food from their fingers, and young men practicing their skills with spears against tree trunks that looked as if they had withstood years of such practice.

Roisin stopped and stared until finally Tilly tugged on her arm. "Come on. If you don't follow, you will never find the right cave." Obediently, Roisin put away her stare and followed Tilly.

"Aelf, I have brought her. I have brought Granny Matilda!"

"No need to yell so, Brenden. I can see with my own eyes." The man that stepped out of the cave was a big man; tall, and well-muscled, his long hair tied back with a leather thong. He swooped in to grab Granny up and swing her around in the air. "Put me down, this very second, Aelf, before I turn you into a toad or something else just as bad." Granny laughed as she pushed against his embrace.

"Can you do that, Granny? Turn people into toads?" The big man laughed.

"No, the truth is, I wish I could. It would have come in handy in the past. It is so good to see you, Aelf. I understand you have a visitor, and I have brought you more."

Aelf had already moved to Tilly, bending to wrap her in his arms. He held her for just a moment and whispered something in her ear. She closed her eyes and leaned against his chest feeling safe and loved.

"Aelf, this is Roisin. She is here to help us and I think before this is over, we will be grateful for her help."

Aelf held his hand out to Roisin who took it shyly. So much love, so much affection all in one place overwhelmed her.

"Let us sit out here in the sun, Granny. There is more room than in my small home which is overrun with bodies. I will fetch Shaen and the others, and I will send for Cormac and Ronan. Be comfortable here, all of you. Shaen will bring cakes and tea. Don't worry, Granny, I will help her. I have learned a thing or two about being a better partner since you were last here." This he said with a grin that split his face in two.

Doiranne was the first to come out of the cave. Granny stood when she saw her and Doiranne fell into her outstretched arms. "Oh, I am so glad to see you, Granny. So much has happened and much of it I don't understand. I need you to help me sort it all out."

She sat next to Granny on the carved bench, still holding onto her arm. Granny nodded toward Tilly, "Doiranne, I don't know how much you know Tilly, my granddaughter. And you know Roisin, I think. I believe you have had conversations with her in the village green."

Doiranne nodded and Granny continued, "I want to know how it is that you find yourself in these mountains. I have tried putting the pieces together, but the puzzle doesn't fit for me. So, you tell me. How did this happen?"

Doiranne sighed and looked down at her feet. "I am the sort of person people don't notice, Granny. I am practically invisible sometimes, it seems. People say things around me, not noticing that I am there. That is all I can think. I heard bits and pieces of conversations, enough to know that Traynor was in our village for a reason, and it was not to sell his goods. In fact, I'm not sure if he sold anything or not. I learned he was looking for someone, and he thought it was Conor. Now, I don't know Conor and I didn't think he would listen to someone like me, so I never thought to warn him until it was too late and he was gone. Then I learned from Roisin that Traynor was gone. I tried to find you, but you were gone to set a broken leg and Erik Tamen was gone to hunt wolves. That left Tilly until her mother told me she was gone as well. I thought to ask the blacksmith, Tomas. He seems to have a fondness for me, if you can believe that, but I didn't think it fair to involve him in all of this. Though I didn't know at the time what all of this was. I just knew that I had to come to the mountain to warn Conor. As it happens, I found him at the cave, not here because I never would have found here."

This all came out in a rush of words that tumbled and fell over each other. Doiranne stopped and took a breath. She looked around at Granny and the others, but they had not moved, their eyes all fastened to her face. "At any rate, I found Conor sitting outside of the cave with his dog next to him. I thought he was asleep, but now I know differently. I hid, not knowing what to do until Sean came out of the cave. Granny, for the very first time since I've known him, I was happy to see him. But he wasn't the same, not the same Sean that I knew. He was thinner and pale it is true, but it was his eyes that were different. His eyes burned with a fire that was full of anger and hate."

Doiranne wiped away a tear. She scrubbed her eyes with the heels of both hands and took a deep breath. "I promised myself I would not cry." She let out an audible breath and straightened her shoulders. "I tried to talk to him, to Sean, but he could not hear me. It was like he was sleepwalking with eyes open. He grabbed me and started dragging me across the clearing toward the edge. I begged and begged him to wake up, to see me, but he couldn't or wouldn't. I don't know. I cried out to Conor, but he never moved, never opened his eyes. I was alone, alone with Sean, a man I no longer recognized."

"We fought, and I kicked out at him. I was so angry, so frightened that I pushed him and pushed him. I kept pushing until I pushed him over the edge. I killed him. Oh Granny, I killed my own husband. What kind of person am I?"

Granny patted Doiranne softly. "No, my dear, you did not kill your husband. You killed a stranger, a stranger who would have killed you if you hadn't fought back. He was under the influence of Ceobhran, he was not himself. I know that the man who stood in front of you looked like Sean, but he had no soul, Doiranne. There was nothing of him left, just a creature doing the bidding of his master. You can feel pity for him, but no blame to yourself."

Shaen came out of the cave at that moment, carrying a tray of cups, balancing them as she walked. Aelf followed closely behind her with a tray equally balanced full of her cakes. Shaen paused when she saw the scene before her. "I am so glad you are here, Granny. Doiranne has been inconsolable with grief, and I have become fond of her. I have tried my best to help her, but her grief threatens to swallow her." She began handing out cups of tea. She nodded to Aelf to offer cakes to everyone.

While they nibbled at cakes and drank tea, Granny tried once more to comfort Doiranne. "The man you remembered was long gone. I think that too much time had passed under the influence of Ceobhran, and like our children, he was not fully released from the grip. They sent him out to do one thing, and I believe that was to kill you. It might have been a test to see if they could control him enough to do that. It could have been anything. I don't know. I do know that if you had not fought back, you would have been the one at the bottom of the cliff on those rocks. Grieve for the Sean we all lost long ago when he jumped into the path of Ceobhran, but do not grieve for the man you fought against. He is no one you know."

Doiranne looked off into space, considering Granny's words. Everyone was quiet, allowing her time to let the words sink in and take root. She nodded her head, took a deep breath, and straightened her shoulders. "I have come a long way in the past months, but I believe I have further to go. With your help, if you will."

Granny nodded, "I think you can count on all of us, Doiranne. We have bigger fish to fry right now, and it's going to take all of us to do it."

"A whale, I'd say, not a fish! We'll need an immense pan!" This drew laughter from everyone and relieved the tension, if only for a moment.

Chapter Nineteen

A Choice

Conor rose from the ground in one smooth motion, standing over Mara who sat quietly next to him, keeping her hand close to where he sat without touching him. She looked up at him and smiled, "You are back with us. Thank the Light, you are back with us."

Conor reached out his hand to help her rise from the ground. She took it, but quickly bent to brush dirt and leaves from her skirt, refusing to look at his face. Traynor, leaning against a nearby tree, watched mother and son closely. He saw how Mara took Conor's hand but refused to acknowledge his help. He nodded to himself as if it was exactly what he wanted to see.

"I'm sure you are enjoying the sunshine and fresh air, but we have work to do and we must do it inside the mountain. Once we are back in the cave, I would like you to make us all tea, Mara. I think we could use some while we talk."

Mara's face knit into a scowl and she opened her mouth to protest, but one look from Traynor and she closed her mouth and nodded. *You see how he discards you once you give him what he wants. Remember that, if you remember nothing else, remember that!*

Conor stood for a moment in the sun, feeling the warmth on his face. *Why go back into the mountain, into the cave? Why not walk away from here, go back to the village or back to the Mountain Folk?. Why follow Traynor?* He watched Mara's shoulders slump ever so slightly as she turned to follow Traynor into the darkness. He watched Jebez's face light up at the sight of Mara's distress and Liam's nonchalance as they followed Traynor. *I don't know why, but I can't leave her here alone. I think she has no one to stand beside her and I think she is going to need someone.* Conor shrugged his shoulders and turned toward the cave entrance.

As he followed Traynor past the stone platforms toward the tunnel, Conor reached out to feel the walls; the water dripping down them, the wetness on his fingers. He listened to the heels of Liam's boots on the cave floor, and the rustle of Mara's heavy black skirts. The sound of her skirts sweeping the floor reminded him of something he heard a long time ago. He frowned, thinking of it. *It almost feels like I should remember something, but it just slips away. I can't hold on to it. But there is something I should know.*

As soon as the group entered the chamber with the tapestries hanging on the walls and pillows strewn across the floor, Mara left to stir up the fire and set out cups for tea. Instead of sitting on the pillow Traynor indicated, Conor walked to Mara's side and took the cups from her hands. He placed them on the low table near the fire and bent to stir the coals. Holding out his hand, he motioned her to hand him some of the small pieces of firewood nearby. With the fire burning brightly, he took the iron kettle from her hand and pushed a flat rock deep into the coals. There, he set the kettle and sat back to wait for the steam to rise from the spout. Using a cloth to protect his hands from the heat, he picked up the kettle and poured the boiling water into the cups Mara filled with tea leaves. He smiled at her as he did this, looking for a reaction, a sign that she acknowledged him. Mara looked into his eyes, and then closed hers as if the sight pained her. Quickly, she turned her back on him to pick up a heavy silver tray from the nearby piles. She held the tray, looking only at the ground, while Conor placed the five cups.

The group sat on pillows and sipped the hot tea, and Traynor began talking. "I don't know how much you recall, Concobhar, but I am going to help you remember everything. Everything that has happened to you in the last many years."

Conor laughed at that. "How old do you think I am, Traynor? Not old enough yet to wed, much less have years and years to remember."

"That's where you are wrong, Concobhar. You count only this lifetime, the one you know now, but you and I have a history together that stretches back for years. Look around you, boy! Do you not see your history displayed in front of you, in plain sight?" Traynor waved his hand to take in the surrounding walls draped with the rich tapestries.

Puzzled, Conor looked at the walls. "I see them, but what do they have to do with me?"

"They are you. Every one of those hangings shows what you have done in the past. The things you did against me. What you did to try to escape your destiny. Every time I created a creature to help me, you destroyed it. Every time. This time is different. You will not destroy what I create. This time, you will help me. You and I will work together to create creatures that will help us rule the world."

Conor stood up and walked across the chamber to stare up at the tapestries, first the one with the serpent, coiled and ready to strike. He then moved to the one with the huge cat, blood dripping from its mouth. Last, he stood in front of the three headed bull, steam erupting from its nostrils. He turned, laughing. "You must have me confused with someone else, Traynor. First, the man in these hangings is older than I am. Second, it would be hard to have a memory of something that happened to someone else. No, you are wrong. Thanks for the tea and the story, but I think it's time for me to go my way. Mara, you don't have to stay here. You can come with me, you know. There are people out there who would welcome you on my say alone." He looked at Mara as he said this.

"Mara stays here as do you if you know what is good for you. You were able to avoid me in your past lives, Concobhar, because you knew your power. Now, you are a fledgling, and you know nothing. You will stay with me and learn my ways, or there will be consequences. You are aware of the consequences, aren't you, Mara?"

At his words Mara looked up with a terror-stricken face, the hint of tears gathered in her eyes. "Please, Traynor, no. Please"

Traynor waved his hand at Mara, and she gasped as if in pain. Her hands clawed at her throat and her eyes bulged. A faint gurgling sound came from her throat, the only sound she could make. Her face paled and her eyes streamed tears. With one hand to her throat, she held the other one out to Traynor as if in supplication.

"Stop it! Stop it now!" Conor roared as he leaped across the chamber to hold Mara. She fell back into his arms, her face a deathly pale, her eyes closed. He snatched her hand from her throat and set her gently on the ground. "Whatever you're doing, stop it now, please." Conor's voice pleaded.

Traynor waved his hand carelessly in Mara's direction. She gasped as she inhaled life giving breath, and color slowly returned to her face. Conor wiped the tears from her face and sat her up. "So, this is what you mean to do? Threaten me with this if I don't do your work."

"Oh, my boy, that is not all I will threaten you with. I have watched you, and I have seen the people you care for, and I tell you they are all within my reach. The young girl with the braid down her back, the old woman with powers of her own, and don't forget the Mountain Folk. Because Concobhar, I have not forgotten them. I will take each and every one of them from you, one at a time. That is the difference between now and then. Then you did not care, now you do. And your caring makes you weak and makes you mine." Traynor set his cup on the ground beside him and smiled at Conor. "You have a choice, Concobhar. Work with me, let me teach you all that I know or watch the people you love leave this world, one at a time. And, dear boy, they will not be easy deaths."

Chapter Twenty

SECRETS OF THE MOUNTAIN

"Power is a strange thing, Concobhar. When you have the power to destroy, you understand that the world will fall to its knees in front of you."

Conor left Mara's side and walked back to look at the tapestries once more. "You say this is me long ago? That I fought these creatures? And they were your beasts? Did you create them?"

Traynor smiled, "So you are interested, after all. No, I did not create them, not really. They have existed in one form or another for centuries. I merely had the power to raise them and bind them to me. I could control their every action, their every reaction."

"And I took that away from you? How?"

Traynor sighed, "You are a draoidh."

Conor sighed and said nothing. He looked at Traynor and raised his eyebrows.

Traynor smiled. "I hoped you would remember that word, Concobhar. It was what we called you, the most powerful word we could conjure up to describe you."

"That answers nothing, Traynor. And I am not in the mood to play childish word games with you. Either tell me what this all means or Mara and I walk away. You and those two over there can stay in this damp cave and play your games together." Conor waved his hand toward Jebez and Liam.

Traynor scowled and his words were angry, "Even in your youth, you are arrogant. I had hoped that you would have learned humility. That you would want me to teach you the things I know."

"How is it you say I did these things and I have no memory of them? If I could do those things in the past, what prevents me from doing them now?"

"I told you. You are weak because you have found people to care for. Once you care for someone more than you care for yourself, you are easy to control. Look at you, already you worry about Mara. This is the woman who abandoned you as a child, and yet your soft heart melts when you look at her. She is your weakness, Concobhar. As are the others you care about. They are your doom, my boy."

Conor looked back at Mara. "Perhaps I don't care as much as you think I do, Traynor. No, I don't want to see you kill her before my eyes, but if I am gone, I will never know her fate."

Traynor shook his head. "Today is a day for lessons." He waved his hand and muttered words that had no meaning to Conor. On the far wall of the chamber, a light appeared that grew brighter and sharper as the moments passed. Conor drew in his breath sharply at the sight of Tilly sitting outside a cave, holding a cup of tea. Granny, Aelf, and Shaen surrounded her. They all looked anxious, troubled even. His heart was heavy to see her look so, but in the next moment, the heaviness turned to terror as she suddenly gripped her head, dropping her cup of tea to the ground. He watched as Granny leaped to her aid. Traynor stopped the flow of words from his mouth and instantly Tilly shook her head and smiled at Granny. The light faded and the shadow of Tilly was gone.

"You see, Concobhar, I don't have to be as close to her as you think I do to cause her pain. I don't have time to keep showing you lessons, but know this, my boy. I control you because I control the fate of the ones you love, even from a distance. I can bring them such pain that they will beg for death. Such is my power."

His body shook as he stared at Traynor. Taking a deep breath, he nodded. "You win. I will do as you say. I have no choice."

"Good, that is settled. Now let's begin with the history of this cave. I discovered it years ago when I found a book from ancient times. A book, by the way I believe you have, Mara. I will need you to return it to me immediately." Traynor turned his gaze on Mara and waited.

Obediently, Mara rose to dig through a trunk at the back of the chamber. She approached Traynor with a book covered with old, cracked leather and bound with iron straps. Silently, she handed the book to him.

"This is how you raised Ceobrhan, I believe." Mara nodded. "I thought as much. You are fortunate that is all you raised, silly woman. When fools play with things they do not understand, they often get burnt. Remember that, Mara!"

Traynor held the book out in his hand, and Liam rushed forward to take it from him.

"I was saying... oh yes, this cave and others like it are full of secrets the book helped me unravel. Ceobhran was only the start. There was Nathair na H-uamha, the great serpent. Using his name, I called him up from far below the earth in a valley several days' journey from here and sent him forth as my scout. He was brilliant, making his way into villages and towns without ever being seen. He brought me valuable information; the number of soldiers, types of weapons, who is on guard and who sleeps when they should be on guard. With the right information, my job was so much easier. Perhaps the child or two that kept his hunger at bay was a small price to pay for the services he rendered. His appetite grew, but what was that to me? As long as he did his job, I left him alone, but not you!"

"The villagers were crying and wringing their hands when they called upon you to save them and their worthless children. They were frightened of the Draoidh, but they hoped you had the power they needed to send the serpent back into the bowels of the earth. And you did, but not with the sword that you wield in the tapestry. I never saw you with a sword in your hand, not once in all the years that I have known you. But the weaver of these portraits cannot understand the power you used, so she put a sword in your hand. You used the power you possessed to turn him into a harmless garden snake. He spends his time catching rats and sleeping off his kill deep within the earth. What a waste of a magnificent creature!"

Traynor ran his hand across his forehead and let it drop to his side. "What a waste!"

Conor pointed to the tapestry with the snarling cat, blood dripping from his mouth.

"Ah yes, Leomhanne Beinne, the lion who lives in the mountains. He marched beside me into battle, and the terrible sight of him was enough to cause even the bravest soldier to flee. A swipe of his paw could bring down the largest charger, the strongest horse. There was something quite amazing about watching him destroy an army. He was my right hand in battle, and I needed no other. Do you know where he is now, Concobhar? Do you know what you did to him? You and your draoidh curses and magical words cast about? He's probably some barn cat, chasing mice for the farmer and hiding in the rafters when the dogs come into the barn. You did that to him."

Traynor bent to pick up his cup from the ground. Holding it out to Mara, he snarled, "Is there nothing stronger in this Light forsaken cave than tea, woman? I need something to fortify me and you offer me tea? Liam, I need something better than tea. Find it and bring it to me."

Liam rose from the pillow where he reclined and walked toward the tunnel leading to the outside world.

"The bull, Traynor. Tell me about the bull."

"The Tarbh, the bull was always behind me. If Nathair na H-uamha was before me, and Leomhanne Beinne was beside me, Tarbh was behind me. With him there, no harm could come to me from behind. I was well protected and invisible. You will help me raise him again, Concobhar. If it is the last thing you do, you will bring him back to me. You sent him back into the earth, you will bring him up again, and he will march with us, both.

Conor shrugged and walked back to the pile of pillows at the far end of the chamber. "I think I prefer my dog, Wolf, beside me, in front of me, or behind me. Your creatures leave much to be desired, Traynor."

"That little rat terrier of a dog, you mean? Watch out that I don't give him something he can't shake off."

Conor shrugged once more. "So, what exactly do you think I can do for you, Traynor? You say I am the one who took those creatures away from you, so I am the one to restore them to you? But tell me this, if I have no memory of them, no memory of ridding the world of them, how do you expect me to bring them back to you? Magic words, Traynor? Is that what you think I have?"

"You do. You held them in your memory of the past, and they are still part of you. When you see that old woman use her powers, you call them a gift. It matters not to me if you call them gifts or a power, they work the same way as far as I am concerned. I know it, and I am going to teach you how to find and use your powers, all of them; the ability to travel and use sight to see people as they will be in the future, the gift of touching people from afar, the gift of knowing how to call up creatures of the dark, and most important, the power to make them do as you wish. These are all powers that you held in the past, and they are part of you forever. You might not know it, you might not be aware of them, but they are there just waiting for you to call them up. You have lived more lives than you know, more than this pitiful life you have now in that forsaken village at the end of nowhere, Concobhar. That is Mara's fault for leaving you there. She is to blame for the life you have now."

Conor shook his head. "I have blamed Mara for that all my life, Traynor, but now that I am here with you, I realize what she did was in my best interest. Leaving me in the village meant it would be harder for you to find me. Isn't that right, Mara? Leaving me behind was a gift, wasn't it? Your gift to me. Hiding me in plain sight. It's just ill luck you ventured into our village, Traynor. You and that daughter of yours."

"Not ill luck, Concobhar. I have been searching for you for years. Your powers pull me as if I were on a tether. I have only to shut out the world and listen to them, and I am drawn to you. It has taken a while, but I think that is because you don't recognize your gifts. You refused to acknowledge them, until now, when you came to spy on us. Curiosity was it? Or something else? Some misguided feeling of love or attachment? Whatever it is, I plan on using it to my advantage.

You will do as I say, Concobhar. You will listen and learn, and you will help me raise up my army once more."

Traynor settled down on the pillows directly across from Conor. "For now, we need meat and drink. Mara, you prepare our evening meal, we will begin at the break of day."

Despite the dark in the cave, Conor was awake before the others. It was difficult to judge time in the cave where no sunlight penetrated to help. He depended on his inner self to direct his waking and sleeping. He stayed on his pile of pillows and thought about Wolf, how much he missed him, how he worried about him. From across the chamber, he watched Mara rise from her place of sleep to stir up the fire.

He rose and walked over to her. "Was I wrong, Mara? Was I wrong to think that you left me there in order to protect me?" Bending to add wood to the fire, he moved the rocks and kettle for tea closer to the still warm coals.

Mara shook her head silently while she laid out cups and measured tea leaves into each. Taking up a jewel handled knife meant more for a nobleman's belt than a meager loaf of bread, she cut thick slices and set them aside. She cut cheese and meat and laid everything on a tray. "No, you are not wrong entirely. It's true I found myself less a mother than I should have been, but I knew what I was looking for and it held no place for a small boy. For years I searched for this mountain, this cave where I could find Ceobhran and more. I always knew you were what he was looking for, and I wanted to be that for him, not you. So yes, I hid you away in that Light forsaken village to keep you away from him, but was it for your sake or mine?" She shrugged. "It is never easy to be honest with yourself, much less with others. I am not the mother you need, Conor. The Light knows, I am no one's mother." She carried the tray of food to the small table in the center of the chamber. Conor poured boiling water over the tea leaves, and she placed the cups on her tray.

"Let's eat and drink our tea while it is quiet and we have peace, because it will be short lived."

Conor sat to eat his morning meal and drink the hot tea. *I will have to bide my time for now. My best weapon is indifference. If I can convince Traynor that I don't care what he does, I can use the time to learn what I can. It's my only chance to keep people safe.*

After morning meal was finished and he helped Mara put away the dishes, Traynor called to Conor. "It's time to start, Concobhar. We'll start by walking deeper into the belly of the cave. Jebez, fix a torch and walk with us."

Jebez obediently pulled one of the torches from the chamber walls and held it aloft. With a lift of his head, Traynor indicated the tunnel that continued on the other side of the chamber. Down they walked, deeper into the earth, with the flickering light of the torch to guide them. Jebez held it high, and Conor could see their faint shadows fell before them and the smoke that curled up from the fire. He heard the scurrying feet of small creatures in the dark recesses of the tunnel. Still down they walked, curving around as they did, until they came to a smaller chamber to one side of the tunnel. Traynor pushed Jebez from behind, moving him toward the entrance. Once inside, he stopped and waited for Conor to catch up.

"Remember this Concobhar. When you come down here, count your steps, and pay attention to the rooms, which way you turn, how many you enter. It is easy to get lost down here as many before you have discovered. I am impressed that Mara could do it. Sometimes I think there is more to her than I know, but then she does something stupid, and I change my mind."

Again, he indicated with his head for Jebez to continue. Jebez walked to the far end of the room and discovered another tunnel leading still deeper into the earth. This one was narrower and it was necessary to duck his head to keep from hitting it on the ceiling. Bent over as he was, it was difficult to keep the torch high enough for them to see their path. Water dripped from the walls of the tunnel and ran across the path. Jebez tried holding the torch out in front of him to light the way, but the ceiling grew lower and lower, until finally his outstretched hand hit a ledge and he dropped the torch. The fire sizzled on the wet ground and went out.

"Fool!" screamed Traynor. "Look what you've done! Here in the bowels of the earth and no light to see by. Fool!"

The darkness swallowed him, stopping Conor in his tracks as soon as the torch went out. He listened to Traynor berate Jebez, but the sound seemed to come from far away as if the darkness added a thick layer to the air that muffled the sound. Closing his eyes for a moment, and then opening them to the same absence of light, he stretched his right hand out to the side, feeling only air. He took one step to the right, still feeling with his hand. Nothing. One more step, still another, until his fingers finally found the cool damp stone. His hands moved across it, feeling the water, feeling for the ceiling, feeling for anything solid in the dark. Now he could easily reach the ceiling; it was so low. He put his back against the wall, feeling the dampness penetrate his shirt, wetting him. He held out his right hand and muttered the words, "Sorcha, shalad sorcha. Shalad sorcha, dimean sorcha." Instantly, there was a ball of light in his right hand. As he muttered the words, the ball of light grew brighter until it illuminated the tunnel, throwing shadows across the walls and floor.

Conor stared at the light in his hand, not trusting what he saw before him. He closed his hand around the ball for an instant, expecting to be burnt. *How could this be? Where did this come from?* It was cool in his palm, but so bright now he blinked his eyes and had to look away from it. Holding it aloft, he turned and went back down the tunnel the way they had come. He never looked back to see if the two men followed, their footsteps on the floor of the cave told him they did. When he emerged into the chamber once more, he waved his hand and the ball of light disappeared.

Traynor threw himself on the pile of pillows and nodded with satisfaction. "It is all inside you, my boy. I was confident that it was there, inside you all along. Jebez, thank you. You played your part brilliantly. I knew you would. You were exactly what I needed to draw him out."

Conor's lips curled in distaste as he looked at Jebez. "You're nothing but a puppet, his puppet. I will remember that."

Jebez met Conor's stare with a flat look, shrugged his shoulders, and turned away.

Chapter Twenty-One

Conor's Limits

Conor sat with his back against a tree, watching the clouds race across the sky in the valley below him. He listened for the sounds of birds, but here outside the cave, no creatures flew or crawled. It was as if even they knew to stay away. His heart was heavy as he thought of Tilly in the Mountain Folk village, pictured Wolf there with her. At least he hoped his dog was near the girl. His heart ached to think of them both, so close but out of his reach. He clenched his fists in anger to think of what Traynor could do to the ones he loved, even apparently from a distance. *How do I defeat that? How can I fight him? I must be patient, not show any anger. My anger makes me weak, and I cannot afford to be weak.*

He looked down at his right hand, remembering the ball of light he held there. *How did I do that? How did I conjure up a ball of light and then send it off with a wave of my hand?* Conor shook his head in disbelief. He remembered the first time that he used his gift to travel into the cave. The sense of wonder that his body could sit outside in the sun with Wolf by his side and yet be in the cave, feeling the wet stone, hearing the water drip. *I need so badly to talk with Granny. I need to understand how this is all possible.* Conor sighed. *Maybe this was something for which there was no explanation. Maybe you just had to accept it and learn to control it.*

Mara stopped at the cave entrance and watched Conor. She saw him hold out his hand and the puzzled look that he gave it. She thought of turning around and returning to the cave, but her body craved sunlight and fresh air so she walked out toward her son.

Conor looked up and smiled at Mara, hearing the sound of her heavy black skirt brush across the sand on the ground outside the cave. She did not return his smile, only looked at him with serious eyes, her brow knitted in a frown. She found a fallen log to sit on and turned her face toward the sun.

"Tell me what happened in the tunnel, please."

Conor sighed and said, "I wish I could. If I understood it, I might be able to tell you what happened. Jebez was carrying the torch when the cave ceiling got so low he dropped it onto the wet floor. The fire went out, and we were in blackness. There was such total darkness in that cave. Even at night, there is the light of the moon or the stars, but in that cave, there is no light, just blackness. Mara, I was frightened. Traynor was cursing him for a fool, and I didn't even think about what I was doing. I held out my hand and words came to me, words I don't remember knowing. Suddenly there was a ball of light in my hand, and even as I said the words, it grew brighter giving me all the light I needed to get out of the tunnel. It seems it was all a plan between your husband and Traynor. He must have thought desperation would push me to do things, remember things. And the Light help me, it worked. I can tell you this, Mara, I'm not sure who was more surprised; Traynor or me."

Mara nodded her head and smiled slightly to herself. "Two things; you are stronger than you know, I think stronger even than Traynor knows. I think down deep, you might frighten him. Remember he's seen what you were capable of doing in the past. He thinks if he finds you in your youth, he can mold you and make you his own. Ever in the past, when he found you, you were a man, grown and aware of your powers, your gifts, as you call them. He is hoping that it will be different this time." She paused and looked off in the distance.

Conor watched her. "And the second?" he asked.

Mara looked quizzical for a moment. "Oh yes, the second. He is not my husband nor your father. He is just a man that I've used these past years, for better or for worse."

Conor smiled to himself. "That is the best news I've had in a few days, Mara. But why him?"

Mara shrugged. "Oh, he was strong enough to keep other men from bothering me, and until now, he was malleable enough for my purposes. Now it seems, he has found a new ally in Traynor, mores the pity. I can't say that I will miss him, but he was useful, and I would rather have him as an ally than an enemy. I'm afraid I lack allies in my present condition; never a good thing."

"You have an ally, Mara. You have me. I just have to figure out how to be that without Traynor knowing I am. I think we need to talk about this, about a lot of things."

Mara looked down and her hands plucked at the heavy black satin of her skirt. "Yes, you are right. I cannot be your mother, I have no right to that, but we can be allies. We must be careful about it; I fear my life may depend on Traynor not knowing we side with each other."

Conor nodded, "I agree. I think from now on, we stay away from each other when we are in the cave."

Mara stood and began walking in a circle in the space outside the cave. She muttered words as she walked, making the circle bigger. "I have placed us inside a small barrier. It keeps anyone from listening to us. They will just see us sitting far away from each other and that's all." She took her seat on the log and folded her hands in her lap. "Do you remember the words that you used?"

Conor nodded his head. He reached out his right hand, but a quick shake of Mara's head brought his hand back down to his side. "I want to hear the words, but do not extend your hand. The words work with your right hand, and without it, they are just words."

"Sorcha, shalad Sorcha. Shalad Sorcha, dimean Sorcha."

She nodded. "You used the ancient words to call up light. These are words that are so old, and the knowledge of them shows how long your lives have stretched across time. The threat of being in the dark cave brought them up, no doubt, without awareness on your part. Know this, Conor, when I tried to do things, it took effort on my part. I had to find ancient books and practice the words, saying them right, doing the right gestures over and over. It took a great deal of effort on my part. You, however, put out your hand and said the words without effort, without even thinking about them. They are such a part of you, though buried deep within you. I wonder if it will always take some threat to bring them out?" Mara sounded thoughtful and once again, looked off.

"I don't know how to remember things I don't remember, Mara. You say these words and gestures are part of me, but there is no familiarity to it. I was surprised to see the light in my hand, and yet, I knew to wave my hand to make it disappear. How did I know that?"

Mara sighed, "You are not just Concobhar, the son of Mara. You are Concobhar, the son of Domiendra, Concobhar, the son of Althene, Concobhar, the son of Nessa, and so many more, I fear. These are but the ones I am aware of. They called us witches; they revered us, they hated us, they feared us. Over time, our role has changed until at last, we knew it was best to keep our powers secret. Usually we have girl babies, but you were different. For hundreds of years, you were the only male issue. You are not a witch or whatever name they choose to call us. You are draoidh. When you were birthed, you gathered all the power from these women, all the gifts, as you choose to call them. And the history you had lives on in you. It always has. For some reason, you find it more difficult to reach it. That is my fault, I think. I left you alone too early, and there was no one there to teach you. I thought maybe that old woman, Matilda, would recognize you for what you were and take you in, but I was wrong. Wrong about so many things."

"You tell me I have lived my life over and over again. How do I tap into those memories, Mara? Are they lost to me or can you help me find them? I think the only way out of this is to find the memory of what I was and become that person again."

"I agree, but it makes me sad, Conor. You were not always a good person, and I fear that bringing back the memory of what you were might also bring back that part of you, the part that was cruel and careless of people. Recall that Traynor has been clear you never found anyone to care for in your past lives. That meant he had no power to hurt you because he couldn't hurt anyone you cared for. That is different now, which tells me you are different now. Not cruel, not careless. Are you sure you want to find that man in you?"

"Yes, I do. There was always some of that in me, even as a child. It was Tilly who changed me, and I don't think I can change back again. She showed me that caring for someone was a wonderful thing, and once I cared for her, caring for others became easier. I don't think touching my gifts will take that away, Mara. Look, I traveled into the cave, using my gifts. Gifts I didn't even know I had. But I still care about you, about Tilly, and Granny, about so many people. I think that cruel man is gone. Maybe with him, the powers are gone as well, but I think not. Will you help me? Will you help me find my gifts?"

"Yes, Conor, I will. But we must be careful not to let Traynor or Jebez know what we are doing. Do you agree?"

Conor nodded and rose to return to the cave. His heart was heavy at the thought of working with Traynor, but he was left with no choice, not yet at least.

Traynor looked up from the book he held. "Good you're back. I want to go back down the tunnel where you found your first taste of power. Just you and me, no tricks this time, I swear. I want to teach you, Concobhar, all the things that will aid you. Mara? Where is she? Ah, there you are. We will have food and drink before we go, Mara."

Mara nodded and began placing dishes and food onto a silver tray. Traynor watched her as she worked, waiting for something. Conor kept his gaze on the far wall where the tapestries hung. When Mara brought him a plate and cup of tea, he indicated a table nearby with his head. He did not acknowledge her in any way, neither with a word nor a glance. His stare at the far wall was cold and distant, and Traynor observed all of that with interest.

They finished their meal and walked toward the tunnel at the far end of the chamber. As before, the ceiling grew lower as they walked, but this time there was no torch to fall into the water that ran down the path. Traynor held the light in his hand that showed them the way. After so many turns that Conor lost track, Traynor turned into a small antechamber filled with books and scrolls packed into shelves and bookcases that lined the walls. From the antechamber, they moved into a large, comfortable room; the floor covered with thick rugs that muffled the sound of their boots and the walls free of dripping water. A low divan nestled against one wall, the fabric embroidered with a rich pattern of flowers and vines. Two low chairs sat opposite, covered in red velvet with gray pillows. Traynor took the divan and waved Conor toward the chairs where he sat upright, his hands gripping the chair.

"Have you and Mara had a falling out? I couldn't help but notice that you seem to be avoiding her."

"No, no falling out. I was looking for something and I thought it was with her, but I was wrong. She was not what I was looking for, that's all. If she doesn't have what I need, I don't need her. It's that simple."

A thoughtful look crossed Traynor's face, and he was silent. "Perhaps I can help you with what you are looking for, if you would just tell me what it is."

Conor stood up abruptly and walked across the room. With his back to Traynor, he shook his head as if in sorrow. "I thought coming to the cave I would find a mother. I would find what I had been looking for, but I was wrong. She is no one's mother, much less mine." His shoulders shook slightly, and he raised his hand to cover his eyes. Wiping at his face, he turned and sat back down.

"Perhaps she is not the one you were seeking after all. Perhaps I could be the one you look for, Concobhar.""You? How could you be the family that I need, that I thought I needed? Perhaps I don't need anyone, after all. Perhaps you were right, Traynor. Caring about someone just makes you weak, and I have the feeling that weakness is not part of my future." The words came pouring out of Conor in a rush, like the river after the flooding spring rains.

Traynor was silent at Conor's words. "I see I have gone too far, Concobhar. I thought to frighten you into submission, but the truth is, I don't what you to submit to me. It is my wish that you work with me; we forge an alliance that benefits both of us. And I want feelings of trust to grow, something I know we will have to work at. I realize threatening people you care about is not the way to win you over. Let us work together, finding and building your powers. Let me guide you, teach you everything I know, and let me show you that you can trust me. Will you try that, Concobhar?"

Conor watched Traynor for signs of deception before answering. "I will try, Traynor. Yes, I will try."

"Good. Now let's start with what you did yesterday to create the ball of light. Do you remember?"

Conor did not answer, he merely held out his hand and muttered the words that he used in the darkness, "Sorcha, shalad Sorcha. Shalad Sorcha, dimean Sorcha." Instantly the ball of light appeared in his hand, cool to the touch but so bright it caused him to blink.

"So much brighter than yesterday. Already your powers grow, my boy! So soon. Now let's try a few more things."

The next few hours were a blur to Conor, a blur in which he moved furniture around the room, created things of light and darkness, brought forth wonders of nature, and revived them after he destroyed them. He traveled down the tunnel and back without leaving the room. He traveled to the larger chamber and listened to Liam and Jebez argue over a game of dice. All these things he did under the watchful eyes of Traynor, who nodded his satisfaction. While stingy with praise, he made it clear to Conor that his progress pleased him. "Is there nothing you can't do once I show you how?" he asked him.

"I don't know what I don't know how to do. It feels as if I can do anything right now."

"Enough for today. Let's return. I believe I sent Liam out for something stronger than tea, and I believe I need the fortification."

Once in the larger chamber, he shouted for Mara to bring him wine. Raising his eyebrows in question, he looked at Conor. "No, Traynor, no wine for me. I need a clear head. I will have tea, Mara."

They sat in companionable silence while Traynor drank his wine and Conor left his tea to cool. At last, Traynor put down his glass and turned his attention to Liam. "This wine is not to my liking. Where did you find this swamp water you call wine?"

Liam stared at Traynor for a heartbeat or two before answering. "There is not much wine to be had in the village, Lord. I brought what I found."

"Hmmm. I am not pleased, Liam." He held out his hand and waved it in Liam's direction. Immediately, Liam's head snapped back as if someone had struck him. He raised his hand to his face and rubbed at the side. "Lord there was nothing else to bring you."

Traynor turned to Conor. "Wave your hand and repeat the words that I tell you."

Conor stared at Traynor and then looked at Liam, still rubbing the side of his face. He sighed and turned his eyes to the tapestries before answering. "I will not."

Traynor started to rise and then thought better of it. "You will not do as I bid?"

"No. This is not how you build trust with me, Traynor. I am not your leashed hound to do your bidding. I will choose what I do with my powers. You will teach me, but it is I who will make the choices when it comes to my powers. You do as you please but leave me out of your petty need for revenge. I will have nothing to do with it."

The silence was heavy in the room, not a breath stirred. Mara's eyes were fixed on the ground and her hands gripped the heavy black satin of her skirt. Liam's eyes darted from Traynor to Conor and back, but he said nothing. Jebez studied the toe of his boot and shrugged as if it were not his business. Traynor was silent and his breath was ragged, his face flushed. Suddenly, he smiled at Conor. "I have found your limits already, it did not take me long, my boy. We will soon see if you can continue down that path."

The morning brought a continuation of his lessons; Conor found that once he began, the memories rushed back to him and the words he needed were at the ready. He moved his cup of tea and his first meal plate from the table to his hand without being told the words. He walked outside the cave and watched the leaves fall in the slight breeze only to be gathered up at his words, piled into heaps and dispersed again at a wave of his hand. There were words that came without bidding now; he had only to think a thought, and the words were there for him. Whatever he did, he could undo with a wave of his hand. He pulled fish from the stream and took them back to the cave. Silently, he handed them to Mara, raising his eyebrows when she looked confused. “Cook them,” was all he said.

As they ate the fresh fish, Conor looked at the tapestries again and said, “I want to know

my past, Traynor. You say I did those things, and my memories are coming back to me, but those up there, those memories escape me. I want to know about them.” He finished the last of his fish and sucked the juices from his fingers. Without looking at her, he held his plate out for Mara to take. He settled back on his pillows and stretched his legs out to the fire.

Traynor smiled at Conor, “Part of the reason you don’t remember it is that those are not real. Those tapestries were created by someone who knew you long ago, someone, I suspect, who loved you. Someone you did not love. You are the same in some ways, Concobhar, but not the same in all ways. In the past, you did not notice people unless you had to. You were content to stay to yourself. You traveled alone, you lived alone. I always thought you had experienced a great loss in one of your lives and the loss made you determined to avoid a similar mistake in your present. I see that has changed. You say the girl, the one with the blond braid, did that to you. I have yet to see if it will be a good thing or harm you. I told you it makes you weak, but there is still iron in you. An iron core that was always there.”

Conor frowned as he continued to regard the tapestries. “Tell me about the person who created the tapestries. You say this person loved me, but I did not love her back?”

“Yes, she did, I’m sure of it. She was a young girl with gifts or powers of her own. She traveled for most of her life, never staying too long in one place. Never, that is, until she met you. I’m not sure how you met her. I wasn’t there, already you and I were in conflict. She saw this immediately and stayed; I surmise to help you if you needed it. She was never a friend to me, I assure you. Still, when you vanquished Nathair na H-uamha, the serpent, she began her first tapestry, depicting the scene as she saw it. Wholly inaccurate, I assure you. As I told you before, you never wielded a sword, to my knowledge. Your weapons were in your words, the wave of your hand, the knowledge you possessed as a draoidh, the most powerful one the world had ever known. My powers paled next to yours, I'm ashamed to admit. But these powers we have aren't something you can develop. You either have them or you don't. The knowledge is there, the work is in discovering them and nurturing them, growing them. I could work with Liam over there for years, and he could no sooner move that table than he could sail to the moon."

Holding his empty plate out for Mara to take, Traynor stood abruptly and strode across the room to stand beneath the depiction of Concobhar battling the huge serpent. "I digress. This woman stayed near you during the time you and I battled, the time it took you to banish my friends and my weapons. After Nathair na H-uamha, you went after my Leomhanne beinne, the lion who lived in the mountains. You took him from my side where he had marched for years. You sent him to chase mice and live a life of obscurity. She began her next tapestry soon after that, completely missing the point. Leomhanne never threatened you, never stood before you with blood dripping from his mouth. But that is how she portrayed him. It took you years to find me the next time. You found us outside a small town. I waited there for Ceobhran to bring me young men from the town and I would march again with Tarbh at my back to protect me. You found us there and sent my bull to some farmer and his family to breed cows again. She started her third and last tapestry." Traynor stared off at the tapestries in thought. "It doesn't matter, Concobhar. You will raise them. Only you can do that because it was you who banished them. You will raise them for me, for us, and with the help of Ceobhran, we will have our army and march again."

"Hmmm. So you say, Traynor. I am not convinced, but that is for another time. This woman. You say she had powers. Could she travel? Did she have the gift of telling?"

"Why do you ask? Why are you so curious about an obscure girl? Is it the flattery that interests you so? Doesn't matter. She is dead long many years ago. No, to answer your questions, her powers were far different from anyone I ever encountered. She had the gift of knowing your past. That's why I thought she created the tapestries as she did. I thought perhaps she had seen you do those things in a past life of yours."

"Knowing the past? How so?

"If she were near you, if she could touch you, she could see things that happened in your past. With you, I think she saw multiple lives and perhaps it intrigued her. I can't say. She did not interest me, except for her work with fabrics. These I kept, in part, to remind you of your powers. To remind you of what you had done and now need to undo."

"Traynor, you say powers, and I say gifts. I'm not sure who is right, but I know I am tired and wish to rest."

Chapter Twenty-Two

A Need

The next day brought a chance for Conor to meet Mara outside the cave entrance. Once more, she walked the circle around them several times, muttering her words that would keep them safe from listening ears. She took a seat on a nearby log but turned her back to Conor so that to the outside eye, it would looks as if they were settled in the sunshine but separate.

"Mara, I need to know about that book you had. The one you gave Traynor. Tell me about it, please."

She was silent for a moment, digesting the kindly way he spoke to her as if the rudeness of the last few days was the odd and this the ordinary. She nodded her head and took a breath. "It is The Book of Words, Conor. It holds the words I use and Traynor uses to call up things, to punish people, to bring things to your hand, everything. I cannot use most of them. I learned to bring forth Ceobhran, but it took great effort on my part. Traynor, on the other hand, had only to read the words once, and he could bring forth anything he pleased. I had to work so much harder to do the things he could do easily and without effort." The last she said wistfully, as if she regretted her lack of strength.

She shrugged and continued, "I learned of the Book of Words from ancient scrolls I found years ago. In truth, I wasn't convinced it was any more than a legend repeated so often that it came to seem like truth. But I found an old lady, quite mad, I'm afraid. She mumbled constantly, odd words that I did not recognize. I pressed her in a moment of clarity. I still remember her laugh, haunting really." Mara looked off into the distance. "She laughed at me, but she told me about the Book of Words and the power it held. I started searching for it, questioning people, reading anything I could find. I will not bore you with the details of my search. You know I took it from Traynor, risking my life to do so. I brought it here to the cave where I could concentrate and practice until I too could do things. And I can, I learned how to hurt Jebez without touching him. A poor power if you ask me, but useful. I could control Ceobhran and the children." She shrugged, knowing that was a painful memory for Conor.

"I have always had the gift of travel, I think that might be the very beginnings of powers for people like you and me. Without it, I'm not sure if we could learn to do anything else. You, on the other hand, were born with the knowledge. In past lives, as soon as you reached maturity, you touched your powers and used them. This time, lack of training and perhaps, being away from your kind, has hindered you. But look what progress you have made."

Conor's voice was urgent. "I have, I know it, but I also know there are far greater depths to what I can do that I don't recall. I think I need the book in order to find the words to defeat Traynor. Where is it now? Do you know?" "Traynor gave it to Liam, and he put it in a chest he keeps locked. Liam wears the key around his neck and as far as I know, he is the only one who possesses a key. I don't think you will ever get him to help you. He cooperates with Traynor because he fears him, and he hopes for great rewards in the future. You have nothing to offer him. I think it is a lost cause."

"I may have more than you think. Thank you, Mara. You help me fill in the spaces in my mind that memory hasn't helped me."

Mara smiled to herself, her back to Conor. *I am glad that I can help him in some small way. I wish I could change the past.* She shook her head and rose from the log. "I will go in first. You stay here for a while." As she walked past him, she laid her hand lightly on his shoulder for just a moment before passing into the cave.

Conor stood and stretched his back and shoulders, the memory of the light touch Mara gave as she passed still on his shoulder. He shook his head and grinned sheepishly. *Will I ever grow up?*

Walking across the clearing, he felt the change in the air. *Fall is coming and with it, winter snows. I do not want to be trapped in this cave with Traynor when that happens.*

He stood silently for a moment, watching the clouds play chase across the sky, feeling the crisp, cool breeze against his face, ruffling his hair. He looked down and saw a bright blue and black butterfly on the path in front of him. It lay in the dirt, its wings barely fluttering; its days spent, its life easing away. Conor picked it up and held it in the palm of his hand. Thoughtfully, he leaned close and blew softly on the creature. It lay still for a heartbeat and then began pumping new life into its wings. It folded its wings back and crawled to the edge of his hand, where it took flight for one more glorious run in the autumn sunshine. Conor watched the creature for a moment, a smile playing across his face. *Will I ever get used to the wonder of these gifts? Maybe that is the answer I missed in my previous life, holding on to the wonder of all of this.*

"Good luck, my friend." Conor turned toward the entrance of the cave.

Once inside and settled on the pillows, he waved Traynor off when he approached. "I am tired, Traynor. Give me just a few moments to rest, please."

He leaned his back against the cave wall and closed his eyes softly. Beneath his lashes, he observed Liam sitting across the chamber, throwing dice in the air and catching them.

Liam. Liam, listen to me but do not look at me.

Liam's head jerked, and he turned toward Traynor. He frowned when he saw Traynor was speaking to Jebez quietly in the corner of the chamber.

Liam, it's me, Conor. Listen to me.

Liam jerked his head around to stare at Conor who gave no notice of him.

I said to listen but do not look at me.

Liam nodded his head slightly and looked down at his dice as if they were the most interesting thing in the world.

Liam, I need that book. The book that Traynor took from Mara. I understand you can get it for me.

Liam gave a slight shake of his head and mouthed the word, 'No!'

I know you are frightened of Traynor. I don't know how you came to be with him but I know you stay because he threatens you. Am I right?

Liam gave a slight nod of his head. He stole a look at Conor, but Conor's eyes were closed and so he did not see the pleading look from the man.

I need you to get that book for me and in exchange, I will protect you from Traynor. I will send you down the mountain to people I know and love who will take you in. Together, you and me, we will find a way to defeat Traynor.

Liam sat quietly, mulling over Conor's words. He looked at Conor quickly and shook his head again, "No!"

You don't have to answer me now, Liam. Think about it. I can help you if you help me.

Liam stood up abruptly and walked out of the chamber.

Conor sat back and took a deep breath. He was taking a risk, an enormous risk that Liam would not take their conversation to Traynor. *He might, but I don't think so. I think he feels threatened by Jebez's friendship with Traynor and Traynor's lack of regard. I'll see what happens. I have to take the chance.*

"I would have thought someone as young as you would have more stamina. Get up, boy, we need to get back to work. I want to show you more of this cave." Traynor stood over Conor, looking down at him, a frown working its way across his face.

Conor stood up slowly, brushing off invisible dust from his pants, taking time to let his mind wander around the cave, searching. He wasn't sure what he searched for, but his instinct told him it was important to know where everyone was. He found Mara in the front chamber, sitting near the entrance while Liam sat just outside the cave. Jebez he could not find, no matter how his mind probed the cave. Shrugging, he followed Traynor down the tunnel leading deeper into the earth.

This time it was Traynor who held up his hand with the ball of light. Conor noted with some satisfaction that the light was not as bright as his light had been. Again, the sense of wonder at his own strength shook him. *I do not want to become the man that Mara described, cold and heartless. What was it she said? Cruel and careless. I'm not sure what that means, but it is not the man I want to become. Does the power do that to a person? Does it change you somehow? If it does, then I want nothing to do with it.*

Traynor led Conor past the place where the ceiling of the cave was so low it was necessary to bend over almost double to pass through it. When they came out on the other side, Conor stopped, his eyes wide, his breath coming in quick bursts. Before him was a chamber ten times the size of the one they occupied. Where that chamber held low tables and soft pillows, an immense pool of water filled this area almost from wall to wall, a waterfall plunging from high rocks above to the water below where it churned and splashed vigorously.

"The water goes underground to a river that runs out of the mountain below us. Where this water originates from, I cannot say, but it always flows, never ending as far as I know. It has its source somewhere up above, and I mean for us to find it. I need you to help me. The path is slippery, not safe for a man alone."

Conor looked above the pool to see the path along a ledge that Traynor spoke of. "Why do you need to know where the water comes from? What does it matter to you where it comes from?"

"Concobhar, do not act the fool. For many of us, water is the source of our power. How often have you touched your power by listening to the river run over the rocks in its path? How often have you used the sight of water in the sunlight to touch your gifts? I think if I can find the source of this water, I will find the source of our power. That alone is worth any price, I think. "

Conor eyed Traynor for a moment, weighing his words. "I thank that is not the reason you wish to find the source, but I'm willing to play along with you. You climb and I will follow."

Traynor nodded and turned to walk along the edge of the pool toward the ledge above. He glanced back to make sure that Conor was following. Conor waved his hand at Traynor. Satisfied that he was behind him, Traynor began the climb to the ledge. The rocks were wet from the waterfall's spray causing his boots to slip, but it was not a far climb and handholds were within easy reach. Once he reached the ledge, he turned to offer a hand to Conor who again waved him off. Gaining the ledge, Conor looked down in surprise at the height they had climbed to reach it. From the ground, it seemed so much closer.

The ledge was not wide enough for a man to walk comfortably forward. So narrow was it, that Traynor put his back to the cave wall and walked sideways, sliding one foot at a time. His right hand still held the ball of light. Conor watched for a moment and then followed suit, a short distance away. The ledge carried them higher and higher toward the top of the cave, the roar of the waterfall making conversation impossible. At last they reached the waterfall itself and Traynor, using hand gestures, indicated they would crawl along the ledge behind the water as it plunged down to the pool. Conor shook his head in wonder. *Why is this so important? And if it was important, why hasn't he come here long before with Liam or Jebez?*

Traynor crouched down and began crawling toward the waterfall with Conor behind him. It was necessary to put away the ball of light while he crawled behind the water that roared past them. The rushing water had long ago hollowed out the wall, so that a small room hid behind the water, the floor wet with spray, the sound deafening. Conor blinked water out of his eyes and raised one hand to wipe the spray from his face. The darkness was so intense that Conor held his breath until they reached the other side, and Traynor once more called up the light. Coming out on the other side of the waterfall, he could see that the ledge went up further toward the cave roof. It appeared that here was another tunnel beyond that, but he could not be sure from where he stood. He shrugged. *What did it matter? I'll humor him a while longer, but if this ledge goes nowhere, I am turning around.*

The ledge was less slippery here, the spray of the water drifted in the other direction. Conor stopped for a moment, feeling the air around him. Yes, he could feel a slight breeze against his skin. He might not have noticed it, but the water that bathed his face cooled as the air blew across it. He stopped and looked up. What it possible there was light above them?

Traynor stopped ahead of him, staring up as well. He waved his hand and the ball of light disappeared. It took a moment for Conor's eyes to adjust to the darkness, but when they did, it was clear this was not the same darkness as in the cave below them. There was not much light in this space, but it was sufficient to see the path in front of him. Cautiously, he put one foot in front of the other, holding his hand out to feel for low rocks. Stopping often to listen to the sound of the waterfall behind them, they slowly made their way ever upward toward the source of the light. The ledge wound its path away from the waterfall, but now it turned and began taking them back toward it, on a higher level. Once again the rocks were wet and slippery, and with the light behind them forced Traynor to bring up the ball of light to see. Again, the ledge turned in a switchback pattern, heading back toward the light, away from the water. Still, they climbed. Conor wondered at the size of the chamber, the height still towering far above them. They stopped often now to catch their breath as the switchback ledge took them higher and higher. Toward the light, away from the light, they crept, always upward. Traynor stopped putting away the light, it took too much effort to call it up each time.

Finally, they reached the point where the ledge stopped at a sheer wall. Craning their necks to look up, they could see that there was another ledge that continued on and upwards, but the space between the two ledges was formidable, with little prospect for feet and hands to climb. Without hesitation, Traynor began the climb toward the ledge across the slippery rocks. "Put your hands and feet where I put mine," he commanded.

Conor nodded and watched him carefully. Slowly he began the ascent, using the same small spaces to fit his feet and hands and pull himself up. At last, the climb up the rock was so vertical that no amount of craning his neck backward would reveal the holds that Traynor used. He struggled to find a place for his fingers to grip, moving first his right hand and then his left, until at last, he found some small piece of jagged rock he could use. With the toe of his boot he felt for a hole big enough to support him, and little by little, inch by painful inch he crawled up the side of the cave wall. At last he could see the top with the ledge in view if he turned his head sideways and looked up. He felt for another hand hold, gripping the slippery rock with hands that cramped with the effort. Moving his right foot, he found a small indentation in the rock that might work. Just as he moved his left foot out to search with the toe of his boot, he felt himself slip, just a fraction of an inch. It was enough to cause him to panic, and he grabbed at air with his left hand. Hanging by only his right hand now, he felt his muscles strain as he blindly felt the rock face for any kind of toehold. Nothing! Not so much as a fraction into the rock could he find for his foot.

Just as he felt his muscles tear and the inevitable downward slide, he felt a hand reach out to grab his right wrist with a strength he found reassuring. "Conor! Grab my hand with your left hand. I have you."

Conor hesitated, using his left hand to try in vain to find a hold, any hold for his fingers.

"Conor! Son! Trust me! Take my hand, please! Take my hand, son!"

Chapter Twenty-Three

All the Difference

Conor reached up with his left hand and grabbed Traynor's outstretched hand. With a mighty effort, Traynor pulled him up, inch by inch until, at last, he pulled him over the edge onto firm rock once more. They both lay across the narrow ledge, their chest heaving, their breath coming in heavy gasps. At last, Conor rolled onto his back and stared at the ceiling, so much closer now than a few minutes ago. Slowly his breathing became even again, and he could find his voice. "I don't know what you hoped to accomplish here, Traynor, but I thank you."

Traynor said nothing. He stood and looked up toward the source of light at the top of the cave. Sure enough, it appeared to be a small hole in which sunlight poured in along with the water that rushed from above. He stood silently for long minutes, slowing his breathing and staring at the hole. At last he shook his head and spoke quietly, "I was wrong to come here. The water source is not in this cave. It is outside somewhere. I was wrong and all I did was risk your life. I'm sorry, Concobhar. I am sorry. We should go back."

Without looking at Conor, Traynor began the descent down, trusting that Conor would follow him. The way down was no less treacherous than the ascent, but the two made their way slowly, stopping to find better hand and foot holds. At last they reached the bottom ledge and began the slow crawl back past the waterfall to the chamber below. Neither spoke on the way until they reached the chamber where once again, Traynor created the ball of light with which they could find their way. Traynor stopped to sit by the pool, gazing up toward the cave ceiling again, toward the source of the light, though from this vantage point, it was not visible to his eyes.

It was Conor who broke the silence. “Is it true? What you said, what you called me?”

Traynor nodded but did not look at Conor. He held the ball of light in his hand, bouncing it up and down gently, watching the light play around the dark chamber. He sighed and said, “I did not mean to say it, Concobhar. I thought I would tell you when I had earned your trust. I thought it might mean something to you then. Now I’m afraid it doesn’t mean much. At least, I don’t think it should, not yet.”

“It makes a difference, Traynor. I’m not sure how or why, but it makes a difference in how I feel. I might not be ready to think of you in that way, but it makes a difference.”

“All I ask is that you think about it, Concobhar. I am not asking you to act on it, just think it over.”

Conor stood and began walking to the end of the chamber. Traynor smiled to himself, bounced the ball of light a few more times, and then heaved himself up from the rocks to follow.

Once back in the smaller chamber, Conor did not look at Mara. He walked through the tunnel to the outside, standing in the cave's entrance until he heard the rustle of her heavy black skirt against the cave floor. Only then did he step outside to sit in the fresh air.

The air had a bite to it that was not there a few days ago. He saw the clouds that drifted across the sky were darker now, full of moisture headed somewhere. The fall leaves had been stripped from the trees by the winds that whistled through the mountains, their bare branches raised to the heavens in an attitude of prayer.

Mara walked her circle around and around Conor, putting her barrier in place before she sat on the log, facing away from him. “Something happened to you while you were gone, Conor. What was it? What happened?”Conor didn’t answer for a moment. He stared at the sky, at the bare trees, and thought about the coming winter. How cold it would be up here. How would they stay warm? How would they feed themselves? At last he spoke. "Is Traynor my father?"

Mara raised her hand to her mouth in a reflexive gesture of dismay. She shook her head and muttered to herself. "The light take his soul, he swore he would not tell you. What happened? Tell me, now."

"Traynor wanted to go deeper into the earth, further down into the cave. We reached a large chamber with a pool of water and he wanted to climb to the top. He said the source of our power was water and he thought that water had its source at the top of the cave somehow. I doubted him, but he said he couldn't reach it alone. It was a dangerous climb, too dangerous to do alone. I agreed to go with him, though I thought it was a foolhardy plan. We reached a section where we needed to climb the cave wall to reach the ledge above. I slipped and would have fallen, but he caught me and pulled me up. When he reached for me, he called me 'son'. I asked him if it was true, and he said it was though he hadn't planned on telling me that way, he said. He wanted to wait until I trusted him, he said."

"He's lying, Conor. He planned to tell you all along whether you trusted him or not. He is using this as a way to pull you in. Please do not be fooled by his act. He planned this all very carefully." Mara begged him.

"So you think he planned on me slipping down the face of the rock in order to save me? Seems a little farfetched, Mara."

"He might not have planned it exactly that way, but he has been waiting for a time when you were vulnerable. I wouldn't be surprised if he didn't somehow cause the slip you felt. Conor, please believe me, he is not to be trusted."

"And you are? You could have warned me. You could have told me yourself. I am to trust you when you withhold the truth, but not trust him when he tells me the truth. Mara, that is sideways thinking. Perhaps it is Traynor I need to put my trust in unless you can convince me otherwise. Why don't you start by telling me the truth, for once."

Mara sagged on the log where she sat, her head in her hands. Slowly she straightened up and dropped her hands to her skirt where she gripped the satin in both hands. "I will tell you everything that I can, Conor. Yes, Traynor is your father. He was your father with me, with Domiendra, with Althene, and Nessa. And countless more, I'm sure. He has always been your father, and he has always tried to use you in one way or another. He left us soon after you were born. I believe he thought I was unworthy and that the child I bore would not be a draoidh, much less the most powerful one on earth. He left us in search of a stronger woman than me. One who he thought could give him the draoidh he sought." Mara stood and walked to the far side of the circle she had created, looking out across the treetops.

"I told you why I left you in the village. I knew that sooner or later he would have to realize you were the draoidh he searched for, and I wanted to hide you from him. I was afraid of exactly what is happening now, Conor. He has a way of insinuating himself into your life, into you. He will try threats and if they don't work, he will try kindness and flattery. I'm telling you, Conor, he is not to be trusted. You have seen what he has done to me, to Liam. He lashes out at us when he is displeased with us. He will do the same to you. And if not you, to someone you care about. He has made that clear."

"You are right. He did try threats with me, but when he saw they would not work, he tried the truth. I wish you had from the beginning, Mara. It would be so much easier to believe you now." Conor stood and walked out of her circle and into the cave.

Once in the chamber, Conor approached Traynor who sat with Jebez on the pillows, playing at dice. "You win again, Traynor. By the Light, I know you use your powers to turn the dice to your advantage."

"And if I do, what does it matter? You have no coin with which to wager so it matters not if I win. I tell you what, why don't you pick out some pretty things from that pile of silver you keep horded over in the corner, and we will make a game of it yet?"

Jebez shook his head and grumbling, went to sift through the pile of silver and brass trays and candlesticks, the result of Mara's thievery with Ceobhran and the village children.

Conor stood above Traynor, looking down at him while he tossed the dice in his hand and caught them. Traynor looked up at Conor with a contemplative look. "I would like to talk with you, Traynor. Away from all of these prying ears."

Traynor smiled and stood to follow Conor down the tunnel. Once again, it was necessary to call up the ball of light to find their way, but this time it was Conor who did it, and the light was so bright their shadows were painted black on the walls of the cave. He passed by smaller chambers until he found one that suited him, one with several small platforms for sitting. There he sat, holding the ball of light in his hand and waited for Traynor to settle.

"I have given it some thought, Traynor. I would like to work with you further. I think you have much to teach me. I'm not sure if my goal is to be the draoidh you wish me to be, but I do want to explore my gifts and see what I am capable of doing. I have two conditions that must be met. If you are willing to abide by my wishes, then we can work together. If not, then I think it best that I leave the cave before the snow flies and return home to my village."

Traynor's eyes narrowed as Conor spoke, but he held his tongue and nodded.

"First, I will not use my gifts to punish anyone. I will not inflict pain on someone for my own purpose. I could see a time when I might have to defend myself or someone I love, and I can't say I would not use it in that way. But not for my benefit alone. Second, I will have no part in raising those creatures you say I defeated long ago. I have no knowledge of them, no knowledge of words I used to rid the world of them, so I see no way I can bring them back for you. I will have no part in raising an army with them to defeat people I don't know."

Traynor was silent, but his breathing was harsh and his eyes were cold as he looked at Conor, but as Conor watched his face, it softened and he almost smiled. "Of course. Those are reasonable conditions, Concobhar. I agree. But if there is ever a time when you change your mind about raising my creatures, I will help you find the words you need. I have them at my fingertips. Sadly, they will not work for me since I was not the one to banish them in the first place. But yes, let us work together to strengthen you, to plumb the depths of your knowledge. But may I ask, what changed your mind?"

Conor looked down at his feet for a moment before answering the man. "It made a difference, Traynor. What you said yesterday made a difference to me."

Conor rose and holding the ball of light, left the chamber. Traynor looked after him thoughtfully for a moment. *My instincts were right, my boy. I thought your weakness would be your need for someone significant. Bless you, Mara, for not being the one he needed. You made my path so much easier.*

Chapter Twenty-Four

Lessons

"We will begin our work by traveling together, Concobhar. You remember what trouble you got in traveling into this cave without a guide. I propose that we travel together so that you learn the dangers and how to avoid them.

"I want to start outside the cave, in the sunlight. I believe you will tap into your powers of traveling easier if you sit in nature. One more thing. You have to go to familiar places, Concobhar. Traveling to an unfamiliar place until you have mastered the art can lead to trouble. If you try to do that, you may find yourself trapped there with no way home, so to speak. There are two simple choices: your village and the Mountain Folk village. The best thing is to start with one and then move to the second. I propose we start with the Mountain Folk village."

Conor started at his suggestion, "Why would you want to go there, Traynor?"

"I don't want to go there, Concobhar. I have no desire to see those cave dwelling, backward people, but it is the closest familiar place to here, and as I said, you need to start with something familiar. I would like to try your village next, but it is quite a distance away, and I'm not sure of your traveling powers. Until I am confident you can travel there and back without worry, I would like to start with something closer to us. Traveling takes a good deal of our powers, and the further away the object of your travels, the more of your power it takes. There have been many of us who have traveled beyond our capabilities and found that we needed power while we were there we no longer had, drained as we were. Do you agree we go to the caves of the Mountain Folk?" Conor reluctantly nodded in agreement and sat with his back against a giant cedar tree.

"Good. Settle back in the sunlight and do as I say please. Picture where you want to go. Put it firmly in your mind, the familiarity of it, the smells, the sounds of it. Now set it aside and find your water source, a river, or a stream. Close your eyes and listen to the sound the water makes as it travels over the rocks, watch how the sun plays across the water, and feel yourself floating along with the water. You are as a leaf, floating, allowing the water to carry you effortlessly along in its current. Your body is light, your thoughts are only of the water, the feel and sound of it."

Conor stood outside the rock wall, the one that looked like a dead end to eyes that were not familiar with it. Traynor stood next to him, a frown playing across his face. "I thought you would be able to find the village, Concobhar."

Conor smiled and stepped past the rock, turning to find the break between the two immense granite walls. Traynor smiled to himself and followed Conor through the gap to find himself in an open meadow, the wildflowers long since gone, the grass tall and golden now. He stared in amazement at the warren of caves dotted across the mountain; the women working in the sunlight, the children laughing and chasing, and the men talking quietly as they repaired tools and weapons.

Without looking back, Conor began the climb to the caves, so glad to hear the happy voices that filled his ears and mind with memories of good times spent among the folk. He climbed past the women who never saw him, never knew he was there among them. He climbed until he came to Cormac's dwelling where he watched his friend sitting outside on the carved bench speaking to a small group of boys who sat at his feet and listened with rapt expressions to his stories. Conor smiled to see his friend engaged in what he did best, teaching the history of the folk to the young.

He left Cormac's cave and walked to the end of the village where Ronan, the healer, took in the sick and the wounded. He stopped outside her dwelling, listening to the voices inside. *Granny! I hear Granny's voice.* The sound took his breath away, and he turned abruptly from the entrance.

Granny sat with Ronan, sifting through herbs, pulling out stems and saving the leaves and flowers in a basket to use for teas. Ronan talked on about her forthcoming wedding to Cormac when suddenly, Granny raised her hand to silence her. Ronan looked with question at Granny, but the old woman's face was frozen in concentration and her body trembled. At last, she lowered her hand and leaped up to run to the doorway. There, she threw aside the woven blanket that served as a door, and dashed to the clearing outside, Ronan on her heels.

"Granny, what is it? You act as if a ghost walked past you."

"Oh Ronan, for just a moment, I thought Conor had come back. His presence outside your house was so clear I could almost hear him calling out to me. Come, we need to go through the village. I have to make certain of something. Please, come with me."

Together they walked back down the trail toward the village, Granny stopping every few feet to test the air as a hunter does, listening intently for any sound. "I want to go to Cormac's dwelling, Ronan. Now."

She increased her speed so that Ronan was forced to run to catch up. Coming around the corner, they stopped at the sight of Cormac with the young boys at his feet. He had stopped talking and sat looking across the clearing as if he waited for something.

"Did you feel it, Cormac? Did you feel Conor here?"

"I don't know, Granny. I felt something and I know I thought of him instantly, but I didn't know if it was him or just a memory of him."

"I don't feel him here. We need to go to Aelf's. Please hurry. Boys, you stay here. I need to be able to concentrate when we get there. Ronan, I need your skill, please."

The three of them made haste to Aelf's dwelling where they found Tilly sitting on a bench outside in the sunlight. Her face was pale and her breath came in short, quick gasps. As soon as she saw Granny, she leaped to her feet. "Oh Granny, he was here. Just now. Conor was here. I heard him call my name and felt his hand on my shoulder. He's gone now. Granny, he was not alone. Someone was with him."

"I know, Tilly. I think he came with Traynor, though I can see no reason for him to do that. I feel the evil that walks with that man still in the air. I cannot think why Conor would bring him here to us."

Doiranne stood in the doorway to Aelf's dwelling, her hand held to her chest and her eyes wide and staring. "He was here, Granny. That man, Traynor, was here, wasn't he? I didn't see him, but I felt the same feeling as before when he watched me in the night."

Conor opened his eyes and looked around him. His heart beat fast with the memory of Tilly sitting in the sunshine. He could almost smell the lavender in her hair if he closed his eyes and took a deep breath. He could feel her shoulder still under his fingertips. The longing for her was more than he could bear. He closed his eyes and leaned back against the cedar.

Traynor watched him through half closed eyes. *I am so close. I am so close to everything I have ever wanted. And you, Concobhar, are going to give it to me. Yes, and willingly before we are through.*

"Are you all right, my boy? Did the traveling hurt you in some way?" There was a look of concern in his eyes and a small frown played across his face.

"I'm fine, Traynor. It was just a memory that overtook me for a moment, but it's gone now. Don't worry about me."

"You left so abruptly I thought you were hurt somehow. I wanted you to stay long enough to test your powers while you were there. I told you that often traveling took so much of our power there was nothing left of it. I don't want you to leave like that again, Concobhar. It's important that we complete our lessons before we walk away from them. Do you understand me?"

Conor stared at him without answering, finally nodding his head.

"Good. Are you up for more traveling? If so, I would like to try the longer distance to your village. I want you to show me where you lived."

Again Conor nodded without speaking. He settled back once more against the cedar tree, feeling the rough bark against his back through his shirt. He closed his eyes without being prompted and began to picture the river, flowing across the rocks, the sunshine playing on the ripples as they crossed. The sound of the river filled his ears and his body became light as he felt the water carry him.

Conor stood outside his humble cottage at the far end of the village. He smiled when he saw the porch, so small but well-built and sturdy. The steps to the porch were cleared of weeds and tall grasses, in fact, his yard looked neat and tidy as if he lived there still. He walked behind the cottage to stare at his garden. The rows of herbs were there despite the cooler fall air, neatly weeded and freshly watered by the look of them. His dill was in full flower, the yellow petals filling the air with their scent. The lavender he planted for Tilly bloomed its final fall bloom, the purple flowers on tall stems reaching for the last of the season's sun. Someone had been tending his garden while he was gone. He wondered if it was Tilly or Granny. He shrugged to himself and turned to climb the steps to his front door.

The door opened with a creak, and he thought of the can of grease he kept for oiling the hinges. His fireplace was swept of ashes and his floor was clean enough to make any village woman to be proud. Conor felt rather than saw Traynor behind him, so he stepped inside the door and stood to one side.

Traynor entered and looked approvingly at what he saw there. He walked to the fireplace and peered up the chimney, nodding his head. Noting the rough table and chairs, the shelves in the kitchen, and the sideboard with the bowl and pitcher resting there, he again nodded his approval as he ran his hands across every surface as if his fingers told him something that his eyes did not. He lingered longest at the table, touching first one side and then the other, where he placed both hands flat and leaned his weight on them. Satisfied with what he saw, he turned and walked out of the cottage, Conor at his heels.

Together they walked down the dusty road into the heart of the village where Traynor stood, looking thoughtfully at the village green where his wagon sat under the trees. His mule was gone, either run off or perhaps someone had taken pity on the poor beast and had him in their barn. He cared for the mule but not to the extent that he planned to trouble himself finding out which one had befallen the creature.

He crossed the green toward Erik Tamen's house, the largest and best built house in the village. The great wide porch beckoned him and he climbed up on the steps to stand outside the door. Conor stood on the path below, frowning up at him.

"I want you to try your powers while you travel. Something small, perhaps. Raise your hand where you are and knock on this door." Traynor's voice commanded.

Conor raised his hand and thought of the door beneath his fist. Sure enough, a loud banging echoed across the porch. A moment later, the door opened and the kindly face of Guin appeared. She looked puzzled at the sight of no one, stepped out of the house, and looked up and down the path before her house. Smiling to herself, she muttered, "Must be the fancy of a tired woman." With that, she closed the door behind her.

"Do it again," commanded Traynor.

Conor shook his head. "I will not pester this good woman. Find me something else to play with, Traynor. It will not be my friends that I bedevil." He turned on his heels and walked away.

Traynor shook his head and smiled. *I catch you again, Concobhar. Is there no one in your world that you do not care for?*

Traynor stepped down from the porch and walked across the green to the blacksmith's forge. He beckoned to Conor to follow him there. "Move the tools in this forge around, Concobhar. Nothing difficult, nothing to bedevil your friends as you put it. Just having some fun."

Conor shook his head but began moving his hands around while looking at the tools hanging on boards around the shop. First, he moved all the tongs, the long, thin, iron pinchers used to hold the metal in the forge's fire. These he put in a pile on the ground before moving to the hammers. The hammers he put where the tongs hung before. Next he walked to the long workbench and, without touching them, picked up the swages and fullers. These he turned over and over in the air, noting the grooves of different sizes used to shape the hot metal. These he put under the workbench. Next, he picked up the heavy anvil, turned it around and set it back down backwards. Last, he piled all the chisels, drifts, and bits into a bucket at the far end of the smithy. When he was done, he turned to Traynor and smiled, undisturbed by the mischief he had wrought.

"Anything else you would like me to try?"

"Yes, from here, ring the bell."

The bell began pealing out its beautiful clear tones, ringing across the green to the ends of the village. Before long, the villagers all came out of their cottages at a brisk pace, looking at each other in bewilderment. "Who would ring the bell? Is Erik Tamen calling a meeting?"

When they gathered at the bell tower, confusion was written across everyone's face. There was no one who claimed to have called them. A giant of a man with long red hair and a great red beard strode through the crowd. "Those pesky boys. If I get my hands on them, they will rue the day they played this trick." He stopped short when he got to the bottom of the bell tower, for there was the rope to the bell, still tied to the tower, higher than any young boy could have reached. The villagers began muttering among themselves, until he called out, "No fuss, folks. It must have been a strange wind that blew the bell round, causing it to ring. Let's go back to what we were doing and leave it be." The man patted the villagers on the shoulders, reassuring them that all was well.

Traynor turned to Conor. "Do it again."

Conor stared at him for a long moment. "Traynor, you weary me with your silly games. Let's walk out into the fields and do something useful instead of playing childish games with folks who are busy." He shook his head as he walked off.

Without giving it much thought, as if drawn by an unseen voice, he began walking toward Granny Matilda's cottage. He hesitated outside her gate, knowing he should not enter without asking permission. Smiling to himself at his foolishness, he opened the gate and walked up to her porch. Traynor stopped just inside the gate, pausing to feel the power here even without Granny's presence. *Oh, she is stronger than I thought. I can still feel her as if she sat on that Light forsaken porch.*

Conor walked to the back of the cottage, stopping at the sheep fold. Opening the gate, he stood still, sending his thoughts up the hillside and the pasture beyond. Traynor watched him curiously, waiting to see what he would do. But Conor did nothing, he just stood there, his hand on the gate, breathing slowly. Nothing but the warm sun-kissed autumn air, filled with the scent of apples and cut hay. Nothing. Until...yes, Traynor could hear the far-off sound of a bell. He watched Conor and listened.

Over the hill came the lead ram, the bell around his neck ringing out a signal for the sheep, the ewes and lambs bleating and following close behind. Conor stood aside to hold the gate as they came filing in behind the ram. Once inside, the ram looked around, expecting Conor to be standing in the corner of the pen. Conor walked to the feed troughs and, waving his hand, brought sweet smelling hay down from the loft to spill into the troughs. Eagerly, the sheep buried their faces and began their evening meal.

Laughing, Conor turned and waved his hand at the gate, shutting it behind the sheep. He left the fold with Traynor behind him.

"Any more lessons, Traynor, or are you convinced that I could keep my powers as I travel?"

"We can return, Concobhar. I am fully aware of your powers now." *And I am aware of so much more, my boy.*

Chapter Twenty-Five

THE JOURNEY BEGINS

Conor opened his eyes and sat still for a moment, thinking of his village and the familiar faces there. The smell of the sheep, rank and pungent as it was made him smile. He thought about his cottage and the garden that someone was tending for him in his absence. *I don't think I knew how much it meant to me. Will I ever see it again except in my travels?*

He looked across at Traynor who watched him with a small smile on his face. The man stood up abruptly and walked toward the entrance of the cave. "Come, Concobhar, we have plans to make."

Once inside the chamber, he motioned to Mara to bring him food and drink. As an afterthought, he commanded her to fix the evening meal for everyone. He lounged on pillows and watched her as she stirred stew in a great iron pot above the fire and set bowls and cups on great silver trays. "Bring wine with mine, Mara." She nodded and set out a goblet in place of one of the cups.

As they ate, Traynor watched Conor and Mara for any sign of friendship but found none. *I think the absence of signals from them indicate the strongest signal they could send me.*

As if he spoke those words aloud, Conor held his bowl out to Mara, "This is not fit for the village pigs. Do you not know the use of herbs to make this stew fit for a man to eat?"

Mara looked embarrassed. "I have not had experience with cooking, Conor. And no, I don't have herbs nor do I know how to use them."

"The next time I go to my village, I will bring some back with me and teach you how to prepare a decent stew. A man could starve to death on the food you fix."

Traynor looked from Conor to Mara, heartened to see the quick dip of her head, the flushed look on her face as she took his bowl to the washstand.

"Concobhar, I have seen that you can travel with ease without a loss of your powers. It is quite impressive what you are able to do when you are only a part of yourself. I don't think there are many others who could do the things you did today.

"I have also seen the number of people for whom you show an affection, I believe. This is unlike the man you have always been in the past. And while I may have a fondness for you, my needs go beyond forming an attachment to you. I have been clear what my needs are and you have been clear what your limits are so we are at a crossroads, my boy. But you have shown me the Mountain Folk dwellings and your village, and once I have traveled there with you, I can travel there any time I wish. I think you know what that means, and while it would pain me to hurt the people you care for, you give me no choice. I will not be denied again. You owe me a certain amount of fealty, and I mean to collect on it."

Conor sat quietly, feeling the bands of iron that were Traynor's words tightening around his body. He shook his head as if he could shake away the feeling, but it did no good. "You still threaten me, Traynor, to get your way? I have told you, I will not help you in your efforts. What you are thinking is madness. You can't think that I will help you bring those creatures back or use Ceobhran to raise an army."

"You will, Concobhar, because you are weak. Your caring has made you weak. You have powers when you travel, but I do as well. What is to stop me from traveling to your village and burning down every house there? What is to stop me from unleashing creatures that will ravage the Mountain Folk village so not a single person is left alive? There is nothing to stop me from doing that and more, Concobhar. Nothing!" Traynor stood over Conor looking down at him, shaking with rage. He strode across the chamber before turning and snarling, "We leave in the morning for your village. Not traveling, going on foot. We will retrieve my wagon and set out from there."

"Set out where? Are you mad?"

"No, Concobhar, I am determined. Determined to have what is mine, rightfully. We leave in the morning, all of us. Pack what you need to carry down the mountain, no more. Jebez, go through those piles of junk you and Mara collected and find objects that are small but valuable. Look for knives with jewels set in their handles or goblets studded with gems. Nothing too big or too heavy, you and Liam will be carrying it all until we reach my wagon. We will need it to pay our way. Be ready to leave when the sun rises. We will carry enough for two days travel. Do you understand, all of you?"

Mara looked at Traynor with steady eyes, but a slight nod of her head showed her agreement. Jebez shrugged and Liam got up from his place to begin packing. Only Conor sat with no expression, an unwillingness to leave his place. Traynor walked over to stand in front of him once more, "Make no mistake, Concobhar. You will be with us when we leave this Light forsaken cave in the morning. Too many people depend on it."

The dawn was cold with a film of slight frost on the grass when they stepped out of the cave entrance. Their breath made a fog in front of them as they walked, Traynor at the head of the line with Conor walking behind him, followed by Jebez. Mara, in a dark green cloak that covered her black satin dress, walked side by side with Liam, Mara talking quietly while Liam listened.

"You know what you need to do, Liam. Conor must have that book. This has gone on long enough and there are lives at stake. This is not a game of stealing from rich men, he means to go to war and you cannot let that happen."

Liam shook his head, looking miserable. "If Traynor finds I have given the book to Conor, my life is over and in the most hideous way he can think, Mara. He won't just kill me, he will find a way to heap torture on me for as long as he can."

"Conor promised he would keep you safe. He will send you somewhere safe."

"There is no place safe from Traynor. Now that he has traveled to the Mountain Folk and to his village, there is no safe place for me to go."

"Put your trust in Conor, Liam. He will keep you safe, I promise."

"You are a fool, Mara to think he can keep anyone safe. I doubt he can keep himself safe. I cannot risk it." Liam lengthened his stride until he was far ahead of Mara. She gripped the heavy fabric of her skirt in frustration, but in her heart she suspected that Liam was right.

Traynor kept a fast pace all day, not stopping for midday meal. As the sun began to set, they reached a copse of elm trees near a small stream. There he unslung his pack and sat with his back against a tree, his legs stretched out in front of him. Liam and Jebez sank to the ground looking miserable. Mara sat some distance from the men, finding a rock to sit on to keep her skirt out of the dirt.

Conor walked to the edge of the clearing and looked back up at the mountain. For the first time, there were no black clouds circling the mountain. The last of the sun's rays illuminated the peak and the sky around it was free of clouds. Conor looked in wonder at the sight. *How long had those clouds been there, ever present, swirling and never leaving? And now they are gone, all of them. What could that mean?*

He sat down and opened his pack to find the meat and cheese that Mara had laid out for him to pack. The meat, grilled over the fire with no herbs was tough and dry. The cheese had bits of mold on it that he picked off before eating it. No bread, no fat cakes stuffed with berries and nuts like Shaen made. No flavor here at all. He leaned back chewing on the tough meat, remembering the delicious meals he once ate with the Mountain Folk. *How could I have been so blind, so stupid to think that there were any answers here for me*? He looked at Mara, brushing crumbs from her skirt, shifting uncomfortably on the rock. *Yes, I have feelings for her, but is it enough to put everyone in danger?* Conor sat back and closed his eyes, thinking of Tilly and Granny. *If I traveled to the Mountain Folk village tonight, would Traynor know it? Would I be able to go there and warn them and come back without Traynor knowing?* He doubted he could do it. The man seemed to know everything before it happened.

Conor finished his meager meal and looked across at his traveling companions. *What a miserable lot we are, and I am one of them!* He raised his voice to be heard across the clearing. "Where are we going? After you get your wagon and mule, that is?"

Traynor sat back and looked at Conor, debating whether to answer him. Finally he shrugged. "There is a valley some distance from your village. Too far to walk, that's why we need the wagon and my mule."

"What is in the valley that you need?"

"The creatures you will raise for me, Concobhar. My beasts, the ones you stole from me. I believe they are there from everything I have felt. Once there, you will raise them and then if you choose, you may go your way. I will make sure you cannot take them from me again. There are wards that I can place around them that will protect them from you. Liam, you have the book, do you not?"

Liam looked up, startled to be addressed. He nodded and patted the knapsack on the ground next to him.

"Good. I will need it when we get there. Jebez, I will need you as well. You will be my scout. No one will notice you, much less question you when you slip into villages and towns. You will help me raise my army with the aid of Ceobhran. Mara, you will do what you do best; feed us and make sure that we have comfortable lodging wherever we go. Conor, if you decide to stay with me, you will be rewarded beyond anything you can imagine. You will sit at my right hand and when this is over, you will live in luxury and want for nothing."

"Traynor, this sounds like the plan of a madman. You think you will have an army that cannot be defeated? With sleepwalking men, controlled by Ceobhran? It makes no sense."

"Oh, but it does, my boy. You have never been under the spell of Ceobhran. I might have to try it on you some day. When he has you, you think of nothing but obeying. You do not feel cold, or hunger, or fear. You have a driving need to obey and that is all. Ask Mara. Ask her what she did with those children of yours. She will tell you. They were hers and hers alone because she directed the fog, as it will be when I command it.

"Think of it - an army that knows no fear. And at the head of it, my serpent, Nathair na- huamha to clear the path for us. Stalking at my side, Leomhanne beinne, my protector. And behind me, Tarbh who spreads fire and devastation in his wake. And if you choose, and I hope you do, your place will be beside me as well, Concobhar. "

Conor listened to his words, maintaining an even expression. His mind recoiled as he listened to Traynor's ravings, knowing he must not reveal any more than he had. *I will go along until I get that book. If he can use the words in that book to put a ward around those beasts, then I can do the same for the people I want to protect. Getting the book is my only chance.*

"Get some sleep. We leave at first light. Mara, you don't plan on sleeping on that rock, do you? I will set a ward to keep everything out of our camp."

Mara sat on the ground with her back to the rock outcropping, wrapping herself in her cloak to keep off the night chill. Conor watched her from his seat, not bothering to stretch out on the ground. He would get very little sleep this night.

Traynor was up before the sun had fully crested the mountains, kicking Liam and Jebez awake. Breakfast was whatever food they had left over in their packs. "Fill your water skins before we leave. We won't be stopping until we reach the village."

The path down the mountain was easier the second day, less steep as it gradually took them into the foothills and the valley below them. The sun was warm on Conor's back and if it had not been for the company he kept, he would have enjoyed the day. His mind drifted back to days spent in the hills with Tilly and Wolf, hiking, talking, with not a care in the world. Again, he berated himself for the fool that he was to have tied himself to Mara and the rest of them. *What was I looking for? A mother, a father? I found them both and now I'm not sure I want either one of them.*

At one point, the path took them through a thick stand of trees; birches, maples, locusts, and oaks, all with their leaves turning brilliant colors and drifting down around them in the breeze. So thick did the trees grow, it was necessary for them to walk single file. Liam stepped in behind Conor at the end of the line. He muttered as he walked and Conor thought he talked to himself until he heard his name. "Conor, I need to know you will keep me safe."

Conor did not answer aloud but sent his thought to Liam, clearly and slowly, *I will send you to the Mountain Folk village. Granny is strong, and she will keep you safe from Traynor. You have to trust me, Liam.*

"I don't. I don't trust that you can do as you say, but Traynor cannot be allowed to follow his path. I saw what happened when he raised those creatures. I saw the death and destruction he brought to innocent people. I cannot do it again."

Let me have the book, Liam, and I can stop him.

"No! He will know the book is gone; the instant I give it to you. The man is tied to the book in some way. He will know if you take it"

Then what do you think we can do to stop him, Liam? I don't have the knowledge. I might have had it once, but it's gone now.

"Pages. I will give you the pages you need. The ones that set the wards to protect you and the ones you will need to send the creatures back where they came from."

I will settle for that, but do it soon, Liam, before we are too far from the Mountain Folk village. I can travel a good distance, but if I am to take you with me, I will need to be closer. No more than my village. Any further than that, and I am not sure I can get you to safety.

Liam nodded to himself. He had no faith he would ever be safe, but he was so weary of following Traynor wherever he went, being at his beck and call. To live a life away from that man! Just to think of it was too much for Liam.

The afternoon sun was sinking in the west when they reached Conor's village. Traynor did not stop until he reached the green where his wagon still sat under the now bare trees. The grass was turning brown, cropped short by the flocks of sheep the villagers kept. Though he looked around, he saw no sign of Roisin or his mule.

"Conor, where is Roisin?"

"How in all the Light would I know that, Traynor. She's your daughter. Keep track of her yourself."

Traynor stared at Conor for a moment before crossing the green toward the blacksmith forge. Once there he stepped inside and called out, "You! Blacksmith! Are you here?"

Tomas came around the corner, wiping his hands on his leather apron. "Who calls me in such a way? Oh, it's you I see. It's been a while since you were here. We all wondered if you were coming back to claim that wagon of yours"

"Never mind that. There was a girl here with me. Where is she and my mule?"

"the girl I could not say. I've not seen her for some time. Your mule, I have in a pen behind my forge. You left him tied up with no grass at his feet to eat. I brought him here and fed and watered him."

"I will take him off your hands now. And I thank you." The last was said reluctantly.

Tomas folded his arms across his chest and leveled his gaze at Traynor. "There is a matter of payment. I expect to be paid for his lodging and food."

"Yes, certainly. Let me get him and I will come back with payment from my wagon."

Tomas looked hard at Traynor. He fully expected no payment would ever come his way. Finally, he shrugged and walked out of the forge. Picking up a halter, he opened the gate and slipped it over Jasper's head. Patting the mule's neck, he led him from the pen and handed the lead rope to Traynor.

Traynor led Jasper back to the green and immediately began hitching him to the wagon. "You, Mara. Get in the back of the wagon and see what food is there. Jebez, you and Liam pack up the kettle and anything else you find. Liam, you know what I travel with. Get it all in the wagon. We leave this Light forsaken place now.""My lord, where is Roisin? We can't leave without her." Fear was written plainly across his face. What would happen to him if they were too far from the Mountain Folk village?

"I don't know where that girl has gone, and I don't care," Traynor snarled as he continued to hitch Jasper to the wagon. "Get moving, now!"

Jebez and Liam gathered up the black kettle and cooking utensils, still strewn across the makeshift table. Mara dug around in the boxes and barrels in the back of the wagon. "There is not much here. Some potatoes and shriveled carrots. Some herbs and tea in paper, but no meat."

"We will take what we need as we travel. Conor, you will ride with me, the rest of you will walk."

Conor looked at Traynor for a long moment. "I will walk. It will not look right to travelers to see a woman in a fine dress walking. Mara will ride in the wagon with you." With that he turned and strode down the path leading out of the village.

The wagon, pulled by the faithful mule soon caught up with Conor and he swung in behind it. Liam and Jebez, both looking weary and miserable walked some distance back. The wagon was soon lost to sight among the small hills and autumn trees. Jebez grumbled as he walked. "I thought nothing could be worse than that cave, but here I am, footsore and hungry. It seems I have hitched my wagon to the wrong mule. Again."

Conor looked sideways at the man but did not answer him. The road was broad here but not frequently traveled. Conor's small village sat at the end of it and except for the occasional tinker, few traveled this far out. Conor himself had never been beyond the boundaries of the village in this direction, always preferring the fields and forests toward the mountains. He was curious to see what he would find.

"You have been this way before," Liam said under his breath. "Many times."

Conor shook his head, "I have no memory of it. I have no memory of anything but my village."

As dusk fell around them, and the light faded into evening, Traynor stopped the mule and allowed the men to catch up to him. "We camp here tonight."

"Why not camp in the green? Why this mad rush to camp in the middle of nowhere?" Jebez whined as he looked around at the road and the trees crowding in on them.

"That blacksmith wanted payment that I did not want to give him. We have enough to buy us food in the next town, but none to spare for him. We camp here and Mara will fix whatever she found in the wagon. Liam, gather some wood and get a fire going. Jebez, bring down that box with the pot and the rest of it."

Liam went quietly to gather the wood, his knapsack flung over his shoulder. He wandered further away from the wagon, slipping into the forest. When he returned he had an armful of dried wood that he dropped on the ground. He left again to gather rocks to make a fire ring. Then, digging around in his knapsack, he found a piece of flint and his knife. Piling the dry pieces in the circle, he struck the flint with his knife until sparks fell on the wood, catching it. He fed larger pieces to the fire and soon had a good blaze going. Jebez brought the boxes and set them near the fire where he laid out a pot with bowls and spoons.

Mara dug around in the boxes and gathered the potatoes and carrots. Conor walked up to her where she stood looking at the pot and the fire. "I have no stomach for another one of your meals, Mara. Go down by that stream and look for wild onions. Jebez, take this pot and fill it with water. Not full, just part of the way. Liam, there is a tripod in the wagon. Set it up and we will hang the pot over the fire."

Conor set to slicing potatoes and carrots. He searched for the herbs he knew he would find and nodding to himself, set them aside. The pot was hung, and the fire blazed beneath it. He added the potatoes, carrots, and the onions Mara silently handed him. Digging in the very bottom of the box, he found some dried meat and with satisfaction, cut it into smaller pieces to add to the boiling water. The herbs he scattered across the top and stirred them in. Before long, the rich smells of meat and vegetables drifted across their makeshift camp causing even Traynor to look up with interest. Conor used the ladle that Jebez handed him and filled each bowl. Mara carried the first one to Traynor who dug in eagerly. There was not a sound in the camp as they filled their bellies with the rich stew. When he was finished, Conor put a kettle on the hot rocks for tea.

"Mara, you will learn to make this meal. I will not eat another one of your poor dishes, not when we have someone who can cook like this. Well done, my boy. Well done." Traynor sat back and almost smiled as he said this. He reached out his empty bowl for Mara to clean. Conor fixed mugs of tea and Mara took them around. She had grown so silent that words no longer seemed to find their way to her lips. In her world with Traynor, she did not speak unless she was spoken to first. She knew this having learned the lesson the hard way. Now it was a habit.

"How far is this valley of yours, Traynor?" Conor sipped his tea, his back against a locust tree.

"A few days travel. It will take us longer since you must walk. Jasper is a good mule, but not strong enough to carry the wagon and heavy men. You will enjoy the valley, Conor. It was once your home. You had a fine house there, marble floors and a wide staircase that ended in a balcony from which you could look down. A fireplace big enough to roast an ox, not that you did that. But you could have. You lived there for two of your lives, I believe. No doubt that is why you sent my creatures there. It will be interesting to see if it brings back memories."

Conor sat quietly, thinking about his words. A home? He had a home there. Somehow the thought sent a queasy feeling through him, as if he might be sick. *Why would I feel this way? Why would this memory make me feel sick?*

He stood up abruptly and went to the fire. Stirring the rest of the stew, he unhooked the pot and set it on the ground. No sense burning it, it would probably be their morning meal. As he worked, he saw Liam edging his way toward the forest. He looked back at Conor once, indicating with his head that Conor should follow him. Conor nodded.

He sent his thought toward Liam, *Wait for me in the grove of maples. I will be there as soon as I can.*

He picked up their water skins, "I will fill these for us. No sense everyone leaving camp."

Liam waited in the grove as directed. He held out pages, folded into a neat square. "These are the ones you will need."

Conor took them and unfolded the first one, smoothing the creases as he did. He read the words with interest and then looked off into the distance. "There is a memory of these. It is not clear, but as soon as I looked at them, I knew I had seen them, used them even."

"You did. Those." Liam pointed to the ones used to banish creatures called forth from dark places. "The other one, I don't know. It has the words of warding."

Conor read the words, muttering them to himself as if to memorize them. Over and over again, he repeated them to himself, not aloud where they would be used, but to himself where he could make them part of him. Liam fidgeted and shifted his weight impatiently while Conor repeated the words to himself. Finally he looked up at Liam, "You did well, Liam. I am grateful. This page you will keep and take with you." He handed the warding page to Liam. "You will give this to Granny Matilda. She will know what to do with it. This one, I will keep. I don't know how I will stop Traynor, but at least I can rid the world of his beasts."

"And me? What happens to me now, Conor?"

"I will take you to the Mountain Folk village tonight. Wait until everyone is asleep and met me here at moonrise. I will see that you are safe. Where is the rest of the book, Liam?"

"I dare not give the book to you, Conor. Please understand that the book is tied to Traynor, and he would know if it were gone. Somehow he would know and my life would be forfeit." Liam pleaded for Conor to understand.

Conor nodded his head. "The pages will have to be enough for now. I thank you. I know what you are risking. I am aware of it."

With a miserable look on his face, Liam slipped out of the grove and walked back toward the camp. Conor sat down on a nearby log and unfolded the second page. Laying it on his knees, he read the words, strange words that made no sense to him. Would he ever remember his past lives? Would he ever be himself, whatever that was?

Reading the words, he suddenly had a flash of memory. He closed his eyes and let it come. There before him was a beast that sent chills down his back. A snake, but no ordinary snake, more of a serpent, large and sinuous, crawling toward him, coming closer and closer. He could feel his heart racing, his breath coming in short bursts. When the serpent was close enough, it coiled, raising its head, its tongue tasting the air in front of it. Its fangs dripped poison, the liquid thick and viscous, tinged with brown. Its eyes glittered as if filled with gold flecks. Conor watched as it swayed slightly back and forth in front of him, tongue flicking, eyes glittering. Its body was immense, thicker in the middle than Conor's forearm, tapering off to a tail that the creature tucked under him. Its eyes bored into Conor, stilling him, freezing his blood. Conor tried to raise his arm, hold forth his hand, but the serpent's eyes kept him as if he were bound hand and foot. In his memory, Conor muttered the words to himself, over and over, each time a bit louder. With each time he said the words, they grew louder in his throat, until finally, they came bursting out. The serpent lunged at Conor, but he fell sideways, slipping away from those deadly fangs. As he did, his arms were freed and he leaped to his feet. Now he screamed the words aloud, his arm upraised and pointed toward the serpent. Again and again, he screamed the words, advancing on the serpent as it tried in vain to back away from Conor. As he hurled the words, the serpent grew fainter, its gold flecked eyes dulling to brown, the colors along its back fading into fog. As he repeated the words over and over, the creature shrank, becoming an ordinary snake, harmless and vulnerable. Conor dropped his arm and his voice died away to a whisper. The snake turned and slithered away leaving no trace of the hideous serpent it once was.

Conor sat bolt upright on the log. Sweat poured from his face, and his hands holding the pages shook. If this is what his memories held, then maybe it was better not to remember. His whole body shook and tears streamed down his face. *Oh Tilly, what have I become? What kind of man am I? What kind of world am I in?* He dropped his head into his hands and his shoulders shook with sobs.

Chapter Twenty-Six

ESCAPE

The moon's light was dim, but Conor stretched out his hand with the ball of light balanced in his palm, and easily found his way to the maple grove. There he discovered Liam, pacing back and forth, wearing a path between the trees.

"I want to go now before anyone discovers we are gone," Conor's words were clipped and forced. He reached out a hand and gripped Liam's arm tightly. Liam started and thought to jerk away, but the next instant, he was standing before a rock wall, towering far above his head. Without a word, Conor slipped around the end of the wall, finding a path between them. Liam followed closely, afraid of being left behind. In wonder, he stared at the open field in front of him, illuminated by the globe of light in Conor's hand.

"Quickly! We have little time." He began the climb to the caves above, not stopping until he stood outside of Aelf's dwelling. Softly he called out, "Granny Matilda. I need you, Granny."

The tanned hide that acted as a door was brushed aside and Granny stood outside. Without a word, she grabbed Conor and held him close. "You are traveling. You don't feel like yourself, Conor, but by the Light I am glad to see you!" Her voice held the tears that were in her eyes.

"Granny, I cannot stay long. You are right, I am traveling which means I am not really here, as you know. This is Liam and he is here as he stands before you."

Granny looked hard at Liam. "This man, I know, Conor. Why do you bring him to us? He travels with Traynor and does his dirty work."

"I need you to keep him safe for me. He will bring you pages for a warding that will protect you from Traynor. It will take him two days to get here, and I don't know yet how to keep his absence from the man, but I will. Keep this man safe, Granny. He has risked his life for me. I cannot explain everything but give me your word that you will protect him and use the words on this page to set wards around the Mountain Folk and our village. Promise me, Granny!"

Granny's eyes searched Conor's face. She could see that he was no longer the carefree young man she knew. Lines were etched across his face that were not there before. She nodded. "Let me see the page so I will recognize the words when he comes." She held out her hand and studied the words on the page. Nodding she handed the paper back to Conor. "I will expect you in two days' time, Liam. You will give me the full account when you arrive. Do you understand me?"

Liam nodded. He took the page from Conor and folding it once more, put it into his pocket.

"The Light carry you safely, Conor." Granny slipped through the hide door on silent feet.

Conor gripped Liam's arm and once more they were in the grove of maples. "Go now. Walk through the night and day. Do not stop until you are there. You will hear my voice in your head along the way to guide you. I will put off Traynor for as long as I can. You must reach them so Granny can set the ward before he realizes you are gone." Conor turned and strode back to the camp, stopping just outside to look for movement. Seeing none, he found his cloak on the ground and wrapped it around himself once more.

Mara watched silently from her place, closed her eyes and smiled slightly to herself.

The morning dawned crisp and cold, their breath making fog in front of their faces as they glumly drank tea and shoveled cold stew into their mouths.

"Where is Liam?" Traynor looked around the camp. "It's not like him to miss morning meal."

Conor looked around as if he expected Liam to appear. He shrugged and went back to drinking his tea.

Traynor stood up and walked around their meager camp. There was no sign of Liam by the wagon or near Jasper. He turned to look at Mara who looked back with an innocent face. "Jebez, where is Liam?"

Jebez grunted a reply, "Don't know."

Traynor grew more agitated as time ticked on. He climbed into the back of the wagon and began throwing things aside, looking for something. When he found The Book of Words, he gave a sigh of relief. "This is good, but it doesn't answer my question. Where is Liam?"

Conor stood up to carry his mug to the impromptu wash stand. "He is likely out looking around. I did say to him last night that some fresh meat would go well in our stew, a rabbit I suggested. I saw him earlier working with what looked like a sling. He's gone hunting, Traynor. You have your book. There is nothing suspicious going on here. For Light's sake, Traynor, let the man bring us some fresh meat for our evening meal."

Traynor stood for a time, considering Conor's words. Finally, finding no fault in what he heard, he said. "Jebez, load the wagon while I hitch the mule. He will catch up to us, hopefully with that meat you speak of Conor."

By afternoon, there was still no sign of Liam as they neared the first town. Traynor grew increasingly agitated, but he could find no outlet for his frustration. His temper was met with blank faces all around him. Before the town loomed too close, they came upon a small farm, the farmer in the field gathering the last of the season's potatoes. His wife churned butter on their front porch in the late autumn sun. Traynor pulled on Jasper's reins to halt him before the field. The farmer looked up, wiping sweat from his brow.

"Afternoon, my lord. You would be in need of fresh well water for you and your lady? I have a trough out back for the mule, lord."

"I require more than that. I need you to leave. Gather your wife and walk away. We will stay here tonight and use what we need. You may return in two days' time to whatever we leave behind."

The farmer looked puzzled and then sputtered in anger. "Why would I leave my cottage for you, lord? This is my home." He picked up his hoe as if he thought to use it as a weapon.

Traynor waved his hand and muttered words. The hoe fell to the ground, and the man's arm hung uselessly by his side. "You have a choice. Leave now or risk the other arm as well. I can see you doing your work with one arm, but not with none. Your choice."

The man looked with disbelief at his arm. He picked it up with his other hand and dropped it, staring at it. He looked at Traynor with pleading eyes. "Please, lord, I have no one to do the work here. Whatever you've done, take it back. I beg you, lord, give me my arm back. We will leave."

"Yes, you will. Gather your wife and go. Now."

The man stumbled out of his field and rushed to the front porch. There he spoke urgently to his wife, who shook her head and started to climb down the steps. The farmer grabbed her with his last good arm and jerked her down the steps toward the road, without looking back. They past Jebez and Conor who were just coming off the road.

"May the Light forsake you all the days of your life," the man muttered.

"Hold on there. What have I done to you?" Conor grabbed the man's arm. When he saw that it hung uselessly beside him, he dropped it with a sorrowful look on his face. "The man in the wagon?"

The farmer nodded and started off toward the town.

Conor met Traynor in front of the humble cottage where he stopped the wagon. "Was that necessary? Did you have to hurt that man?"

Traynor shrugged. "I asked him to leave, he said no, so I persuaded him. Now we have food and shelter for the night. We will wait for Liam to catch up to us with that rabbit you promised and we will eat and rest. Jebez, see if this ignorant farmer has learned to make cider from those apples I see hanging from the tree. Mara, finish churning. I have a craving for fresh butter on my bread."

Conor stepped off the porch and unhitched Jasper from the wagon. He walked him to the back of the cottage where he found a small lean-to. "No pen for you, Jasper, old boy. Let's see if there are hobbles here to keep you from wandering."

The atmosphere in the cottage was tense that evening. There was no sign of Liam, rabbit or no rabbit. Conor found meat and potatoes for a stew. Loaves of freshly baked bread sat on the board in the kitchen. These he sliced and laid out on wooden plates. Mara scooped butter out of the churn and heaped it beside the bread. Still no Liam.

Traynor was in a fit by evening meal, walking out onto the porch to stare down the road. "If he was out hunting, he is a poor hunter to have taken this long."

"Traynor, eat. You don't do any of us any good stomping around and yelling."

Liam stood outside the immense granite wall, staring up at it. It looked the same, but it was barely moonlight when he saw it last. He walked to the end and slid his hand along the cool stone. Sure enough, around the end, the first wall stopped and the second began. He slipped between the two walls. Breathing a sigh of relief he practically ran across the field toward the caves.

He had not gone far when a young man ran down to meet him. "Are you Liam?" Liam nodded. "Follow me quickly. I am to take you to Granny Matilda in haste. She will skin me if we tarry anywhere along the way."

Liam's legs wobbled as he climbed. *Would he ever feel rested again?* He followed the boy to the same cave he remembered from so long ago, it seemed. Granny Matilda stood outside, tapping her foot, an anxious look on her face. She held out her hand, and without a word Liam took the page from his pocket and gave it to her. She scanned it quickly and then motioned for him to enter the dwelling.

"Neall, get Ronan as fast as your legs can carry you. She is to meet me above our caves, in the high cliffs. Do you understand where that is?"

Neall nodded and raced away. Granny climbed past the caves, finding only a deer path barely visible to her eyes to follow. When she came out on the top, the trees were fewer, stripped of leaves in the waning autumn light. Ronan, her skirts gathered in her hand, joined Granny, panting with the effort of the climb.

Granny held out the page. "I think it will take both our gifts to be strong enough to ward the village from Traynor. I may be able to do it myself, but why take the chance?

"We will link ourselves by holding one hand together. Raise your other hand and read the words with me." Ronan nodded and gripped Granny's hand with hers. She raised her other hand to the sky and looked at the page Granny held out in front of them. Together they read the strange words, repeating them as soon as they came to the end of them. Three times they said the words and then stopped. Granny stood still, listening, barely breathing. Ronan looked questioningly at her, waiting. At last Granny sighed. "I believe we did it. Our work is not done. We must get to the village and do the same thing again. Are you up to it?"

"Of course, but I would like to know what is going on, Granny. Can you tell me?"

"I wish I could, girl. Not yet. There are too many questions only someone else can answer for us, but I cannot take the time to hear him. I will explain everything I know on the way to the village, but we are going to have to walk day and night to get there. If Conor is right, it is important we ward my village just as we warded yours."

"Warded? Granny, you are scaring me."

"I don't mean to, Ronan, but I think it's best you be frightened. The man who might be coming here is worth being afraid of. Now let's go."

The path down the mountain quickly faded in the evening darkness, making it difficult to find their way. Granny would not stop, not to light a fire or a torch. "Better no one knows we are about," she said through gritted teeth. The dark brought a chill to the air and only their fast pace kept them warm. Ronan slipped often until finally Granny turned to her, "Do you need a light? I would rather not, but I would also rather you not break a leg on the way down."

Ronan grimaced, "I'm sorry, Granny. I am right behind you. Please don't stop on my account."

Granny shook her head but continued down the mountain in near dark. At last the moon rose in the night sky, shedding its white light on their path giving them enough to find their way. By the time the moon had set and the sky began to show the signs of sunrise in shades of pink and orange, the two women stood on a small hill overlooking the village.

"This will do quite well, Ronan." Granny pulled the folded page from her skirt pocket and held her hand out to Ronan. Just as before the women held their free hands to the sky and repeated the strange words three times. As before, Granny stood still and listened until she was satisfied the ward was in place.

"We can walk more slowly back, if it pleases you, Ronan. But I don't want to stop until we get to your village. I need to hear what that man, Liam, has to tell me."

Ronan nodded her head wearily but turned without a word and headed back up the mountain. Granny smiled to herself as she watched the woman's back. *She has some nerve, that one. No wonder she is such a good healer.*

As the sun grew warmer, they stopped to drink from a stream that slipped across rocks and sparkled in the autumn sunlight. Granny sat for a moment, legs outstretched, her head tilted back so that the sun shone on her face, warming her.

"Granny, how do you know the ward is in place? I can't see anything or hear anything. You seem to be listening for something, but I can't imagine what it is." Ronan picked at the last of the autumn leaves strewn on the ground around her.

Granny shrugged and looked off toward the valley. 'I'm not sure I can tell you what I am listening for, because it's not a sound it is the lack of sound I try to hear. Once the ward is in place, nothing can go in but nothing can come out as well. I should have heard the first stirrings of the villagers, the bleating of the sheep or the sound of the ram's bell. Anything to tell me the village was awake, but there was nothing. Not a sound and that tells me more than anything else could tell me. The ward is in place and the village is safe, for now. I hope that answers your question, Ronan."

The woman smiled, “It makes perfect sense in a world that often doesn't.” She stood and brushed the leaves and dirt from her skirt. Without a word, she turned and found the path upward once more.

Chapter Twenty-Seven

Liam's Story

Once Granny and Ronan made their weary way back to the Mountain Folk village, they nearly collapsed outside of Aelf's doorway. Neall saw them first and ran to find his da.

"I need that man, Liam, Aelf. I need you and Shaen, Cormac to hear what he has to say. Bring him out here to me, please." Aelf nodded and ducked back inside his dwelling, calling for Neall to fetch his uncle.

They gathered around Granny and Ronan. Granny looked at them, apprehension written across everyone's faces. "Where is Tilly? Doiranne? Roisin? Aelf, you don't understand. I need everyone here. Now. And bring me that man. Now." Aelf gestured to his other sons and set them running to do as Granny bid. He left to bring Liam himself.

Granny sat back and leaned her head against the rock behind her, too exhausted to say any more. Before she could catch her breath, she felt a hand touch her shoulder lightly. Opening her eyes, she saw the cup of tea that Shaen held before her. A smile of gratitude touched her lips as she took the steaming cup. Shean carried the second one to Ronan who accepted it with her own smile.

Before she was finished with her tea, Tilly and Roisin joined them. "Where is Doireanne?"

"Granny, I think she is out walking with Wolf. She has grown quite fond of Conor's dog."

"I will not say one word until she is with us. We would very likely not be here had it not been for Doireanne and her bravery. Do you all know what that woman risked helping Conor? I think not. He would mostly likely not be among the living if she hadn't taken it upon herself to track him to the cave. Now someone go find that woman for me, please."

Tilly rose immediately and went in search of Doireanne. Granny shook her head and mumbled, "I do not think they understand what is at stake here."

At last they were all gathered around Granny, Doireanne standing in the back until she was motioned forward by the old woman. Aelf walked behind Liam, nudging him when the man faltered.

"Stand over there. My name is Matilda, Granny Matilda to the people here, but not to you. Let's be very clear that I don't trust you, not for a hair's breadth. I'm not sure why you are here, I'm not sure why Conor thinks he can trust you, but I want you to start talking and don't stop until I tell you to stop."

Liam nodded his agreement and took a deep breath. He squared his shoulders as best he could and looked at each of the people gathered around him. "My name is Liam and I have been in the service of a man named Traynor Gill for as long as I can remember. Lifetimes, not just this one, but many. I have been bound to him through his powers and my greed and cowardice. That is the truth. With Traynor, my life was easy, at first. There was a good place to live and food on the table. I wore rich clothing and had everything I needed. Before he took me in, I was used to being poor, never having enough food to eat, never knowing where I would sleep that night. No matter how much I struggled, I could not change my life. Traynor did that. He changed everything for me. But as time passed, those things began to trickle away. I don't really remember how or when, but in this lifetime, I have been treated differently. Traynor has been a man possessed, determined to find something. I wasn't sure what. He used me to track people, find them and bring him to them or them to him. It didn't matter. As long as I obeyed him, I was not hurt. My search took me to the cave, the one where Mara and Jebez held your children and called up Ceobhran. She had something that he needed. A book, a book I have been guarding since he took it from her. It is the same book that I ripped the pages out to give to Conor. He asked me for the book, Matilda, but I couldn't do that. Traynor would know the instant I gave it to him. Don't ask me how, but he is connected to that book somehow, and he would know I took it. My life would be over." Liam's look was pleading, begging them to understand.

Granny looked at him without expression. "I told you not to stop until I told you to stop. What is he up to? What does Traynor want with Conor?"

Liam bowed his head before answering, "Matilda, Conor has something that Traynor needs. You are right, there is so much more to the story. Some of it I don't know, some of it has been erased from my mind, some of it I guessed at from conversations I overheard. Please bear with me if it doesn't all make sense."

He took a deep breath and without asking, found a place to sit; an old tree, cut in two and planed smooth to make a seat. "I told you I have been with Traynor for many lifetimes. So many that I have lost count. In these lives there have been things that have been repeated, some I remember, some I do not. One thing I remember is that Conor has been there before, but not as he is now. He is not a child, but he is not a man full grown. In the past he has been a man, a powerful man. More powerful I think than Traynor even. Traynor has had one goal, to conquer and rule. And he has used his powers to bring up creatures from the dark. These creatures look like something you and I have seen, but they are different. Larger, stronger than anything we know. Traynor uses them as part of his army, and he uses Ceobhran to raise his soldiers. He tries this over and over again, but to my knowledge he is never successful because of Conor. Conor sends his creatures back to the dark or somewhere, I can't say. All I know is, he finds Traynor and destroys his army, over and over again. Traynor thinks this time might be different because he thinks Conor is different now. Before, there was a coldness, a hardness about Conor. He was never close to anyone, he had no one in his life. Now he does. He has you. All of you. Traynor reckons that makes him weak. He thinks to even use Mara against Conor. I don't think there is much love between Conor and Mara, but I don't know for certain. She is his mother, after all. It's why Conor wanted the book. He thought to use it to keep you safe. I wasn't sure you would be able to use the warding. It takes a powerful person, and I wasn't sure you were strong enough, Matilda."

The look that Granny gave Liam would have bored a hole in stout wood, but he met her look without flinching. "I had help to set the wards. Don't worry about how strong I am, Liam. I am stronger than you think."

Liam shrugged, "All I know is it takes a great deal of power to protect a place as large as this. I hope it works, for my sake as well as yours."

"Continue," Granny demanded.

"Traynor thinks Conor will raise up his creatures. He is the only one who can do it. The last time he banished them, he locked the door on them so Traynor cannot raise them. He needs Conor to do that. And, like I said, he thinks Conor will do it to keep you safe, all of you. Matilda, you do not know the things that Traynor can do to a person. I have seen with my own eyes how he can blind a man or take away the use of his arms or legs. I have seen him wither living things that stood before him. He has the book that allows him to do things that are beyond your imagination. Please believe me, you will never be safe. You can't live inside a warded village forever. What do you think you can do against Traynor?"

Granny didn't answer. She motioned to Tilly to go stand next to Liam. The girl did as Granny asked and put her hand on Liam's shoulder. She closed her eyes and was so still even her breath seemed suspended. Liam looked puzzled but under Granny's look did not move. Time stood still as the group watched Tilly and Liam. After a few moments, Tilly opened her eyes and nodded at Granny. "I see the things he has told us. I saw him as a very poor merchant, I think. I saw his conversation with Traynor, the hope that Traynor offered him. I think it is as he says, Granny."

Granny looked thoughtful for a moment. "Tilly confirms what she can by reading your past, but she cannot tell us if what you say about Traynor's plans is true. I am worried about you, Liam. I worry that you have too long been a tool of Traynor's to ever be trusted."

Liam looked down at the ground between his feet. "I don't deserve your trust, Matilda. I understand that, and I am grateful that you have let me stay here for the past days. There have been so many years that I have not felt as safe as I have felt in the last few days, I nearly forgot what it was like. If you ask me to do something and it is within my power to do it, I will. Please understand, I cannot take the book, but I can tell you what is in the book. Know this; Traynor believes this time will be different. This time Conor will not interfere, will not send his creatures away. I have seen versions of Conor myself, and I know there is something in him now that was never there before. At first, I thought it was because of his youth, but I'm not sure. I think it might have more to do with you people and if it is true, than all is lost. You will be his doom"

"You said you gave a page to Conor other than the warding page. What was it?"

"The page that he needs to send the creatures back to the dark. The creatures and Traynor.""Hmmm." Granny's sigh said it all, the sadness, the frustration.

"Matilda, there is one more thing."

Granny's eyebrows rose and she pursed her lips together. What was the man keeping from them still?

"Traynor is Concobhar's father."

Chapter Twenty-Eight

The Book of Words

There was not a sound from the group of Folk and friends; the shocked silence that Liam's words caused was broken by no one until Granny stood up abruptly. "I suspected as much. You've gone a bit toward earning my trust, Liam. I was wondering if you would tell us that." Granny looked around her group, "You had to have known it yourselves. How else would Conor have had more lives than a person should have? Why else would Traynor need him so badly. You had all the information in front of you to figure that little piece of the puzzle." She turned to Liam, "Mara still his mother, I suppose?"

Liam nodded but said nothing.

"I need now to know about this cursed book you keep waving in front of my face, so to speak. The one you took the pages from."

"It is called The Book of Words. It is an ancient book, leather bound with iron to hold it. It is in the ancient tongue. I cannot read all of it, but I can read some of it. Traynor has always had it until Mara stole it and took it to the cave. He knew she had it, but he also knew she had his child so he had to bide his time until he was sure he could get the book without harming Concobhar somehow. He is tied to the book in an old way so he knows when the book is taken. He knew the instant she had it in her hands." Liam shook his head at the memory. "He was in such a rage. I thought he would blame me for the loss and do something dreadful to me, but he didn't. I cannot tell you why, I will never guess.

"I used the book to track Mara and Jebez to the cave. Long ago, Traynor put words to the book to help him keep track of it. When Mara took it, he used words on me so I could track it myself. He called me his bloodhound," Liam said ruefully. "His bloodhound." The man took a deep breath, "It took me a very long time to track them to the cave. I can't explain how it works, I just feel a pull, a force that pulls me in one direction. I cannot fight it, I cannot resist it."

Granny searched Liam's face, seeing the pain written across it. "Let me ask you this. Why did Mara only use the words to call up Ceobhran? There must be many more words she could find useful in that book."

"Yes, but Mara is not that strong. I think she could do little things from the book but calling Ceobhran would take every inch of her power and then some. Concobhar did not get his power from Mara."

"We call them gifts, but then, we use them as gifts not as powers to harm or control."

Liam thought about Granny Matilda's words for a moment. "I have never known anything but the power he used to control me, to hurt me and others. The power Traynor would use to conquer and rule. There are times he wields his power like a cudgel, beating people until they submit or die. Other times, he wields it as a sword in battle. Matilda, he could bring the mountains down upon you if he wanted to. Keep the wards up."

"I will, but we are going to have to leave here and soon. There is too much afoot with that man and Conor to sit around knitting. Liam, leave us to talk please. Take a walk, but do not climb too high or you will be out of the warding."

Liam got up to leave and Granny watched his back as he walked down the path toward the main part of the village. "I want us to go inside. We will make tea and food, if you will allow us, Shaen. We have much to talk about.

Traynor's ragtag group left the farmhouse early in the morning before the sun had warmed the thatch on the roof. As they traveled toward the valley, Traynor grumbled and cast about with anxious looks, constantly turning in his seat on the wagon to look through the dust at the road behind them. The day was a long one, made much longer by his abusive words. Mara made no reply, merely gripped the side of the wagon until her hands ached with it. As with everything, the day finally came to an end and Traynor pulled hard on the reins to halt Jasper. Jumping down from the wagon, he threw the reins in the direction of Jebez and stomped away. Jebez grabbed the reins and began to unhitch Jasper, jerking his traces as he did.

"Leave off, man." Conor took the leathers from his hands and gently unhitched the mule. He led him to a place under a tree where grass still grew green and full. There he rubbed the mule with handfuls of dried leaves and hobbled him where he could crop the last of the grass.

Traynor sat in the back of the wagon with The Book of Words in his lap. Thoughtfully, he closed his eyes and reached out to search for Liam. Nothing. No sign of the man.

In frustration, he threw the book down on the bed of the wagon and bellowed for food and wine. "Jebez, you make a fire. Mara, pour me some wine and heat the last of the stew from last night's meal. Mara, now, if you please. I will have silence and peace. We leave in the morning.

The sky was a pale shade of gray when Traynor kicked at the fire, stirring up sparks and raising smoke. "Mara, morning meal and tea, if you please." The pleasantry he attached to his words belied the snarl in which he delivered them.

Conor stood up and stretched. "We are in a good humor this morning, I see."

"Do not tempt me, boy. I want to know where Liam is, and I want to know now. I think you have more to do with this than an innocent suggestion of fresh meat and hunting. Out with it. What have you done with Liam?"

"Traynor, your ill temper bores me before morning meal. I will help Mara with firewood and when we have proper food in front of us, we can talk. I would like to know how far we must travel to find this mysterious valley you spoke of."

Traynor stared at him and Mara ducked her head to hide a smile. *Where does he get the nerve to talk to Traynor like that?* She shrugged and began pulling food and tea out of the boxes stacked in the back of the wagon. Before long, Conor had a fire burning high, and he pushed rocks into the flames to heat them for cooking. When Mara brought a platter of sliced meats, he seasoned the meat with a packet of herbs he took from his pocket. The kettle of water he laid on the hot rocks near enough to the fire to boil the water. Mara poured tea leaves into cups and handed them to Conor. He pulled his sleeve down and doubled it over his hand to pull the hot kettle from the fire, pouring the water over the leaves to steep. The meat he turned with a fork and lifted the pieces off to the platter where they continued to sizzle. Mara cut bread and cheese and placed them on plates where Conor divided the meat. Mara smiled to herself but did not say a word. She carried a plate to Traynor and took hers to a nearby log to sit. Jebez was forced to come and get his own plate after Conor made it clear he would not carry it for the man.

Stuffing meat into his mouth, Jebez grunted some sort of compliment around his food. Traynor nodded as he took his first bite. "You have a better way with meat than Mara, Concobhar."

Conor shrugged. Finishing his morning meal, he sat with his back against a tree and held his steaming cup of tea. "You don't think Liam is off hunting?"Traynor held his plate out for Mara to take before answering. "No, I think he has used it as an excuse and has gone his own way. He thinks to never come back, is my guess. I have him marked with words to track him, but I cannot feel him anywhere, no matter where I travel. I don't think he would be fool enough to go to your light forsaken Mountain Folk, but I want us to travel there and see for ourselves. It is a long two-day journey for a man walking and I don't see Liam doing that on his own without good reason."

"I won't," said Conor.

"What do you mean, you won't? You won't travel there to help me find him? I could wander around that village and their caves for days without finding him if I can't sense him. I need you to help me search."

"I won't," was all Conor would say. "You go if you want. Liam is not important to me, not worth troubling myself with his whereabouts. You want him, you go find him. I will stay here with Mara. I doubt Jebez would be much help to her if trouble were to wander into this camp. No, better I stay here, and you go." This was said with a smile and an innocent look.

Traynor stared at Conor for a moment, but Conor got up from his seat to carry his dish to the wagon, paying Traynor no mind at all.

"If you think for a moment you can do something to me while I travel, think again, boy. I will place wards around me that will prevent that, you know."

Conor shrugged, "It makes no difference to me if you travel from here, Traynor. Do as you please and I will do as I please."

Traynor stood up and stomped away from the fire. He climbed into the back of the wagon and retrieved his book. Turning the pages impatiently, he found what he was looking for. Mara watched as he muttered words and waved his hand. Then he was silent and she could tell that only a shell of him remained, the rest was traveling to the Mountain Folk, she thought to herself.

Traynor stood outside the granite wall, the one that appeared to block his way in. He smiled to himself knowing he had to only turn the corner and find the narrow passage that led to the caves. He held out his hand to trace the wall, but it stopped of its own accord. Puzzled, he held out his hand again, but again it stopped before it reached the end of the first wall. *Never mind, I don't need to feel my way, I know how it goes.* He pushed his body against the end of the wall, but nothing happened. It was as if the granite wall did not end as it had before. He tried to see around the corner of the wall, but there was nothing but a thick haze as if a fog had settled over the passageway. He pulled back and screamed his anger to the sky.

He jumped from the back of the wagon, and stormed over to Conor, "It's warded! The Mountain Folk village is warded! How did that happen, Concobhar? How is it that your Folks' village is warded?"

Conor shrugged, "That is not hard to figure out, Traynor. Granny Matilda must have done it. Why do you think you are the only one with powers? You've been around her. You can sense the power that comes off that old lady. Use your head. She would know you would come after them. She saw me there. She must have known I brought you and now she is taking precautions against you. Against me, for all I know."

Suspicion was written across Traynor's face, but he had no good answer for Conor. "It still doesn't bring me closer to finding Liam. By the light, I need that man near me." He stared into the fire, thinking. *I need Liam more than I thought I did. Without him, I can feel a loss I did not expect to feel.* He stood up and walked toward the mule, picketed in the nearby trees. "Load the wagon, Jebez. We travel to the valley this day."

Conor and Jebez walked behind the wagon, passing fields of wheat and straw cut short for the coming winter. The trees, bare of leaves, raised their branches to the sky as if they entreated the heavens for a blessing. "I'm not sure why you have tied yourself to Traynor, Jebez."

Jebez looked sideways at Conor. "I warned you to stay away from him, stay away from us. You didn't listen as a boy and you don't listen now. Mara never did anything for me." The last came out as a guttural growl from the heavily bearded man. His hair still hung in ragged, greasy locks around his shoulders. His beard, too heavy and thick to be handsome, was more threatening than anything. His eyes, too small and set close together were drawn into a frown.

Conor smiled to himself, "I would have thought she would be easier to work for than Traynor. He seems unpredictable"

"And you thinks she isn't?" Jebez growled. "Think again, boy!"

"I just wonder if we couldn't form some sort of alliance. You could be useful to me, and you know I have defeated Traynor before which means I can do it again."

"Not as long you have any kind of attachment to those people, though the Light only knows what you get from them. And don't think I don't know that you had something to do with Liam's disappearance. I haven't figured out what you did, but as soon as I do, I go straight to Traynor with my thoughts. Stay away from me, boy. I don't need your trouble. I see myself taking Liam's place, so I ought to be grateful to you, but my gratitude doesn't buy you much, so stay away. And if you are smarter than you look, you will stay away from Mara as well. She is not to be trusted, not by you, not by Traynor. She has always been for herself and no one else."

Conor's face did not bely the shock he felt at hearing so many words pour out of Jebez. *This is the man who mostly grunts his answers, and now, the words pour out like water from a pitcher.*

The day passed slowly as the group wound their way down from the hills and into the valleys. The mule was steady but slow ,and there were times that Traynor lost patience with the animal and took out his whip. At those times, the mule loudly brayed his unhappiness with the treatment, but picked up his speed for the next few minutes. Before long, he was back to dragging his feet in the dirt. Evening finally brought them to a small valley tucked between two hills. A stream ran through the narrow cut out, and that is where Traynor stopped the wagon and jumped down. "Mara, you know what to do. Jebez, you unhitch Jasper. Find his oat bag and give him his supper. Picket him over there between the trees. I will be in the wagon." Traynor jumped into the back of the wagon and dug through the knapsack until he found The Book of Words. Conor watched him as he went about gathering some firewood. *I need to distract him before he discovers the pages are missing.*

"Traynor, I can see that you are busy, but I was hoping we could practice some things I have been thinking about?"

Traynor waved him off, "Not now, boy. Later." He continued turning the pages, careful to avoid damaging them. So thin and fragile were some of them that it was clear that those pages were older than others. As he turned, a frown appeared on his face and he began muttering to himself. He turned the pages more quickly now in a frantic effort to find what he was looking for. At last he closed the book and bound it with the iron straps. Sitting very still, he placed his hand on the worn leather cover and closed his eyes. Breathing deeply, he felt for the inside of the book, for any wound the book had suffered. He opened his eyes and the book once more, turning the pages more slowly until he found what he was looking for, a missing page. "Concobhar, here to me now!"

Conor looked up from the fire and shrugged at Mara whose look was one of terror. He ambled over to the wagon, "Are you ready to work on the things I was thinking about?"

"No," snarled Traynor. "I want to know about this missing page. There is a page gone from The Book of Words. What do you know about it?"

"Nothing. I have not held that book in my hands, not once. If there is something missing, it is not on me."

"Mara, you had this book in your possession. Where is the missing page?"

"I don't know. I don't know anything about missing pages. I cannot read half of what is in that book, so I wouldn't know any page to take, Traynor. I swear it. Liam must have done it. He's had that book in his bag with enough time to look it over any time he wanted to." Her voice pleaded.

Traynor looked up at the sky for a moment before answering her. "I am so very tired of you all. You refuse my simplest requests, you scheme behind my back, you do something with my most trusted servant, and now you steal from me. I am so very tired of you, Mara." He raised his hand and began to say words. Mara backed away from him, her face twisted in terror. Conor leaped to his feet and stood in front of her. He raised his hand as if to shield her, outraging Traynor still further.

"Let's talk about this, Traynor. I have ideas, and they might include Mara being in good health. Don't be hasty and act in anger. I don't know what is missing from your book, but perhaps Liam took it for some reason. Maybe he thinks to profit from it. At any rate, whatever you are missing, Mara has no use for I think. Her powers are not that strong, I am told."

"Who tells you that?" Traynor's hand fell and he stopped the flow of words.

"Jebez. Jebez told me she only does what benefits her and how would this page, any page benefit her? I think you are on the wrong track. I lay this at Liam's feet. He had control of the book since you took it from Mara. Let's be reasonable here, Traynor. There are few of us and sticking together might be a better plan than losing any more of our group." Conor's voice was soothing and steady. His hand held out in front of him was strong and sure.

Traynor stared at Conor and through gritted teeth said, "We will find the valley tomorrow, Conor and by the Light, you will do as I wish. You will raise my creatures and Mara will call up Ceobhran, and I will have my army or you will all pay the price."

Mara wiped the tears from her face, smearing dirt from her hands across her skin. Her shoulders shook and her hands trembled, but she knelt at the fire to stir up the coals and begin the evening meal.

Conor walked out of the camp, too tired to be around any of them. He felt the folded page in his pocket, the one Liam ripped from the Book of words to give him. Walking until he found what he was looking for, a tall tree, hollowed out about five foot from the ground, he took the page from his pocket and stuffed it as far back in the hole as he could reach. Raising his hand he repeated the old words three times to protect the page from harm and allow it to bond to him. He did not trust that Traynor would let him sleep through the night without searching for the page. Early in the morning before the others were up and around, he would slip away from camp and retrieve the paper before they began their travels.

The next morning's sunrise found the group on the road, winding through land barren of good grasses and trees. The hills had the appearance of burnt ground as if a fire had ravaged them and the valleys between. The burnt skeletons of trees, blackened and twisted into torturous shapes, were the only things that rose up out of the scorched earth. The smell of smoke lingered in the air making Conor's nose twitch. Traynor's face was set, and he drove the poor mule with no mercy, using the whip constantly. Jebez and Conor quickened their steps to keep up and Mara held tight to the side of the wagon to keep from being jostled out. Jebez's eyes slid from side to side, taking in the desolate landscape. Conor began whistling a tune, anything to replace the silence that dogged them. No birds' songs here, no insects' hums met their ears so he filled the air with his own tune.

The road was rockier now and the wagon wheels groaned as the mule pulled the wagon across them. There was the scent of death as well as smoke, and finally even Conor grew silent. They reached the floor of the valley and here Traynor pulled on the reins to halt the wagon. "This is my valley," he said. The small group looked with dismay at the land before them.

Chapter Twenty-Nine

A Meeting, a Plan

The group met in Aelf's dwelling he shared with Shaen and their three boys. Aelf, with a quiet word sent the boys outside, cautioning them that they could not leave the village. Tilly and Doiranne helped Shaen brew tea for them, and Cormac looked through the rock shelves for some of Shaen's cakes made of berries, seeds and nuts held together with rich bear fat. Shaen smiled at him when he brought the cakes over. "Sister, do you mind?" She shook her head, and taking the cakes from his hands, placed them on a tray carved from maple, smooth to the touch and brilliant with the colors of the wood.

As they sat to drink their tea and eat her cakes, Granny was thoughtful. *How do I do this? How do I keep them safe from Traynor and still have enough of us to rescue Conor?*

"I don't have any plan yet. I am hoping we can all come up with something that sounds like it has a feather's chance of success. I know this; I am going to need people with power to be with me. I don't know if I can defeat Traynor on my own. But I am not willing to risk people's lives who have no power to help me. I cannot ward everyone, and I don't want to take the chance of losing anyone.

"I am thinking that Tilly and Ronan should go with me. The rest of you stay here where the ward is set."

An immediate reaction of outrage and denial met Granny's words. Voices all raised at once in defense of their willingness and ability to help. Granny raised her hand to keep the onslaught at bay. "Please, one at a time. I beg you."

Cormac stood first, "You will not take Ronan without taking me. I forbid it!"

Ronan's peal of laughter surprised everyone. Such a serious moment, and here she was laughing out loud. "Almost husband, you surprise me. I would not have thought you would ever be so stupid as to try to forbid me anything. Would like to think of your words again?"

Cormac looked abashed. What was he thinking? "I am sorry dear wife to be. My words escaped me before my mind could settle on the right thing to say. Here is a more measured approach. Granny, please do not ask Ronan to go without taking me. I know I have no powers, but I am still good with weapons and a good guide. I could not breathe if you took her away from the village, from me toward such danger. I will not be able to breathe." Cormac sat down and gripped Ronan's hand. The slight pressure he felt from her hand reassured him that his impetuous outburst was forgiven.

Roisin stood next. "I don't think I have powers, Granny, but I have lived with Traynor since I was too young to remember anyone else. I know him. I know what the man is capable of doing, and I could advise you along the way. Please do not leave me behind. I beg you."

Shaen stood and Granny shook her head. Would no one be sensible and stay home and stay safe? "We went to the cave with you to recue our children. We faced Mara and Jebez with Ceobhran. Would you leave us out of helping Conor? Would you deny us that, Granny Matilda? We would not rest knowing you were out there and we were here, sitting on our hands doing nothing." She folded her arms across her chest and sat down abruptly. Aelf leaned over and kissed her softly on her cheek. "You spoke for both of us, dearest heart. Thank you."

Liam appeared in the doorway, brushing aside the deerskin that acted as a door. "I know I am not allowed in here, but I must ask you. There is a lifetime of wrongs for me to right, and the only way I can do that is to help Conor. I watched him defeat Traynor before, and I know he is different now, but I know how to help him. Remember, I gave him the page, but I know how to use it." He stood quietly, just inside the door, expecting to be rebuked. No one said a word.

There was silence across the dwelling as Granny looked from one to the other. At last her gaze fell on Doiranne, and as she expected, the woman stood and walked to stand in front of Granny. "I have never been a good person, Granny Matilda. I have been selfish and greedy, thinking only of my needs. I have killed my own husband. I know, I know, you say it was justified, but it still weighs me down some days so heavy it is hard to lift my head. I came to the cave to help Conor, and with your permission, I would like to continue that quest. There will be danger, I know this. Part of me would like to run home to my cottage and pull the quilt over my head, but I can't. Even if you tell me no, I will walk behind you all the way." She too folded her arms across her chest, but in a less defiant way than Shaen did.

Granny nodded to herself and then motioned to Tilly with a slight wiggle of her fingers. Tilly looked confused but rose to stand behind Doiranne. She leaned in to whisper in Doireanne's ear and then laid her hand lightly on her shoulder. Time passed slowly until at last, she took her hand away, looking confused. "I am not sure what I am feeling, Granny. But there is some sort of power there. I tried to read her past, her dreams, but she blocked me as if she knew what I was doing."

Granny raised her eyebrows in question at Doireanne. "Keeping secrets, are we?" she asked.

Doireanne looked puzzled. "I don't know what you mean, Granny. For certain, I felt something when Tilly put her hand on me, like a firebrand being held to my skin. I blocked it with my mind without even thinking."

"You have some sort of power, Doiranne, but I don't recognize it and we don't have time to work with it. You will come with us." She let her gaze go to the people in the chamber, even Liam who still stood in the doorway, looking nervous. "We will all go together. I am not sure it is the best thing to do, but I don't think you are leaving me any choice. When we find them, it will be necessary for Tilly, Ronan, Doiranne, and me to work together to fight him. I don't know what Conor's thinking is right now. Cormac, he came to talk with you about something before he went hiding off to the cave. What was it?"

Cormac looked thoughtful for a moment before he answered, "Granny, he's been searching for something, himself, I think more than anything. I know he wanted to know why Mara abandoned him at a young age. He wanted to know why she didn't love him. He also was afraid that his gifts came from her and he didn't know how to deal with that knowledge. It seems that was a waste of his time. It turns out it was Traynor all along who gave him his gifts, not Mara." Cormac shook his head.

"Don't be so sure of that. I am not convinced that gifts are passed on from father to son or mother to daughter. I don't know if I will ever know why some of us have gifts and some don't. I am finding out more people have gifts than I have guessed." She looked at Doireanne when she said that. "There is no clear reason for Doireanne to have a gift. So sorry, my dear, to be blunt."

"No offense taken. I am as surprised as you are, Granny, and I wish I had known. Maybe my garden would have grown a little better if I had applied a gift to its planting." Doireanne smiled as she said this, and Tilly gave her shoulder a quick squeeze.

"Liam, I have a job for you, if you are up to it. I know you cannot steal the book, but surely you might know if there is anything else in the book that would help us. Think on it, man, and let me know. Meanwhile, you know the way to this Light forsaken valley Traynor means to go to?" Liam nodded.

"Good. You and Cormac will guide us. He knows these mountains and will get us out the easiest way. We will be fighting snow and trapped until spring if we don't leave now. Pack up what you need but only what you can carry. We will need to hunt along the way. That's where you come in, Aelf. There is no better hunter among the Mountain Folk than you. No fancy dishes, just warm clothing and stout shoes for walking. Bring a walking stick; it helps to get down the mountain with a stick by your side. Ronan, you pack herbs and ointments for healing. Pack ointments specially for sore muscles. There will be plenty of those before we get off this mountain. Tilly, you divide up the pack from Ronan so she is not left carrying everything. Cormac, you are to deal with weapons that don't count on our gifts. Bows and arrows, spears, and hunting knives, I think. You will know best. Shaen, we will need tea to keep us warm and help us sleep at night. Bring what you need for that. Who will watch your children while you are gone?"

Shaen smiled at Granny, "The whole village. You know that, Granny. They won't be able to take a step without the whole village knowing about it."

Roisin stepped forward. "What do Doireanne and I carry, Granny?"

"Knowledge of this man who has passed himself off as your father and Doireanne apparently brings gifts I knew nothing about. Pack well. We leave at morning's first light."

Chapter Thirty

A Loss

Night time found the group halfway down the mountain, much to Granny's dismay. She fidgeted at every stop for water or rest along the way. Aelf grumbled that for such an old woman, she set a fast pace. Shaen smiled at her husband who had grown used to sitting by the warm fire working on his carvings, only venturing out to hunt when the meat supplies grew low. Her legs were strong from her endless search for berries, nuts, and the herbs she used to season their food. Ronan too, kept up the pace without complaint, Cormac at her side or behind her when the path narrowed. He would leave her to guide them when needed, but the deer and other animals had marked the trail well, and he was only needed to show a shortcut here and there that he knew from his years in the forest.

Doireanne helped Roisin and Shaen fix the evening meal. She had learned much in the way of cooking, the use of herbs and the way of cooking meat so it did not dry out. Roisin's stews were the best she had ever eaten and she dreamed of making Shaen's cakes for Tomas someday. In fact, she found herself thinking often of Tomas, wondering if he knew what had happened to her. She wondered if he missed her, until she realized she was being a foolish woman. Why would a man like Tomas look at a woman like her? And yet, had he not said he had feelings for her? She shook her head and put her mind back on the evening meal.

As they sat around their fire, eating and drinking steaming cups of tea, Tilly brought up something that she had been worrying about. "Granny, I know we have a few of us here, but I can't help but remember what a help Erik Tamen was when you rescued us from Mara and Jebez. I wish he was here with us now, Granny."

"So do I girl, so do I. It was his plan to divert Mara and Jebez that gave us the time we needed to release you from Ceobhran. Without his bravery, I'm not sure we would have been able to do what we did. I too, wish he was here with us. He is such a mountain of a man, like Aelf, he just inspires confidence in me. I hope I do not live to regret letting you all come with me, but the truth is, I find such comfort in your presence, I am not sure I had the strength to deny you."

"Granny, is there any way we could go the village and bring out Erik Tamen?" Doiranne's question was one that was on many minds.

"Yes, we could. We could drop the wards long enough to go in and get him but is the reward worth the risk? I want him along, but I have no way of knowing if Traynor is near the village. He could be there, he could be at the Mountain Folk. I think even as he travels, his powers are not diminished." She shook her head. "I do not risk it, Doiranne."

Doiranne nodded to herself. She understood but in the chance that Granny had agreed, she planned on going to the village with her to see Tomas. Her heart ached for the man, and she wondered if she would ever see him again.

"Liam, I would talk with you, please."

Liam had expected Matilda would call on him again. He had given it much thought, what The Book of Words could hold that might help them. He hadn't come up with much, more of the book than not was out of his reach, the words strange and incomprehensible. Still, he had one thought.

"Have you given my request any thought, Liam?"

"Yes, Matilda, I have. Please understand I cannot read much of the words on the pages, but over time, I have learned some words and I see them repeated. I can guess what they mean when I string them together." I had seen the pages for warding, creased and used as they were. I watched Traynor cast the warding, so I knew which page to give you. I have guessed at the page I gave Conor because I see the names that he calls the creatures on the page. And yet, they are not the calling up words, so I believed them to be for another purpose. There is a page

I have seen used in the past, a very long time ago. Traynor needed to join with someone, and he used words to make them more powerful together than apart. I know you and Ronan used the warding words together and it helped, but I think this is even stronger. I think it is not two people working for the same end, but two people joined to become one power. When Traynor used it many lifetimes ago, his power was beyond anything I had seen before or since. The man he joined with died, completely burned from within. Too much power, I'd say. I think there is a terrible risk to using this to join your powers. I tell you because I would not see you or anyone harmed."

Granny took a deep breath. She looked over at Ronan who sat with her head on Cormac's shoulder, talking quietly and smiling up at him. She looked at Tilly, her head bent to the arrows that she fletched by the firelight. She watched Doiranne with Roisin and Shaen, talking quietly about herbs and spices they used for cooking. Could she risk these people to save Conor? Was it just Conor she hoped to save or more than just him? Could she live with the fire and destruction that Traynor threatened to bring to innocent people? "I thank you for your honesty, Liam. I will think on it and let you know my decision in the morning."

Liam stood to leave, but Granny reached out a hand to hold him, "My friends call me Granny Matilda, Liam. Please do so if you like."

Liam froze for a moment, and when he turned to her, she could the tears the shone in his eyes. "I thank you, Granny Matilda. You honor me more than I deserve."

First light saw them huddled around the fire in a vain attempt to warm themselves. Shaen and Doiranne passed around cups of tea, the steam making small clouds above the cups in the frigid air. They ate cold meat and cheese to fortify them.

Granny spoke up over a mouthful of bread made from ground rye seeds, "Liam knows of a page that would help us join together to become one far more powerful person. He says it carries great risk, and I believe he is right. But I have thought of it overnight, and I believe we can avoid the risk if we are careful not to pull on our gifts too strongly. If I try to pull on my gifts more than I should, I know it can cause me harm. I can feel the destruction of myself just around the corner. However, if we join, we will not have to pull too much into us. There is a risk so I must ask you to consider it. The risk involves Ronan, Tilly, Doiranne, and me." Granny looked at each of them in turn and one by one, they nodded their agreement.

"The rest of you will need to stay away from us in the chance I am wrong, and things go badly for the four of us. Aelf, you and Shaen and Cormac need to help us in another way. I don't want Mara or Jebez sneaking up on us and causing us trouble. Aelf, will you and Cormac stand guard over us? Liam is going to try to get that page for me, and I don't want any more exposure for him. I fear that will be enough. Shaen, you can handle any weapon the men can handle. Will you stand guard as well? Roisin, you will watch Traynor from the hill without being seen. Keep a close eye on him and if he does something you think is a threat to us, warn us immediately. Enough eyes on everyone and we should be all right.

"Cormac, your role in this is vital since you've chosen to come. Once we reach the valley and Liam takes us to where they are camped, I will need you to scout for us. We will need a hill that is guarded but overlooks their camp. Our best position will need to be above them, looking down, I hope in a place that they cannot see us. Tall enough, you see?" Cormac looked down between his feet, drawing circles in the dirt with a stick. At Granny's words, he looked up at Granny and nodded his head.

Granny continued her plan, "Shaen, Aelf, and Cormac will set up in a circle around us, Roisin will make the part of the circle looking down on the camp. You will watch, but you will not want to be seen. We will stand on the hill and, if Liam can bring us the page, we will join, and see if we can't send Traynor to a place where even the Light cannot illuminate his days."

Each person in turn looked at Granny and nodded their agreement. They knew the risks, at least, they thought they did. Liam watched them all. *Foolish people, they have no idea what that man can do to them. They are like the village idiot in their ignorance.* He shrugged to himself.

Aelf put his arm around Shaen and pulled her close in the morning chill. "I want nothing more right now than to be on our sleeping platform, wrapped up in our furs with my arms around you, dearest heart. If we get out of this with our skin still on our poor ragged bodies, I do not plan on leaving our village again." Shaen leaned her head on his shoulder. "Speak about your own ragged body. Mine is holding up just fine, love of my life. But yes, when we are back home, I say we stay back home."

Doiranne collected the cups and cleaned up the food that was left over. Aelf and Cormac gathered their bows and tucked arrows into their belts for hunting. Everyone got up on weary feet and gathered their walking sticks. "This day should see us out of the mountains and down by our village. Keep a close eye out for anything odd or out of place." Granny set off with her usual brisk step, confident the others would follow.

The day passed slowly, each step harder than the one before. The group soon lapsed into an exhausted silence and Granny did nothing to change it. *Better not to waste energy on talking.*

By mid-day, Granny stopped and they filled their water skins and ate their meal of bread and cheese. Cormac and Aelf joined them each with a brace of fat doves for their evening meal. Shaen took the birds and set about cleaning them by the stream where the remains could be washed away. She laid them out on a large rock and digging around in her pack found the herbs she was looking for. She sprinkled the birds liberally and wrapped them in a cloth. Stowing them back into her pack she would roast them over the fire later that evening.

The hills were easier to walk through, the wind not so cold against them. The grasses were golden and cut short, the trees barren of leaves, but they enjoyed the feel of the warm sun on their backs as they headed east toward the valley. Liam walked with Granny to show them the way, Cormac behind them to point out shortcuts only he knew.

Evening found them at the base of the hills, the village lights visible below them. Both Tilly and Doiranne sat watching the lights blinking on and thought about their homes. Doiranne wished there was a way to send a message to Tomas, anything to let him know she was safe so far and he was in her thoughts. Tilly thought of her da, Quinn's strength that she must draw on now.

Aelf built up the evening fire and gathered sticks to roast the doves. Using his belt knife, he whittled sharp points on several of them and found sticks with good forks to hold them. Carefully sliding the sharp points through the birds, he rested the ends in the forks with enough to act as a turning handle. Shaen watched everything with a critical eye. Those doves would make a good evening meal if Aelf did his job.

"Two more days travel by Liam's reckoning," Granny said through a mouthful of tender meat. "Shaen, Aelf, Cormac, thank you for providing this meal for us. The meat is welcome to give us strength and as always, Shaen, you have a way of making everything taste delicious." The group voiced their opinions and Shaen blushed at their praise.

"Granny Matilda, I may speak?" Liam's familiar address of Granny caused heads to swivel in his direction. Their eyes went immediately to Granny, expecting the rebuke she would heap on his head, but none came his way.

"Of course, speak freely."

"I wonder if I shouldn't walk on ahead of you to reach the valley. I think that would give me time to find The Book of Words and locate the page I believe will help you."

"Yes, I'd thought of that, Liam. But I also thought you might be too valuable to lose. To lose to Traynor that is."

"Me, valuable? No, Granny Matilda, I have done nothing in my life to be valuable to anyone except Traynor, perhaps. As his errand boy, his bloodhound, his whipping boy when he needed one." Liam shook his head and looked off in the distance when he said this.

"Be that as it may, you are valuable to us, Liam, whether you believe it or not. But yes, I see the wisdom of you having the page in your hands when we get there. I'm just not sure if we know how to get there without you."

"I will sit with Cormac and draw out a map from my memory. I've been to this valley a number of times, and I know the way as surely as I would know my way home if I had one."

"Agreed, then. You give the map to Cormac and indicate where we should go when we arrive. You go and the Light be with you, Liam. You will leave with the morning sun?"

Liam nodded as he walked to sit with Cormac. Together they bent their heads over the ground where Liam drew his map in the soft dirt.

Ronan came to sit with Granny. "I'd feel a sight better if we had parchment to draw a map on, Granny. I know Cormac is a good tracker, but still, a piece of parchment to hold in his hands while we travel would be a comfort, even to me."

Granny smiled at her friend," Have faith in your near husband, Ronan. He has an eye for this sort of thing. We will get there, the Light help us when we do." She rose up from her seat, "First light we travel, my friends."

Shaen was up before anyone, even the morning sun did not shine on her as she built up the fire and heated the water for tea. She took all the pieces of leftover dove meat and warmed them on her flat rocks, turning them with her stick and sliding them onto plates. Her rye bread she heated as well and took the pieces of meat and laid them across the warm bread. Lastly she laid thin slices of cheese on top and warmed them over the fire. These she handed out with steaming cups of tea. Roisin rubbed the sleep from her eyes and smiled up at Shaen when she took the morning meal from the woman. "I will come and live with you and you will teach me how to cook, Shaen."

"I hear enough to know you are a good cook in your own right. I saw the packets of dried herbs you keep with you in your pack. Anyone you carries her own cooking herbs must know a thing or two, my girl. But yes, you come and live with us when we are finished here. I have a son, you know, and he will be needing a wife soon." She winked at Roisin whose face turned every shade of red there was. Tilly watched and smiled to herself. *Not much chance of Shaen's son making hay with Roisin, not if Conor is anywhere around.*

Granny called Tilly over to where she sat near Liam, talking quietly with him. "I want you to try something for me, Tilly. I read about this years ago in my granny's ancient book, but I have never known anyone who could do it. You are able to connect with people with your gift, see their past and know them, sometimes more than they know themselves. You haven't had any time to work on this, but our circumstances are such that I am going to ask you to try to do this." Tilly looked questioningly at Granny, "If I am able, you know I will. What is it, Granny?"

"I want you to try to link with Liam so that when he is gone, you will know where he is and what he is doing. I ask this, not because I don't trust him, but because I fear for him with Traynor and Mara. I don't trust Mara any further than I can see her walk away, and with these poor old eyes, that isn't very far. I know you have your own methods of reaching your gift, so you tell me what we might need to do to help you." "Granny, I have no idea how to link with someone. I know if I am touching my gift and I touch a person, I can read his past, but that is not the same as linking with someone." "I know, but will you try? Touch your gift and then imagine an unbroken chain between the two of you. A chain only you can see and feel, but a chain that is every bit as strong as any iron. Try that and see what happens."

Tilly sat obediently next to Liam. She reached out to touch his arm and shuddered as she did so. But she closed her eyes and reached for her gift. She thought of a chain, strong and unbreakable, and she held it in her hands and looked it over carefully. The chain she clipped to a bracelet and the bracelet she placed on Liam's wrist. The other end she hooked to a second bracelet and placed it around her wrist, shuddering again as she did. She kept her eyes closed and felt with her mind the links of the chain, the bracelets. In her mind, she pulled on the chain and tested the bracelets. Unbroken. The bracelets were one smooth piece of metal with only an eye through which the chain traveled. There was no latch, no hook that anyone could see to fasten the bracelet. Once it was on, there was no way to remove it, save with her gift. She opened her eyes and nodded toward Granny. "It is done. It is in place, and we are linked."

"Good." She replied. "Liam, through this, Tilly will know what you are doing. Most often, she will feel you, know where you are. But if she needs to, she can pull on her gifts to see what is happening to you. Do you understand?"

"I do. I will leave now. By traveling alone, I will be much faster than you. It is my hope to find Traynor's camp before you reach the valley." He rose from his seat and without a backward glance, lengthened his stride out of the camp and down the road.

As the day wore on, and their travels took them further from the mountains and their village, a deepening gloom seem to settle on the group. There was little chatter among them. Once again, Cormac and Aelf left to hunt fresh meat for evening meal.

As she walked, Tilly felt overwhelmed by the sense of Liam through their link. She felt his anger and his frustration. She felt something else as well, a deep shame that she did not understand. Over midday meal, she asked Granny about it.

Granny chewed her bread and cheese carefully before answering. "I'm not surprised, Tilly. Liam has lived a life that we cannot imagine, indebted as he was to Traynor. What did he say he was; a bloodhound for the man and a whipping boy if need be? Liam is recognizing his life and in his own way, faltering and hesitant as it might be, is trying to make amends. I'm sorry to ask you to link to him. He is not the most pleasant person, but please understand that he is trying to change, trying to be a better person, I think. Sadly, I am convinced that the road he is on will not end well for him, but I think he knows that too. Strangely, I believe he welcomes it."

Tilly walked alone that afternoon, feeling Liam's pain as she walked. Toward evening, a strange thing happened. She felt something other than pain and shame. For an instant, she felt warm sun and the scent of good earth, rich and full of life. She paused as she walked to try harder to feel what Liam was feeling. She smiled to herself. *He is enjoying his freedom, the sun on his face, and the good smells around him. He is actually feeling happy.* She marveled at the thought, but she had no real way to understand what was happening to the man.

That night around the fire, they once again enjoyed the fruits of Cormac and Aelf's hunting, this time in roasted rabbit, seasoned with herbs and covered with the last of the wild onions Shaen found near the stream by their camp. Roisin shared her herbs and together the two women made a meal that satisfied the group. The sun had no sooner set than everyone was wrapping themselves in their cloaks and finding a patch of ground with no rocks to sleep.

"Tomorrow should bring us to the valley, according to the map Liam drew for us." Cormac said as he lay down next to Ronan. No one replied, their bodies too tired for words, their thoughts too worried to put into words.

Traynor stretched his feet to the fire and yawned, an enormous, satisfied sound. "We will travel into the ground at first light, Concobhar. We go to bring Nathair na h-uamba, my beloved serpent from his hiding place. Now that I know you can use your power even as you travel, it will be the safest way to find him. It is far too dangerous to try to climb down into the earth. Once you have raised him, you will bring us all back out. Then we will make plans for the other two."

Conor made no reply. Moving his fingers only, he felt for the page in his pocket. It mattered not that it was still there. He had held it and read it so many times the words were now part of him. He might raise the serpent, but he also knew how to rid the world of it. *Knowing that I can do it is the only way I can live with this until I find a way to rid myself of Traynor.*

The morning was dark with heavy, black clouds roiled overhead, thunder rumbled in the distance, the threat of rain in the air. Conor could smell the lightening on the wind without seeing it. *It fits my mood.* Conor drank his tea but ignored the morning meal set in front of him by Mara. She tried to catch his eye, but he ignored her efforts.

Traynor was in good spirits, looking forward to the day's work. "We will need the ball of light you make while we are in the earth. I will call to Nathair and when he comes you will raise him."

"If he comes when he is called, isn't he raised?"

"Not in his true form. The words you spoke over him reduced him to a mere snake who dwells beneath the earth, feeding on whatever comes his way. He is meant for so much more than that as you will soon see."

"I have seen the tapestry, Traynor. I have an idea of what kind of monster he is."

Traynor shrugged. "To you he is a monster, to me he is my beloved pet. And I will have him today, Concobhar, or there will be a price too heavy for you to pay."

Traynor motioned for Conor to follow him, and they walked some distance down the barren valley floor, past trees bent in tortured shapes, blackened rocks strewn in their path making it difficult to walk. They came to a large hole in the ground, half filled with a landslide of rocks and debris making it impossible to climb down into it. Traynor gripped Conor's arm and he found himself under the earth inside a huge chamber. He stumbled into boulders that blocked most of the tunnels leading deeper into the belly of the earth and there was a smell of death, fetid and decayed all around them. Conor held out his hand and instantly the ball of light appeared showing him a scene of devastation before him. Bones scattered about the chamber were a testament to the beasts that once inhabited this space, their leavings piled everywhere. Chains, rusted and long neglected, hung from rings driven deep into the rock walls. It was not hard to imagine the torment that took place here so deep underground that the wails of the tortured would never be heard, not by human ears at least.

Traynor emitted a high-pitched noise that shook Conor to his bones. His instinct to cover his ears was so strong that the globe of light in his hand wavered. "Hold it still," snarled Traynor.

Conor swallowed but steadied his hand. Somewhere in the distance he heard an answering cry and Traynor fell silent. A sound of something being dragged across the ground met Conor's ears and he looked in the direction from which it came. A snake, brown with a black and tan design, slithered across the boulders, making a rasping sound as if its belly was rough. It raised its head and tasted the air with its tongue, darting in and out, flickering this way and that way until it seemed satisfied. The snake continued its forward motion until it came to rest at Traynor's feet.

Traynor smiled down at the snake before he turned to Conor. "Say the words here. On this page. Only you can bring him back to me. Say the words, now!" He thrust a page into Conor's hand and bent to pick up the snake. It coiled into his hands, wrapping around his arm, flicking its tongue in and out.

Conor unfolded the page and looked at the words. They swam before his eyes, and for a moment, he could not focus on them. As if from a great distance, he heard Traynor's voice, loud and demanding. He looked from the page to Traynor, his face eager and greedy, like a child reaching for a sweet. More than anything, he wanted to crumple the paper in his fist and throw it to the ground, but what of the people he loved? Did he dare risk their lives, not knowing if they were safe? Not knowing how they were going to live. Or did he raise this creature and watch the devastation Traynor meant to wreak on the world? Conor felt as if he stood apart from the person holding the page, felt as if he watched him make the decision. He glanced down at the page and willed his eyes to see the words clearly. In a loud voice, he spoke the words written on the page.

"Again!"

Conor repeated the words three times. No sooner were the words out of his mouth and in the air than the snake began to change. The colors along its back became bright and vibrant, its eyes now flecked with gold darted around the chamber, its fangs glittered in the light from the globe he still held in his hand.

The group entered the valley in the early morning hours. They stood for a moment looking at the wasted land spread out before them; trees blackened and bent, the earth torn up, the great rocks strewn across the landscape. An ominous feeling hung over the valley, as if even it warned them to stay out. Cormac quickly found a small hill overlooking the land he thought would give them an advantage. From its small height, they could see Traynor's camp, Mara and Jebez sitting by the fire, the wagon with Jasper the mule picketed nearby. Not a word was spoken as they set about finding spaces to clear the rocks. "No fire tonight." Aelf cautioned. "No talking unless absolutely necessary." Granny's voice was the smallest of whispers that somehow still carried to their ears.

Tilly sat quietly, nibbling on her hard bread, feeling for Liam. She knew he was in the camp below, she could feel his fear. A cold sweat covered her face, and she wiped it away with the hem of her skirt. Her heart beat faster, the sound in her ears harsh. Abruptly, she stood up and walked to the far side of their small hill, quietly slipping down the back side and around. In this way, she came to the back of Traynor's camp where she stood soundlessly, straining to hear anything that might be a threat to Liam. Hearing nothing, she approached the wagon where she found Liam on his knees, something before him on the wagon bed. He looked up at her approach. "What are doing here? This is too dangerous. Tilly, go back, please."

"I felt you, Liam. I felt your fear. What can I do?"

Liam sat down, his knees drawn up near his face, his arms around them, hugging them close to him. "Nothing, Tilly, nothing. You have already done more for me than you will ever know. When you linked with me, I knew you did it to keep track of me. Granny told me you would be able to know what I was doing. But what she didn't tell me is that I would feel you, Tilly, and I have felt such happiness from you in the last day traveling here. You are a strong young woman and all of what you are seeped into me. I have never felt such happiness in my whole life. In any of my lives." Tears ran down Liam's face and for a moment he buried his face in his knees. Finally, he wiped his face and turned away from Tilly. She saw then, The Book of Words before him. He tore the page out and handed it to her. "I cannot take this to Granny Matilda. You do it for me, Tilly. Go now! I beg you!"

Traynor grabbed Conor's arm, and they were once again under the dark clouds, where Traynor dropped the snake to the ground. It coiled at his feet, its forked tongue flickering, tasting air that was no longer fetid and full of death. Before their eyes, the snake began to grow, its sinuous body curving one way and then another as it stretched into its new length. Traynor's eyes were half closed as he watched his creature regain its form, his face relaxed in a small smile of ecstasy. The serpent reached its full size as Conor watched in horror, the gold-flecked eyes watching him, the heavy coils wrapped around each other, the tongue constantly flicking in and out. The serpent was never still, always coiling, always searching the air with its tongue. Its head turned toward the wagon, its body uncoiling, the movement suddenly slow and inexorable. Conor caught the flash of something out of the corner of his eye and he darted toward the wagon, ahead of Traynor and the serpent. There he saw the flash of a skirt, the swish of a long blond braid and he stopped, his heart in his throat. Tilly whirled for just a moment and looked at Conor. He held out his hand to her, his eyes lit up, but she whipped her head violently back and forth and the look she gave him was one of fury. She turned and was gone in a flash around the end of the wagon and out of the camp before he could call her name.

The serpent followed Conor and coiled once more, piling its heavy body on itself, raising its head and half its enormous body toward the wagon where Liam stood frozen, holding The Book of Words clasped to his chest. His eyes were sad as they met Conor's eyes, and he shook his head softly back and forth as if to tell Conor there was no hope.

Traynor rounded the wagon, shocked to see Liam standing with the book held tightly against his chest. "So, you've come back to me but only to steal from me? After everything I have done for you, you desert me and then return to steal from me?" Traynor's voice was tight with anger and his face grew colder with each word. "Get down from that wagon, Liam. Hand me that book."

Liam obeyed without a word, handing the book to Traynor. His face held a look of resignation, the same look he wore for the many years he served Traynor. He refused to look down, refused to look at Conor, but stared straight into Traynor's eyes. "You can have the book for all the good it will do you, Traynor. You can have me for all the good it will do you."

"I will have you, Liam. You are mine until I no longer need you."

"No, Traynor, I am no longer yours. I have tasted freedom for the first time in so many long years, and I have felt happiness for the first time in my life. I will not give those things up, not for you, not for my own life. You can try to keep me, but I will steal from you, I will work against you at every opportunity, I will never be your servant again. You will never be able to trust me." Liam's words were quiet but firm. His eyes held a sadness in them, but with each word his face almost glowed and the half smile that touched his lips was peaceful. Liam stood still, quietly, his arms at his side, no measure of defense about his posture. His mind felt for Tilly through the link, the chain still strong, the bracelet around his wrist felt cool against his skin. *Let me go, Tilly! Let me go before it's too late.*

Traynor lifted his hand and motioned to Naithar, still at his feet. The serpent uncoiled and moved his enormous body toward Liam, its tongue tasting for the man, its gold flecked eyes narrowed. Liam looked at the serpent in horror, but did not move, not a flicker even of a finger. His eyes sought Conor, and he held his stare while the serpent pulled him to the ground. The serpent's mouth yawned widely, its fangs searching for the man's flesh. Finding what he sought, the serpent sank deeply into Liam's body. Liam gave out a great cry and his body shuddered, but he did not fight as the serpent dragged him to the ground. There it wrapped its coils around the man in an embrace of death.

For an instant, Tilly felt a pressure around her chest, one like she had never felt before, her heart and lungs squeezed until no air or blood could pass into them, and in that same moment she heard Liam's voice. She closed her eyes and reached for the chain, ripping it from the bracelet. The bracelet she tore open and let it drop from around her wrist. She sank to the ground, holding her chest, and drawing in great mouthfuls of air, filling her lungs, feeling her heart quiet. She sat for a moment, her head bowed in grief for the man she had grown close to through their link. Her hands were on the ground beside her, and she beat the ground with them, feeling the rough earth. Finally, she wiped the tears from her face and pushed herself up, touching the page in her pocket as she did.

Traynor allowed Naithar to do his work and when it was done, he motioned for the serpent to take the body of Liam away, the man's eyes open and staring without sight at the dark sky. "Naithar has not eaten. He will need his strength."

Chapter Thirty-One

A Confrontation

Conor stood with fists clenched at his side, his face contorted with rage. "You are a monster, Traynor. You and that creature are both monsters. I will not be your son. I will not help you. I will not be a part of your madness."

"Oh, but you will, my boy. Your people are just over the hill. I can feel them from here. I will have them if you do not fulfill your obligation to me. And don't forget, there is still Mara to consider. Our work together has just begun." Traynor strode off with The Book of Words held in the crook of his arm. Conor stood still, undecided, touching the page in his pocket.

Traynor called to Mara, "You did this didn't you, Mara? You turned Liam against me. It had to be you who hid him from me. Did you think to be everything to me, you and that worthless Jebez? Did you think you could take his place, you stupid woman?" He raised his hand and began to point it in her direction.

"No, Traynor, I swear. I said nothing to Liam, ever. It was Conor. I swear it. It was Conor. He wanted The Book of Words, but Liam was afraid to give it to him. I think he gave him pages from it. It was Conor who hid him from you."

Tilly ran until she had no more breath to run, reaching their small camp on the backside of the hill. "Granny, get up! We need to act now. Liam is gone, he is dead. I have the page and we need to act now." The words spilled out in a torrent, the folded page clenched in her hand.

Granny took it all in in one short breath. She called out to Doireanne and Ronan. Together they gathered their skirts in one hand and dashed to the top of the small hill overlooking the camp below. What they saw down below froze them. Conor still standing by the wagon as if he were asleep, Traynor with The Book of Words in his hand, and Naithar, the giant serpent swallowing Liam, one bite at a time.

Doiranne screamed when she saw the serpent., and Granny whirled on her in a fury. "Hush, Doiranne! Do not alert him to us. For the Light's sake. Aelf, it's time. Get into position."

She grabbed Doiranne's hand in hers and motioned her toward Tilly. Tilly took her other hand and grabbed for Ronan. Granny held her free hand above them with the page held tightly.

Traynor heard Doiranne's scream and raised his head toward the sound at the top of the hill. He dropped The Book of Words and raised both hands in defense. Shielding himself with a ward, he called out to Mara to join him.

The four women stood tall, their hands held so tightly that it felt as if their bones would be crushed. They drew on their gifts, pulling into them all the light they could reach. Together they said the strange words, words that made no sense to them. More and more they pulled, saying the words, Ronan's free hand directed at Traynor and Mara. Her hand wavered and her knees buckled slightly. She shook her head and gripped Tilly's hand tighter. Her breath came in ragged gulps and her head felt light and dizzy. Without saying another word, her knees buckled completely and she fell to the ground. The link between them was broken for only an instant, but it was enough for their world to change forever.

From his place on the hill, Cormac saw Ronan crumple to the ground, and he leaped up from his hiding spot. Aelf, in desperation grabbed at him, "No Cormac. No! You must not!"

But the man would not be denied. He raced across the short space to Ronan's side. Traynor saw the woman fall and instantly dropped his ward. He raised his hand toward Cormac as the man ran, bent over to make himself as small as he could. The power Traynor wielded hit Cormac full on and he fell, his hand stretched out to touch Ronan, a touch that would never be fulfilled.

Once more, Tilly grabbed at Doireanne's hand and the women began to say the words through gritted teeth.

Conor reached out for the water, the water that carried him across the rocks and into the sun, but it was not peaceful water he called on now. This water tore through its banks, raged over the rocks, throwing waves high into the air, mud and debris carried along in the torrent. This water poured in a rush of mud and limbs torn from trees and bushes, rocks and Conor, carrying him along in its path. He felt more than saw Jebez grab a hammer from the ground and rush toward him. He whirled and raised one hand, drawing fire from the very depths of his being. Jebez fell in a heap of ashes, the hammer dropping harmlessly to the ground.

Traynor turned toward Conor, pulling his ward tightly around himself and Mara. "You cannot do this, Conor. You cannot do this! Naithar, come!"

The serpent moved slowly now, his body engorged from his meal. Conor did not need the page, but he pulled it out of his pocket to show Traynor that he held it. He threw back his head and screamed the words, over and over that would send the creature back to its own hell, deep within the earth. Traynor cried out in frustration as he watched Nathair grow smaller with each word Conor uttered. The serpent became the snake once more, but Conor did not stop with that. He held out his hand again and pulled on the fire that was within him. The snake became a flame and was gone, leaving a pile of smoking ash behind.

The women on the hill grew silent as they watched the scene unfold, shocked at the power that Conor drew. Granny's hand with the page fell to her side and she released Doireanne's hand.

Roisin darted down the hill toward Conor, her hand raised, her long red hair flying behind her. She reached Conor just as he turned toward Traynor and Mara. Clutching his arm, she shook him screaming, "No, Conor. Stop. You will kill yourself. Stop!"

Conor turned on her with a snarl, "Leave off, Roisin. Leave me!" He shook off her hand violently.

Roisin grabbed him again, "You must stop, Conor. Please, stop" She shook him with all of her strength, trying desperately to reach the man that was still inside Conor, the man she knew could reason.

Traynor watched Roisin and Conor, gripped in the struggle to save him from his own power. He dropped the ward around him and seized Mara's hand.

Conor pushed Roisin to the ground and turned to face Traynor and Mara. He watched as the ward disappeared and Traynor grabbed at Mara. Gone in an instant, gone from his sight. He stared down at Roisin, on her hands and knees now, struggling to get up. He raised his hand toward her, but from a distance heard someone call his name. Confused he shook his head, and the waters that carried him in their mad rush receded. He looked down at Roisin and then up at the hill where Granny stood, still calling his name, her arms outstretched pleading with him. The strength drained from his body and he dropped to the ground next to Roisin. On her knees, she wrapped her arms around him and held him tightly. When he could move again, she pulled him to his feet, and taking his hand, drew him toward the hill, as a child who needed to be led.

Ronan knelt in the dirt next to Cormac, breathing into his mouth, massaging his chest, over and over again, calling his name. "Please, my heart. Cormac do not leave me. Please stay with me, please stay with me, Cormac" She breathed again and again into his mouth, her hands working across his chest. Granny pulled softly on her shoulder, calling to her. "Ronan, please. Stop. Let him be. He is gone from us. Let him be."

Ronan collapsed across Cormac's body, her sobs shaking her as if she had a fever, her hands gripping his body. Conor stood over them both, looking stunned. He dropped to the ground next to Cormac and reached out to touch him. Roisin stood over him, her hand still on his back. Conor breathed on Cormac, again and again, until finally Roisin begged him to stop. "You don't understand. I can do this. I've done it before. I can do this." He turned to Cormac's body again, but his breath would not work its magic on Cormac as it had on the butterfly so long ago, it seemed.

Aelf gently raised Ronan from the ground and held her to his chest for a long moment, his hands soothing her back in long strokes, until at last, the big man bent down to the ground and gathered up the body of his brother. He held him close to his chest for an age, tears streaming down his face, and then he carried

Cormac to their camp. Shaen spread their cloaks on the ground, and Aelf gently laid Cormac on them. He brushed the hair from across his brother's forehead and kissed him on his cheeks, his forehead, and lastly his mouth. Shaen bent and kissed him in the same way. "We will carry him back to the Mountain Folk village and bury him there. You all will come with us. Ronan, you will lead us, and I will bring my brother."

That is what they did, the small sad group of them. Aelf cut stout branches and formed a litter with the ends long enough for him to haul on. Shaen wrapped their cloaks around the shafts to make a bed and they placed Cormac on it. The group was silent, there were no words to say. Conor looked toward Granny but she shook her head. Tilly would not meet his eyes.

The journey back from the valley seemed shorter than before, each person wrapped in a layer of grief so deep and heavy they moved as sleepwalkers, unaware of their surroundings, unaware of each other. They passed their village on the way through the hills, and Granny and Tilly stopped above it to release the ward that guarded their friends and family. Tilly looked down at the village, so peaceful, so safe, and she vowed to herself she would never leave it again. Never leave the comfort of family and friends.

When they reached the Mountain Folk village they did the same so they once more could enter. The Mountain Folk gathered around the somber group, silently watching as Aelf dragged the litter with Cormac's body up the path to the caves above. Ronan indicated Cormac's dwelling and Aelf acquiesced, carrying his brother's body into the darkness. There he laid him on his sleeping platform and Ronan gestured for him to leave. She asked Granny to heat water and bring her soft cloths, she would wash his body and dress him in the finest doeskin pants and shirt she had made for their wedding day. Granny did as she asked, adding a small bottle of aromatic oil that she carried in her pack. Ronan accepted the gift gratefully, knowing she had no way to anoint the body of the man she loved.

The next day was bitterly cold as heavy black clouds brought the first snowfall of winter to the mountain. The Mountain Folk men, under Aelf's watchful eye, had broken the earth with their tools and carved out a place to lay his body. A great mound of rich, dark earth stood nearby, covered with evergreen branches to be placed on his body. Ronan directed the men to put his body on the litter that had brought him home, and this they did, taking turns carrying it to the site.

The frigid wind whipped the Folks' cloaks in a wild frenzy, and they clutched them close to their bodies to stay warm. Ronan wore no cloak, her hair now undone from the braid that fell down her back, blowing around her. She wore a beautiful dress of the softest deer hide, tanned to a golden brown. Beads woven among the fringe along the bottom danced in the wind. She watched silently as the men tenderly laid Cormac's body next to his grave. When they turned to her, she nodded her head toward the earth, and they placed his body in the ground. Slowly, she walked to the mound of earth and gestured to Aelf to pick up an evergreen branch. Bending to pick up more, she held them out to Aelf's sons, to Conor, and to Shaen. In this way, Cormac's family buried him beneath a blanket of fragrant branches, the cold air bringing the scent of pine to the Mountain Folk. "We have no flowers for my beloved," Ronan's voice rang clear and loud to reach everyone gathered. "We honor him with evergreens so that he may ever be in our hearts and minds."

The Mountain Folk did not say words over their dead like the people in the valley. Instead, one by one, they called out a word or two that came to their minds as they dwelled on Cormac's life. Keven was the first to call out, "Stories." Aelf, through his tears, called out, "My brother." The area around the grave rang with words, tears, and even laughter as the Mountain Folk remembered the man who kept their history, their stories safe. Conor shook his head, "My friend." At last Ronan spoke her words, "My best beloved." With that she bent to pick up a handful of dirt and threw it on the boughs that concealed Cormac's body.

CHAPTER THIRTY-TWO

AN ENDING, A NEW BEGINNING

The morning was cold with heavy snow clouds drifting across the mountains when Conor sought Tilly and asked her to walk with him. Reluctantly, she agreed. "You are angry with me. Why?"

"Oh Conor, I am not angry with you, I am just so utterly tired of all of this. This madness, these gifts that seem like a curse to me. I am not sure I even know who you are anymore." She shook her head and brushed tears from her eyes.

"Let's sit. Please Tilly. You are my best friend, and I need you right now. Tell me what you need, Conor. Just tell me what drew you to that Light forsaken cave."

Conor looked off in the distance. "I'm not sure I can say it all, Tilly. I felt something calling to me, something drawing me. I thought maybe it was a longing to know where I came from, who my mother and father were. But I think maybe it was more than that. Truly I did not know what was going to happen. I did not know what I was, and now that I do, I hate it. I felt as if I had a hole in me, and I thought I would fill it by going to the cave. I am sorry, Tilly. I can never right the wrongs that I have committed."

"Let's be clear about this, Conor. You did not kill Cormac, Traynor did that. He came to our village looking for you, you did not go looking for him. I have talked to Granny, and she helped me understand that you may have been drawn to that cave, to those people, without you even knowing it. I saw your past life, Conor. One of them, at any rate. You were a different man in that life. I don't know. Maybe there are powers here at work that we cannot understand. I know you are back, and I am glad."

"I am sorry about Liam as well." Conor looked off in the distance and he thought about the man he hoped to save.

"Liam did what he did to save his soul. I believe that, Conor. I linked with him. Did you know that?"

Conor shook his head.

"I did. The intention was to keep track of him, make sure he would bring Granny the page she would use to join us all. But something interesting happened along the way. He could read me as much as I could read him, and he said it changed him. For the first time in a very long time, he was happy."

Conor nodded. "He told Traynor the same thing just before Traynor set his serpent on him. He told him he had tasted freedom and happiness and he wouldn't let it go. The serpent that I brought back." Conor put his head in his hands.

"I know. You are taking a lot of the blame on yourself, but I don't think that is where it needs to rest, Conor. Traynor was driving this wagon from the beginning and we were just trying to catch up to him. There is so much grief now in the Mountain Folk village. I saw the boys, Keven, Brian, and Neall. They don't know how to let go of their uncle. Aelf grieves, and Ronan is past grief into something I have never seen before. I am glad she is a healer because it gives her something to take her mind off Cormac's death."

"I think what needs to happen now is we need to allow time to do its work on us. Hold each other and give time a chance to heal us." Tilly looked sad as she spoke.

"Perhaps. I am not sure of that, Tilly. But I am so sorry, and I believe you have forgiven me."

"Yes, Conor, I have forgiven you. Everyone has forgiven you. Time for you to forgive yourself. And Conor, take some time to talk with Roisin. I think you might be glad you do."

They gathered that evening around the fire in Aelf's dwelling, watching the snow fall outside his entrance. Shaen cooked for everyone and they passed around the cups of steaming tea and platters of wild dove, cooked golden brown. Ronan looked down at her food without really seeing it. Doireanne leaned close and whispered something to her. Ronan smiled at the woman before picking up some of the food and ate it without tasting it.

Granny sat with the three boys and listened to tales of their uncle and his tricks. Keven told of the time Cormac had taken him to hunt his first bear. He wiped tears from his face as he told the story. She put her arm around his shoulder and he leaned his head on her.

"Where do we go from here?" Granny's voice shocked them out of their silence. They all began to speak at once, denying that there was anywhere to go at all. "Nonsense." Granny's voice rose above them. "I am a very old woman with not too many more years in front of me, far more behind me. I can tell you I do not plan on spending them staring into a fire and doing little or nothing. We are grieving, but one of the bits of wisdom my granny gave me was that action and a plan were often the best medicine for grief. So I ask again, where do we go from here?"

Keven was the first to speak. "I want to tell the stories that my uncle told us. I am so full of our history and the reasons for what we do. I want to learn to take his place and pass his knowledge on to the children. I know I am too young, but who else has sat at his feet since I could crawl there to listen to him?" Keven looked pleadingly at Aelf. "I cannot take your brother's place, but if you will allow me, I would like to learn to be what he was for the Mountain Folk, for all of us."

Aelf looked up startled from his silence. He turned to Shaen, who quietly reached out her hand and slowly nodded. He turned to his son, "Keven, there is no one more fitting to take his place than you. I have watched you choose to sit with Cormac when the other children were running and playing. You, of all of us, know what he knew. You honor his memory and our family with your decision. I will proudly take it to the council."

Doiranne raised her hand slightly. "I once thought if I could ever find my way out of the Village at the Edge of the Valley, I would never look back. Sean frustrated me so with his lack of ambition, and I shunned the village women and the way they took joy in the smallest things. My selfishness and greed kept me from being a part of my own village. How stupid I was! Now, I want nothing more than to go back to our village. I want to see if Tomas remembers and still holds an interest in me. Perhaps, try to help my neighbors and be part of the life there." She fell silent.

Tilly spoke next. "For as long as I could remember, I hoped for a gift like my granny, something that made me special. It is not a gift that makes me special, it is being myself, caring for you all. When I had given up hope, that is when I found my gift. I would like to work with you, Granny; I want to discover how to use it to help people. I would like to make up to my mother and hug my father so tightly I squeeze the air out of him."

Aelf looked down at Shaen. "Shall we tell them, love of my life?" Shaen nodded although she looked at Ronan with a worried look. "Boys, your ma and I have news for you. We have decided that three is not enough and we will add a fourth child to this dwelling when the gardens are in full bloom."

Ronan threw her head up at that news, shock written across her face. She saw the look of joy on Aelf's face and the calm look on Shaen's and she took a moment before replying. Drawing in a deep breath, she smiled at them. "Cormac would be pleased. I would be pleased to be your child's aunt. All of your children. You will allow this?"

"You are my sister in all ways, Ronan," growled Aelf.

"And you, Ronan. What will you do with your future?" Granny's voice was soft.

"I will heal, Granny. I will learn. I will grow. I will never stand still, unless I choose to stand and listen to the wind for that is where I will hear Cormac's voice." Granny smiled. "I will teach you. You will be the best healer, far better than I."

Everyone was quiet, looking now from Conor to Roisin. Conor looked up from the fire. "I will go hunting. I have to. Tilly has shown me enough of my past to know I cannot allow it to be repeated over and over again. I will hunt Traynor and Mara and put an end to this once and for all. You all know I cannot go back to the village and pretend this didn't happen. I will go hunting."

Roisin reached out and touched his arm lightly, "I will go with Conor. Who knows Traynor better than me? We will take the wagon and Jasper and we will find the man."

Granny looked at the two of them with searching eyes. "Conor, I beg you to stay with me for just a while. Let me work with you so you learn your gifts and how to use them. Give me time to guide you. I hesitate to remind you what happens when you go hiding off without a clear thought."

"Gifts or curses, Granny? I wish I could, but his trail grows colder as we sit and mourn. We will leave at first light." He stood and the others followed suit. He grasped Aelf's arm and Shaen gathered him up in hers. The boys wrapped themselves around Conor and held onto him. Farewells were murmured and Granny promised to make up a pack of herbs and ointments for their journey.

The full moon bathed the Mountain Folk village in a soft, white light, the snow having moved down into the valley. Roisin slept with Doiranne on the sleeping platform, warm furs pulled up around their necks, their breath made small clouds in the frigid air. Conor sat by the fire, a fur wrapped around his shoulders, his pack between his legs. He looked around the dwelling to make sure everyone was sleeping, and then he opened his pack and from it drew a book; the worn, cracked leather cover bound in iron. Quietly, he turned the first page, and read the words to himself. He repeated them over and over until the words crept into his very being and became part of the man named Concobhar. Only when he was sure that the words were now him, did he turn the page and begin again.

The End

About the Author

K E Meuir grew up in the deserts of Tucson, Arizona with two sisters and three brothers. Her father, Ernest FitzGerald, was one of the most influential people in her life. As a chef and a lifelong gardener, he inspired her love of digging in the dirt and the joy that comes from preparing good food for those you love. Her mother, Josephine Baker, instilled in her a love of reading that has lasted a lifetime. Evenings spent listening to her mother read A. A. Milne and his beloved Winnie the Pooh left its mark.

Ms. Meuir traded the deserts of Arizona for Nevada where she attended the University of Nevada, Las Vegas earning degrees in education. Teaching became her passion and her classroom opened the door to discovery for many students. Ms. Meuir was active in the Southern Nevada Writing Project, a mentor to young teachers, and a representative in the Nevada Teacher's Association. She retired from teaching and moved to a small farm on the Olympic Peninsula in Washington where she raised chickens, rode her beloved mare, Rosie, and learned to garden in a world with abundant rainfall.

Life is full of surprises, and the best was yet to come. In a turn of events never imagined, Ms. Meuir met the love of her life, Mark. Together they began a new life together. Ms. Meuir lives in Henderson, Nevada.

Ms. Meuir and her late husband raised four wonderful children along the way. *Conor's Quest* is her second novel.

For more information or to follow KE Meuir's projects, go to her website at

www.kemeuir.com

www.ingramcontent.com/pod-product-compliance
Lightning Source LLC
LaVergne TN
LVHW050535160826
845677LV00011B/2038